THE PRIME SUSPECTS

Flo gazed at her pad for a moment. She looked up and surveyed the room. "We have a hand's worth of people who might have wanted Beverly Ruchart dead." She ticked names and reasons off on her fingers. "Ron inherits."

"So he says, anyway," I pointed out. "He could be just assuming he gets Grandma's estate."

"Granted," Flo said. "Then there's Isadora with her anger about the potential of losing half her own inheritance."

"I've met an Isadora." Derrick gazed over my head out the window as if he was thinking. "She always seemed to wear expensive-looking things."

Flo went on. "We also have Eli, who might or might not have hated Beverly."

"Gin, you also mentioned Beverly acted really drunk last night," I said, "and that she said she wasn't feeling well."

"Somebody at the dinner probably poisoned her with a substance mimicking being intoxicated," Derrick said.

"Maybe. But what substance?" I asked. "What poison can do that?"

Books by Maddie Day

Country Store Mysteries
FLIPPED FOR MURDER
GRILLED FOR MURDER
WHEN THE GRITS HIT THE FAN
BISCUITS AND SLASHED BROWNS
DEATH OVER EASY
STRANGLED EGGS AND HAM
NACHO AVERAGE MURDER
CANDY SLAIN MURDER

Anthologies
CHRISTMAS COCOA MURDER
(with Carlene O'Connor and Alex Erickson)

Cozy Capers Book Group Mysteries
MURDER ON CAPE COD
MURDER AT THE TAFFY SHOP

And writing as Edith Maxwell
A TINE TO LIVE, A TINE TO DIE
'TIL DIRT DO US PART
FARMED AND DANGEROUS
MURDER MOST FOWL
MULCH ADO ABOUT MURDER

Published by Kensington Publishing Corp.

Murder at the Taffy Shop

MADDIE DAY

KENSINGTON
PUBLISHING CORP.

www.kensingtonbooks.com

KENSINGTON BOOKS are published by

Kensington Publishing Corp.
119 West 40th Street
New York, NY 10018

Kensington Books Mass Market Paperback Printing: April 2021

ISBN-13: 978-1-4967-3169-2
ISBN-10: 1-4967-3169-7

ISBN-13: 978-1-4967-1509-8 (ebook)
ISBN-10: 1-4967-1509-8 (ebook)

10 9 8 7 6 5 4 3 2

Printed in the United States of America

For Dru Ann Love, who, with her Dru's Book Musings blog, has done more to promote the cozy mystery than almost anyone else. Thank you for your dedication to our stories and for your friendship!

Acknowledgments

So many people help with the writing and publishing of a book. As always, the crack team at Kensington, headed up by John Scognamiglio, produces a well-edited and gorgeous product. Thanks to my agent, John Talbot, for connecting me with Kensington.

Sherry Harris again gave the book a sanity and reality edit—thank you, dear Wicked. She and the rest of the Wicked Authors—Jessie Crockett, Julie Hennrikus, Liz Mugavero, and Barbara Ross—are my backup crew and sounding board, and we hope you'll visit our blog, wickedauthors.com.

For this book I consulted the fabulous *Book of Poisons: A Guide for Writers* by Serita Stevens and Anne Bannon. My friend Kathleen Stearns kindly gave me access to her African gray parrot, Jewel, and took note of some of the things she says for me to use. I so appreciate the Wi-Fi–free West Falmouth Quaker retreat house, where I worked on this book and ones in the other series that I write, and where I soaked up Cape Cod scents, sights, and sounds. My consultant on Massachusetts police procedure, Lieutenant Kevin Donovan of the Amesbury PD, provided me with several key tips. Any errors in procedure are entirely of my doing.

Gratitude always to my menfolk: Allan and JD, my bicyclist sons and biggest fans; and Hugh, who helped with astrology in this book and who makes me laugh. To Sisters in Crime, without whose support and inspiration I never would have achieved whatever successes I have gained. And to my mystery-fan sisters Barbara and Janet, and all the readers and librarians out there—thank you for enabling me to enjoy this best and last career. I hope you'll check out my Edith Maxwell author hat, too, and keep letting me know when you've read and loved one of my books.

Chapter One

In my opinion, only the coldest heart could resist a puppy. Beverly Ruchart apparently possessed an arctic heart. She marched through the gap in the hedge between her property and my parents' yard behind the church parsonage. Beverly held the wriggling, yipping three-month-old puppy at arm's length. My father had acquired Tucker for his granddaughter, my niece Cokey, to play with when she visited. A curly-haired rescue, the little guy was all sweetness, energy, and enough wile to slip his collar and go exploring.

"This, this *creature* has been digging in my garden." Beverly's crisp white shirt bore dirt smudges. Her florid neck contrasted with her cap of silver hair, which was definitely not as perfectly styled as usual. She caught sight of me where I sat with my mother, our brightly colored—but empty—plastic margarita glasses in hand.

"Good evening, ladies." Beverly was a regular at Mac's Bikes, my bicycle repair, rental, and retail shop here in our small Cape Cod town of Westham.

"Hey, Beverly." Mom smiled, ignoring Beverly's tone. "Have a seat. Can I fix you a drink?"

"No, thank you." Beverly kept her arms extended.

My father, Joseph Almeida, took the puppy. "We're very sorry, Ms. Ruchart. He slipped out of his collar. It won't happen again." He stroked Tucker's silky dark coat and smiled kindly at his irate neighbor.

"Please see to it that it doesn't. I pay good money to my landscape service and I grow prize-winning roses."

"Tucker! Bad boy." Cokey, with a five-year-old's frown, shook her little finger at the pup. Her curly blonde hair was pulled back in a ponytail, but escaped ringlets framed her face like angel curls.

"The dog was extremely bad, young lady. I don't intend to have my grounds ruined by him again." Chin held high, Beverly turned and slipped back through the hedge a moment later. She'd bought the property adjoining the Unitarian Universalist Church years earlier and had had the house and grounds renovated to her expensive liking.

Cokey stared. "Am I a lady, Athtra?" she lisped to her grandmother, who loved Cokey, calling her Astra instead of Grandma.

"Of course you are, honey," Mom said.

"I guess she doesn't like puppies," I said, gazing after Beverly. "Have you had trouble with her before?" I looked from Mom to Pa and back.

"I don't believe she thinks much of our modest lifestyle, but we haven't had this kind of run-in prior to today." My father gazed at the gap Beverly had disappeared through. "I'm wondering about installing a fence, Mackenzie. What do you think?"

"So Tucker can run around freely?" I asked. "Sounds like a good idea."

"Yes, and so Ms. Ruchart won't have cause to complain again. Fences make good neighbors." Pa, the UU minister, had a steady, quiet presence reflected in the deep tones of his comforting voice.

"I hear you," I replied.

Cokey dashed off. She came back to us holding Tucker's leash and collar. "Abo Joe, here." *Abo*, the Kriolu word for both "grandfather" and "grandmother," came from Pa's father's Cape Verdean heritage. Pa had grown up speaking the language with his father.

Pa knelt and helped Cokey securely refasten the collar. From the lawn chair where he'd been sitting, he picked up the little harness that went around Tucker's chest. "We have to put the harness on every time, Coquille, not just the collar. All right?" He was the only person in the family who used Cokey's full name, bestowed on her by her French mother.

She nodded solemnly. "Cuth I don't want that lady mad at uth anymore," she lisped.

"Neither do I," he said. Together they fastened on the harness, which framed the puppy's white chest, and hooked the leash to it.

Mom, otherwise known as Astra Mackenzie—thus my first name—piped up. "I'd be willing to bet she's an Aquarian. Not the most touchy-feeling of signs." Mom was a professional astrologer and was astonishingly accurate in assessing personalities. She leaned over and refilled my glass from the pitcher, which she'd lifted out of an ice chest.

"Thanks, Mom." I didn't believe in astrology myself, but it's a big world, and my mother's profession made her happy.

I stretched out my legs. I often stopped by my parents' place after closing the shop. Mac's Bikes, which I'd opened a year and a half ago, kept me busy, especially in the height of the season, but it was thriving, and I liked the multifaceted challenge of keeping a business afloat. I sipped the frosty, citrusy drink. A cold drink at the end of a busy mid-summer Saturday and a dose of family was almost never the wrong choice.

"Where's Derrick?" I asked. Cokey's single-parent dad worked in the rental-retail side of my shop. "He left work at five today."

"He's at a meeting," Pa said.

"Good." I nodded. Derrick, my older half brother, was a recovering alcoholic but was stable again. Attending AA meetings regularly was much of the reason why. Pa's being a solid support for his stepson was another. I watched Cokey walk the puppy around the yard. "Derrick's doing great, isn't he?"

"He sure is." My mom stood. "Are you eating with us, Mac?" She tossed back her nimbus of flyaway blonde hair that included more than a little gray.

"Thanks, but no. Tim's cooking for me. I'd better get home and clean up so I'm not late." I glanced at Tucker, who had run toward us with Cokey barely managing to hold on to the leash. Tucker, a Portuguese water dog, rubbed against my leg and I didn't have to recoil. Pa had been careful to find one of the few breeds of dog that didn't make me sneeze, wheeze, and reach for my antihistamine eye drops.

"Titi Mac, I want to go to Tio Tim's, too," she said, using the Cape Verdean words for aunt and uncle.

"Not tonight, *querida*." When I saw her lip push out, I added, "But he wants to meet Tucker, so we'll get together soon, okay?"

Her expression brightened. "Hold Tucker, Athtra, so he doesn't get away." She thrust the leash at my mother and ran over to the swing.

Life was good in August here in Westham. I had family and a thriving business, not to mention a devoted—and handsome—boyfriend. What more could a woman want?

Chapter Two

Tim and I walked hand in hand along the beach at nine the next morning on another cloudless summer day. A sea breeze brought a fresh tang of salt and seaweed, and kept the sun from feeling too hot. Tim had taken off his shirt, and I wore only a tank top and my EpiPen bag with my shorts, a pink cap over my short black curls. I normally power walked with Gin Malloy, a friend from the Cozy Capers book group, early in the mornings, but I saved Sundays for Tim. He also took precedence over attending the UU services my father conducted, about which I felt the tiniest jab of guilt.

"I'm glad your assistant baker is working out." I squeezed his hand. My guy owned Greta's Grains, an artisanal bakery in town. When we were first going out, he had to be at the bakery by four every morning, including Sundays. He'd finally found another baker to take over weekend mornings.

"Me too."

"How's your training going for Falmouth?" A row of plovers at the water's edge ran ahead of us, poked sharp beaks into the wet sand, and ran again when we approached. Tim had entered the Falmouth Road Race, held next week, but he'd be running straight ahead and fast, not zigzagging like these energetic little birds.

"Eli is a great running buddy, and we push each other. I think I'm ready for the race."

"It's a week from today?"

"Yep, and Eli thinks he might actually place in the top ten."

"Wow. He must be fast." The race was a big deal on the Cape, with a seven-mile route that started hilly but also led along a beach on Martha's Vineyard Sound before heading back into town. It had been taking place since 1973 and attracted over ten thousand runners.

Tim laughed. "He just turned forty, so he's the youngest in his age category. That makes it easier to place in his age group than me in my thirty-to-forty group."

"World-class runners come to compete, don't they?"

"They do. Some well-known, elite racers are coming this year. Mostly from Kenya and Ethiopia, as usual."

"Do you know what Eli does at the Woods Hole lab?" I asked. Tim and I had done a little matchmaking with my friend Gin and Eli. They'd only been dating for a month, but Gin seemed pleased with the guy.

"He's some kind of marine researcher at the Oceanographic Institute. I'm not quite sure what his area is." He pushed his shoulder-length dark blond hair back off his face, but the wind blew it back again. "I should have tied my hair. I'm going in the water. You?"

I shook my head. "You go." I plopped onto packed

sand and set my arms on my knees. I hadn't brought a towel. Anyway, I had to open the shop at eleven and didn't want to have to shower again.

He jogged in and dove when the water was deep enough. Here on the bay we didn't have waves except small ones lapping the shore like a caress. Tim popped up and ambled back out. He was an extraordinarily fine specimen of his gender. He kept his abs toned and pulled in, and had broad shoulders, with a small patch of chest hair at his sternum. He had a luscious set of lips—and knew how to use them—and big baby-blue eyes. More important, he was kind and smart and adored me. I wasn't quite sure how I'd lucked out.

He leaned over, shaking the water out of his hair. He tossed his head up, tucking his hair behind his ears, and sank with grace to sit next to me.

"Better?" I asked.

"Much."

A boy and a girl a little older than Cokey dashed by in front of us, shrieking as they chased a seagull. I held my breath, waiting to see if Tim would bring up the question of starting a family yet again. Every few weeks he raised the issue, and every time I said I wasn't ready. My life was good. Happy, busy, in order. I wasn't sure I wanted to disturb the status quo by getting married, getting pregnant, figuring out how to live with a baby. It wasn't like I wanted to be with anyone else, and I supposed one day I'd want a family. Tim, on the other hand, couldn't wait. And I probably shouldn't, either. I was thirty-six to his thirty-two, and my eggs weren't getting any younger.

But the moment passed. We sat quietly looking out to sea, our lives at peace for the moment.

Chapter Three

*U*h-oh. Here came possible trouble. Beverly Ruchart wheeled her Diamondback hybrid bike through the door of the repair side of my shop at one o'clock that afternoon. Derrick was busy explaining our rental policy to a family of five. My mechanic, Orlean Brown, was deep in a bike tune-up in the repair shop. I'd finished showing our array of brightly colored shirts to a serious cyclist who explained he'd ridden down from Boston and wanted a souvenir of the Cape. Another group of tourists waited to rent bikes, and we had a big sign out front asking people to leave their bikes outside. Now was not a good time for an imperious customer who thought she was so entitled she didn't have to follow the rules.

"Excuse me, Ms. Ruchart." I intercepted her. "Please leave the bike outside." I smiled but blocked her way into the shop.

Her nostrils flared. "I always bring it in. Ms. Brown never has a problem with me doing so. This is a valuable bike and someone could steal it out there."

It was a very nice bike, true, although not particularly valuable, and the customer should always be right. However, this was my shop, and procedure was procedure. "I'm sorry, we simply don't have room in here. I'll come out and give you a ticket, and then we'll store it where we keep the other bikes waiting for repairs." I glanced over at Orlean. Technically the areas of the shop were different rooms, but they were all open to the others, except my office and the bathroom, of course.

She'd looked up from her work and now raised a blue-gloved hand black with grease. "Hey there, Bev. Come see me after Mac gets you all set." She lowered her gaze to her work again.

Bev? I'd never heard anyone call her anything other than Ms. Ruchart or Beverly.

"Very well," Beverly said to me. She wheeled the bike back outside and stood tapping her fingers on the handlebars.

"I'll be right there." I hurried over to the desk and grabbed the repair book. "What do you need done?" I asked her once I'd joined her.

"The front tire keeps going flat, and something's rubbing the rear tire. I inadvertently ran over a big stick yesterday. It had fallen onto the trail during that windy night Friday, I believe. It must have knocked things out of alignment."

"The Shining Sea Trail?" The lovely, flat trail ran along the coast on the former rail bed and was a popular locale for walkers, runners, and cyclists. I jotted down her name and what she'd said on the ticket.

"Yes, I ride it in its entirety every day. My cardiologist recommended vigorous daily exercise."

"The trail is a good place for it. And a twenty-one-mile round trip is a decent ride. Can I have your phone number, please?"

After she told me, I added it and tied the ticket to the handlebar. "I'm not sure when it'll be ready. Depends on how many are in front of you. I'll get to it myself tomorrow if I can."

"I will need it as soon as possible." She pursed her lips, which made a little row of lines appear above her top lip.

"I understand. We do repairs in the order in which we receive them, however." She had to already know this. She'd been a customer here ever since she'd moved in three summers ago.

"Very well. Now, Ms. Almeida, I have another matter to bring up with you. I must say I am increasingly concerned about the riffraff who frequent that soup kitchen you all run at the church."

I stared at her. *The riffraff?* Despite the steady stream of tourists with money to burn and the affluent folks who summered here, Westham had local residents who were hungry and even homeless. The soup kitchen Pa ran out of the church basement several days a week, along with the food pantry he hosted, made all the difference to those down on their luck. I was a regular volunteer at both, as was Gin, who owned and ran Salty Taffy's candy shop at the other end of the main drag from here.

"They have left trash in my front yard and sometimes loiter about smoking cigarettes. I meant to speak to your father about it yesterday, but that dog had me too rattled to remember."

I did not have time for this. "Ms. Ruchart, we feed the desperately needy. Often it's their only meal of the day. I'll let my father know your views. If you'll excuse me, I have customers waiting inside." I turned to wheel the bike around to the back.

She called after me. "Please call me as soon as my bicycle is ready."

At least she'd said please. I stashed the Diamondback in the walk-in shipping container serving as repair storage. The space wasn't great, but acquiring it had been a lot cheaper than adding on to the building after I'd bought the business last year. I'd run electricity into the container and painted the inside white so we could see which bike was where. Customers not picking up their repaired or tuned-up bikes promptly were a real problem and meant we provided free storage for them. I was thinking of a way to penalize anyone who left it more than a week unless they had extenuating circumstances.

I hurried back into the shop. Beverly had, in fact, gone back in to talk with Orlean on the repair side. My mechanic was a normally taciturn employee, stopping a few millimeters short of being dysfunctional. She was so talented at fixing bikes, though, I forgave her almost anything. Since Derrick was now helping the second group of renters, I moseyed over and straightened the nearest merchandise so I could listen in on Orlean and Beverly's conversation.

"I got a nibble on my Colby line," Orlean said. "Found the town records for 1903." She hung a blue-handled wrench on the hook in the middle of the set, arranged in order of size. She kept her work bench tidy, a sight dear to my neat-freak heart. Tired straw-colored hair peeked out of the Orleans Firebirds ball cap she wore every day.

"Good work," Beverly said. "And I might have un-earthed that missing aunt on your maternal line we were talking about."

Orlean nodded. "We're meeting again Tuesday night, right?" She grabbed the curly blue air hose hanging from the ceiling. It hissed as she half inflated the tube she was checking.

"You can count on it." Beverly smiled at my no-nonsense mechanic.

I wasn't sure I'd ever seen Beverly smile. Also—town records for 1903? A missing aunt? It sounded like they were talking historical research. Or . . . of course. Beverly Ruchart was a professional genealogist. I'd known her occupation, but it had slipped my mind. What I hadn't known was that Orlean was interested, too, and apparently good at finding old records. Beverly's expertise must have been the trigger to get Orlean to open up, as well as their mutual love of bicycles. Beverly sounded polite and respectful speaking to Orlean, quite a change from my interactions with her this weekend. But I was a staunch attender at the church of Live and Learn, and happy to witness Beverly's good side.

Chapter Four

I'd finished my closing checklist at five o'clock and had locked the door to the shop when I spied Gin hurrying down Main Street toward me. I waved and waited for her to reach me, which took a minute as she dodged tourists and a friendly pair of dogs on leashes.

"What's cooking?" I asked, smiling.

"I'm going out tonight, so I thought I'd check in with you about tomorrow." She was breathless from her fast walk, and her thick brownish-red hair was straggling loose from its ponytail.

"Do you have time for a beer?" I asked.

"Absolutely. Today was nuts at the shop." She shook her head.

"Same here." I led the way through the yard behind the shop, past the picnic table under a big tree where I often ate lunch, and through a break in the low hedge to my

350-square-foot tiny house. Once inside, my African gray parrot, Belle, started talking.

"Hi, Mac. It's about time. Belle's a good girl. Belle wants a treat. Hi, Mac."

I stepped out of my sneakers and padded to her cage. "Hi, Belle." I opened the door, scritching her head before she hopped out.

Belle cocked her head at Gin. "Hi, gorgeous. Give Belle a treat?" She let out a perfect wolf whistle. "Belle's a good girl. Grapes?"

Gin laughed. "Does she ever shut up?" She took off her own shoes and came in.

I liked to have a no-shoes policy in the house. It kept the floors clean, and I had a basket with a few pairs of spare slippers for the wintertime. "Sometimes. But not when I first come in." I pulled out Belle's cherished frozen grapes and put a few in her cage before opening two cold Pilsners for the humans. I handed Gin a full glass and clinked mine with hers. "Cheers." I sank onto the two-seater couch and pointed to the small upholstered chair opposite. "Take a load off."

"I know we can't complain about great business, but boy, it's exhausting," she said after sipping the beer. "My best high school employee had asked for the day off and the other one, well, she's not very good at retail."

"I ran my tush off today, too." I took a long sip from my glass. "Mmm. Beer sure goes down right. So what are you doing tonight?"

"Date with Eli." Her cheeks pinkened.

My friend had been divorced for years, and her daughter was grown and lived elsewhere. I was happy to help her love life along. A few months earlier I'd tried to get her and my brother together, since they were both in their early forties and single, but he was raising Cokey and Gin was all done with child-rearing. She and Derrick went out once but seemed to have agreed not to take it any further.

Gin went on. "Eli is taking me to some fancy dinner party he was invited to."

"At a restaurant?"

"No, at some lady's house. She's the one who owns the really nice property just beyond the rectory."

"Beverly Ruchart? Interesting. I've seen her twice this weekend."

Belle hopped up on the arm of the couch and to the back near my head. I reached up and stroked her. She started humming the tune to "Happy," bobbing her head with the rhythm.

"Beverly summers here, and she's been bringing her bicycle into the shop for service since I opened," I said.

"That's her. She's Eli's former mother-in-law."

"I didn't know she had children. She doesn't seem particularly maternal."

"Well, it takes all types, right?" Gin took another sip of beer.

"Is Eli divorced?"

"No, his wife died some years ago. He has a stepson a little older than my Lucy. I haven't met him yet, but he'll be at the dinner. The kid, Ron, is apparently living with his grandmother this summer."

"Is Eli over his wife's death?" I asked.

"He seems to be. It's been a while. Remember the rich guy who stayed in my Airbnb in June? He's going to be at the dinner, too."

"Wesley somebody." I couldn't remember his last name.

"Farnham. He bought a property in Pocasset and is

having it renovated. I guess he's living there during the construction."

"So what are you wearing tonight?" I wasn't much of a clothes horse, but Gin loved both clothes and the shopping required to obtain them.

She smiled. "I got a really sweet hand-painted silk tunic at the consignment shop last week. It goes perfect with my white rough-silk capris."

"Cute."

Belle flapped up to the roost on top of her cage. "Really sweet. Really sweet," she muttered in an uncanny imitation of Gin's voice. "Really sweet."

"By the way, I wouldn't bring up the soup kitchen in your dinner conversation tonight," I said. "Ms. Ruchart called the people we serve riffraff. She as much as said they're driving down property values."

Gin's mouth dropped open. "Hungry and homeless residents of our sweet town are riffraff? You've got to be kidding."

"No joke. Her words. I know, it's disgusting."

"Ugh." She drained her glass and set it down. "We're walking tomorrow, right?" She and I walked every weekday morning at seven, rain or shine. Not if it was too cold or icy out, but at this time of year, we were as regular as a metronome in the Cape Symphony's rehearsal room.

"Absolutely."

Belle laughed to herself.

Gin tilted her head. "Was that the parrot?"

Belle laughed softly. "Okay, love you, see you soon, bye," Belle murmured and laughed some more.

"Exactly." I pointed at the bird. "She has a recording of my phone calls in her brain."

Gin snorted. "She's amazing. So, have you finished the book yet?"

I shook my head. "No, but I have time to read tonight. And we're not meeting until Thursday." We were both charter members of the Cozy Capers book group. The collection of local shop owners and others read one cozy mystery per week and met to discuss the book on Thursday nights, often in the lighthouse where my brother was caretaker. We took turns making a recipe from the foodie cozies. This week's book was Liz Mugavero's *The Icing on the Corpse*, one of her delightful Pawsitively Organic pet food mysteries. The recipes were all for animals, but we'd found they tasted delicious for humans, too. This summer we were working our way through the calendar year, each week's book moving ahead a month, and had selected *Icing* because it was set in February.

"I haven't finished it, either. I'll tell you, it's awfully nice to be reading about February New England temperatures when it's hot out. I think the AC in my shop is about to go. As if I need a big expense like a new appliance." Gin grimaced as she stood. "Thanks for the drink. I'm off to get cleaned up so I can brave the rich and not-so-famous."

"Have fun. You'll have your new man at your side. How bad can it be?"

Chapter Five

My leaving-home ritual took a little longer than usual the next morning. I always felt compelled to leave everything clean and in its place before I left the house. One could argue that doing so was a near necessity for someone who lived in such a small space. Or, as others had pointed out, my obsession with cleanliness and order was borderline clinical. I'd earned my Neat Freak badge several times over. Mom had attributed it to my having both my sun and my moon in Virgo, of course.

Regardless of the diagnosis or the cause, I was a few minutes late to meet Gin for our walk. I grabbed my EpiPen bag and slung it across my chest. After a near-fatal meet-up with a wasp a few years earlier, I never left home without a double dose of the lifesaving medicine. I locked the door, stuck the house key in my shorts pocket, and headed out.

The day had dawned sunny and cloudless again. Good for those of us in the tourism business, not so good for local farmers. I hurried down the length of Main Street. I passed the fragrant smells of baking emitting from Tim's bakery and the blessedly quiet Westham police station. Only two cars passed me on my way to where Gin lived above Salty Taffy's at the other end. A quick shudder rippled through me at the memory of our close call with death in the shop's kitchen in June, but I shook it off.

Apparently, Gin was running late, too. She wasn't stretching her hamstrings in front of the shop. I glanced up at her windows but didn't see a light on, not that she would need one almost an hour and a half after sunrise. I checked down her driveway on the right side of the building, but she wasn't there. The back of her small yard abutted the municipal parking lot, and on the far side of the shop was a new walk-in health clinic.

I headed around the front of the shop to the clinic side. The owners had planted a particularly lovely flower garden facing the street, and both Gin and I always liked to check out what was newly in bloom. I had a brown thumb, myself, but that didn't mean I didn't appreciate others' talents in the plant department.

But when I cleared the shop, I gasped and froze in place. Gin knelt on the walkway between the buildings. Next to her lay the crumpled figure of Beverly Ruchart.

"Gin, what . . . ?" I hurried to her side.

She gazed up at me, her eyes as wide as saucers. "She's dead." Her whisper was barely audible.

"Are you sure?" I asked even as I took in Beverly's open and unseeing eyes, her skin devoid of pink, and the way her lips stretched back from her teeth. I brought my hand to my mouth. The poor, poor woman. Her heart issues must have caught up with her.

"I'm sure. Her skin is cold, Mac." Gin's eyes welled with tears. "I can't believe it. I was at her house. I ate dinner at her table only twelve hours ago. She was alive, and now she's not."

And poor Gin. I doubted she'd ever seen a dead body before, at least not like this. "Did she seem well during dinner?"

Gin opened her mouth to speak, but I held up a hand. "Wait." What was I doing asking about dinner? First things first. "Did you call the police?"

"No." Gin sniffed. "I just found her a minute ago."

"We have to let someone know. You know, like we've read about so many times? It's an unattended death. The police need to be informed." I hauled my phone out of my back pocket and pressed 9-1-1. When the dispatcher answered, I said, "This is Mackenzie Almeida in Westham. We, um, found a dead body next to the walk-in clinic on Main Street."

"Is someone else with you?"

"Yes, Gin Malloy. She owns the taffy shop we're next to."

"When did you encounter the deceased?" the dispatcher asked next.

"Just now. A couple of minutes ago."

"Do you feel safe?"

I checked with Gin. "Do you feel safe?"

"Of course," she whispered, staring at Beverly.

"Yes, we feel safe," I told the dispatcher.

"Someone will be there shortly."

"Thank you." I disconnected and sank down to sit next

to Gin, who had wrapped her arms around her knees. The walkway was cool and hard under my rear, and the taffy shop blocked the morning sun. I shivered, then put my arm around her shoulders and squeezed.

"Yesterday Beverly said she was seeing a cardiologist," I murmured. "She said that was why she biked so much. I'll bet her heart just gave out on her."

"You asked how she was at dinner last night. She seemed like she was getting really drunk, and by the end of the night she said she didn't feel well."

The sound of a siren rose into the air. Why had it taken them so long? The station was only two blocks away.

"Why do you think she was here, Mac?" Gin asked plaintively. "Her house is way down at the other end of town."

I pointed to the shiny new sign on the building next to us. "Walk-in clinic is my guess. Maybe she thought they were open all night. It's closer than the hospital."

"But why didn't she call nine-one-one if she was feeling so bad?" Gin kept her gaze on Beverly's still form, as if guarding it.

"I don't know. Maybe she didn't feel sick enough for an ambulance and it hit her all of a sudden. Plus, ambulances are super expensive." Not that that would have mattered to Beverly. A scarcity of money never had seemed an issue for her.

Two dark blue Westham police cruisers whooped to a stop on the street in front of us, followed immediately by a boxy red Westham Fire Department rescue vehicle. All three vehicles kept their rooftop lights strobing red and blue but turned off the sirens. A bicycle officer rode up, too, in a helmet, light blue polo shirt, and navy shorts, the department's summer uniform. I scrambled to my feet, but Gin stayed sitting next to Beverly. A woman in maroon scrubs emerged from the clinic's front door and stared, her hand to her mouth.

Officers climbed out of both cruisers, and two paramedics jumped out of the WFD vehicle, red bags in hand. The one I wished hadn't heeded the call was Westham Police Chief Victoria Laitinen, a woman with whom I had a long and slightly rocky past. She strode up and stood with her arms crossed on her navy-blue-clad chest, gazing down at Gin. And at Beverly's body. Since Victoria was barely five foot one, she didn't have far to look.

"Morning, Mac, Ms. Malloy. Were you two together when you came across the deceased?" Her pale-blonde, nearly white hair was pulled back into a neat bun at the nape of her neck, as always.

"Morning, Victoria," I said. "No, Gin had found her before I got here."

Victoria narrowed her eyes at the corpse. "Is this that lady who lives near your father, Mac?"

"Yes, her name is Beverly Ruchart."

"Thought so. She's always calling in petty complaints."

No surprise there. Including calls about the soup kitchen riffraff, I'd guess.

Victoria beckoned to one of the waiting paramedics. He hurried up, squatted, and laid a gloved finger on Beverly's neck for a minute. He leaned over and sniffed in front of her mouth. He felt her skin with the back of his hand, then put both hands near her ears and tried to turn her head, but it was unyielding. He must have been checking for rigor mortis, the stiffening that sets in a few hours after death. Which I only knew about from reading crime novels, of course. He stood.

"Deceased, Chief."

"Thank you." Victoria directed a few officers to secure the scene and told the one on the bike to call the medical examiner and the state police. One officer attached yellow police tape to the clinic building, out to a lamppost at the curb, and along to a post in front of Gin's shop.

"Now, ladies, if you don't mind?" Victoria ushered us away from Beverly and along the sidewalk to the driveway at the far side of Gin's shop. "We'll need a full statement from each of you, but for now, please tell me exactly how you came to find the deceased next to your shop, Ms. Malloy."

I watched as the officer ran the tape from the lamppost to the corner of Gin's shop. He disappeared along the side of the shop to finish blocking the perimeter of the secure area. If the tape stayed up for very long, tourists would have to step into the gutter to keep walking on this side of Main Street.

"I came out here at seven," Gin told Victoria. "Mac and I go walking every weekday. She was a little bit late, so I went over to check out the flowers in front of the clinic. I saw Beverly there and I rushed up to her to see if I could help."

"Did you touch the body?" Victoria angled her stern look upward. Gin was almost as tall as my five foot seven.

"I only touched the skin on her neck. I hoped I could find a pulse. But I couldn't." Gin hugged herself, shivering despite standing in full morning sun.

"You called her Beverly. Did you know her?" Victoria asked Gin.

"I met her last night for the first time. She threw a dinner party and the man I'm seeing invited me. She was his former mother-in-law."

Victoria groaned. "How many people at this soirée?"

"Let's see. Me, Eli—"

"Last name?"

"Tubin. Then there was Ron Ruchart, Beverly's grandson; Wesley Farnham, and Wesley's daughter, Isadora."

The chief sighed. "We'll get those details in your statement. Did Ms. Ruchart seem ill last night?"

Gin glanced at me. I gave her a little nod.

"I was telling Mac. Beverly seemed to get drunk really fast, and by the dessert course she said she wasn't feeling well."

"Did she seem more drunk than the amount of alcohol she consumed might have merited?"

"I think so," Gin replied.

Victoria turned to me. "You, Mac?"

"I didn't touch her. I showed up maybe five minutes after seven. Beverly had told me she was seeing a cardiologist, just so you know."

"Were you at this dinner party, too?" she asked.

"No, not at all."

Victoria narrowed her eyes as if she didn't quite believe me. "When was the last time you saw the deceased?"

The deceased. Beverly had a name. It was Victoria's style, though, to play by the rules, and her terminology must be police culture.

"Yesterday in my bike shop," I said. "I think it was at around one o'clock in the afternoon." A rumble in the distance grew louder, turning into a group of gawking motorcyclists who slowed to a crawl when they saw the police activity. These were shiny, decked-out bikes ridden by men with white ponytails, each with a skimpy Harley helmet, a leather-fringed woman seated behind him, and an entirely insufficient muffler.

Victoria waited until they passed before opening her mouth to continue. She didn't get far.

"Good morning, ladies. I caught this on the scanner and thought I'd stop by," Lincoln Haskins said as he strolled up. State Police Detective Lincoln Haskins, that is. He gazed at Beverly's body through dark-rimmed glasses before shifting his eyes to Victoria, who stood a full foot shorter than him. The fabric of his tropical-patterned, square-hemmed shirt was in somewhat louder colors than he usually sported.

She frowned at the detective. She and I had been debate team rivals in high school. Even though I hadn't ever hung out with her, I knew her well enough to pick up resentment in her expression. "Unattended death. Found by these two responsible citizens." She lifted her chin.

Lincoln stuck his hands in the pockets of his khakis. "Carry on, Chief." He rocked back on his heels, his expression as implacable—bordering on inscrutable—as ever.

"Either of you have a theory about why Ms. Ruchart was here next to Salty Taffy's?" Victoria asked us. "Had you argued with her, Ms. Malloy?"

"What?" Gin pulled in her chin. "No! We thought maybe she was trying to get to the clinic because she didn't feel well."

"Had you had conflict with the deceased, Mac?" Victoria's pale-blue eyes sparkled, as if she was eager for me to say yes.

I put my fists on my waist. "Why are you asking if we didn't get along with Beverly? Surely she simply had a heart attack. She was alone. She died. Why do you think it's more than that?" Maybe I simply didn't want it to be anything other than a natural death.

"Mac, sometimes an unattended death is 'simply'"— Victoria surrounded the word with air quotes—"a matter of a heart attack."

Haskins silently followed our back and forth like he was watching a beach volleyball match.

Victoria continued. "Other times it's much more complicated."

"Yes, much." The detective's face was a somber mask.

No. My mouth pulled down. "Do you mean suicide . . . or murder?"

Gin's eyes widened.

The chief folded her arms. "We can't rule out either of those until we rule them out."

Chapter Six

Gin and I were ushered into separate interview rooms at the station to give our official statements. Lincoln didn't appear in my room, and I wondered if he was questioning Gin. The officer interviewing me wasn't someone I'd encountered before. He asked me to identify myself and my address for the recording, and I complied.

"Please relay exactly what happened this morning." He looked about thirty, more or less my height, with short-cropped dark hair and some of the longest natural eyelashes I'd ever seen.

I peered at his name badge. "It was pretty simple, Officer Jenkins. I went to meet Gin Malloy in front of her shop for our daily walk."

He checked some notes. "That would be Salty Taffy's, correct?"

"Exactly. I didn't see her, so I went around to the far

side near the health clinic to look at their flowers. Gin was kneeling on the walkway next to Beverly Ruchart's, uh"— I swallowed—"body."

"Was she touching the deceased?"

"No, but she told me Beverly's skin was cold."

"Did you confirm that?"

I shook my head.

"Please answer verbally, Ms. Almeida."

"No. She looked dead. I didn't need to touch her skin."

"Did either of you attempt resuscitation?"

"No! She wasn't alive." I stared at him. "And probably hadn't been for a while."

He was unfazed by my outburst and continued in his calm, smooth voice. "Were you acquainted with the deceased?"

"She brought her bicycle to my shop for servicing, and she lived behind my parents. Behind the Unitarian Universalist parsonage on Main Street."

"That would be Mac's Bikes, correct?" he asked, looking at the notes again.

"Yes."

"When was the last time you saw Ms. Ruchart?"

"Yesterday afternoon in my shop."

"Did you happen to argue?"

I pressed my eyes shut for a moment. *Keep calm, Mac.* "No, we didn't argue." I gazed at a mirror in one wall of the room. A two-way window? Probably.

"Did Ms. Malloy have any disagreements with the deceased that you know of?"

"No, as far as I know she'd never met her before the dinner last night."

"Were you at this dinner as well?"

"No, but Gin had told me she was going."

He finally ran out of questions and dismissed me. I hurried out but sat on the front steps to wait for Gin.

"Even though a walk would calm my nerves, for me it's too late today," I said to her when she emerged a few minutes later.

"Same here. Get a quick coffee at Greta's?" Her face was pale and her voice quavered.

"As long as coffee includes one of Tim's pastries, I'm game." I didn't feel too steady, myself. The image of Beverly's dead body floated as an overlay on everything I looked at.

"I could use some sugar right about now," Gin said.

Inside Tim's bakery we ordered at the counter. I waved to Tim when I spied him through the pass-through window to the kitchen. Five minutes later, we sat at a sidewalk table out front, coffees and pastries in front of us. The bakery was halfway between Gin's shop and mine.

"Was Detective Haskins in your interview?" I asked in a murmur so the few other diners near us couldn't hear.

"No, it was some junior officer I'd never seen before."

"Same here."

Gin frowned at the table. "What if someone killed Beverly?" She kept her voice low, too.

"All those questions made me think the police think it's possible. We imagine that murder only happens in the cozies we read. But as we've seen, Westham isn't exempt." A mottled brown immature seagull perched on the nearest lamppost and eyed our pastries as if hoping the crumbs would be her lunch. "And you have to admit, Beverly wasn't universally liked."

"I know. That's the thing, Mac. There were so many weird undercurrents at the dinner last night."

I leaned forward across the round wrought-iron table.

"Like what?" I took a bite of my *pain au chocolat*, a puff pastry with a piece of dark chocolate baked into it. I'd eaten the pastry in France and was positive Tim's version was even more delicious.

"Like Beverly's apparent dislike of Eli," Gin said. "I don't know why she even invited him."

"The old son-in-law/mother-in-law dynamic? No man is ever good enough for my daughter kind of thing?"

"Maybe. But the wife has been dead for years. She and Eli didn't have children together. And he's a really nice guy. You've met him."

"Only that once when we double-dated with you and him, when we introduced you. He does seem nice. What else went on last night?"

Gin tapped the table. "Things between Wesley and our hostess didn't seem problematic, not that I picked up. On the contrary. They seemed, I don't know, kind of flirty. I learned she found a birth son for him, one who he knew about but had never known how to locate. The two apparently had a loving reunion."

"Beverly does . . . I mean, did genealogy, right?"

"Finding long-lost parents and children for people was apparently her specialty. That, and writing her clients' family histories for them." She sipped her cappuccino.

A tall shadow fell over the table, and a strong, warm hand descended onto my shoulder. "How are the most competent businesswomen of Westham doing today?" Tim asked.

I gazed up at him. "We're having a delicious fresh-air breakfast, thanks." I didn't have it in me to give him a big smile.

"Hi, Tim." Gin worried the edge of her paper cup. She hadn't touched her cheese Danish, although she had dosed her coffee with lots of cream and three sugars.

He looked from her to me and back. "Problem with the pastry, Gin?" Tim asked, his voice solicitous.

"If the pastry were only the problem," she whispered. She finally took a bite.

I tugged on his shirt and beckoned him to lean nearer. "Gin found Beverly Ruchart dead next to her store this morning, right before I showed up for our walk."

His thousand-watt smile slid into darkness. "I'm sorry to hear that, man. Was she . . . I mean . . ." He studied my face. He'd been with me right after I'd discovered a murdered man on the biking trail. He knew how hard it had been, what a shock.

"We don't know yet how she died," I replied, keeping my voice low. "No signs of anything, um, out of the ordinary." I raised an eyebrow. I hoped he knew I meant we hadn't seen blood or a weapon.

"Gin, listen," Tim said, ever gentle. "You need help, you come to me if you can't find Mac, okay?" He laid his other hand on her shoulder. "We're all on the same team."

She nodded, her eyes filling. "I know." Her voice was barely audible.

"You take care." He wiped his hands on the half apron tied around his waist. "Back to the ovens for me. Talk to you later today, darlin', okay?" he asked me.

"Perfect." I smiled inwardly watching him greet other sidewalk diners before heading back inside. That man could warm my insides like nobody's business. I forced myself back to the here and now.

"You know Tim is a national treasure, don't you?" Gin munched on her pastry, watching the door he'd disappeared through.

I laid my hand on my heart. "I do. He's pretty awesome any way you look at it." But even while thinking about Tim, Beverly's death refused to leave my brain. "Gin, you were talking about the interactions at the dinner last night. If you're okay to keep talking about it, did you notice anything else?"

"I guess I'm all right talking. Okay, let's see." She swallowed. "Wes's daughter, Isadora? She wasn't very nice to Beverly at all."

"Is her last name Farnham?"

"Yes," Gin said.

"Why was she rude to her hostess?"

"Frankly, I think she's upset her daddy now has another heir. Which means she won't inherit everything when he goes. She's pretty spoiled, like she'd been given everything she'd ever wanted in life. An only child, or so she thought. Entitled. Said she works part-time at a dress shop in Falmouth. What's it called? Macbeth's?"

"Maxine's, I think. Not that I shop there." I rolled my eyes. A high-end clothing shop wasn't exactly my style or in my modest budget.

"Yeah, me neither. And then there's Ron Ruchart, the grandson. Tats up one arm and down the next. He works at Game's Up here in town but seems kind of sketchy."

"Interesting group."

"Probably the worst part of the dinner was how rude Beverly was to me." Gin grimaced. "She had the nerve to insult me for being a candy maker."

"At a dinner party? You're kidding."

"I'm not. Eli and I left soon after."

"What did she say to you?"

"We were having an amazing chocolate mousse and little glasses of port. She was rude to Eli in the same breath. She said she couldn't believe he would replace her daughter with a candy cane, and she looked right at me when she said candy cane. I told her I made all kinds of high-quality chocolates and saltwater taffy. In fact, I had brought her a box as a hostess gift. She sniffed and said something about owning a candy shop not being much of a career. I guess her sainted daughter was a doctor."

"Geez." I shook my head. "Did you put all that in your report, Gin?"

She wrinkled her nose. "No, not that part."

"You're going to need to tell Lincoln, you know." I waited until she nodded before going on. "So Victoria asked you about Beverly's intoxication and her alcohol consumption."

Gin popped in the last bite of her Danish and swallowed before answering. "It's hard to tell, you know? I mean, she could have been drinking Scotch all afternoon before we arrived as far as I know. She served Manhattans before dinner, we were offered lots of wine with the meal, and everybody finished off with sweet liqueurs afterward. I had only a small glass of each, myself. With our busy season, the last thing I need is to be hung over in the morning."

Victoria hadn't seemed happy at the news that now-dead Beverly had hosted a dinner party last night, and she'd hinted an unnatural death was a possibility. What if the chief was right? Almost anyone—barring Gin, of course—could have slipped Beverly some poison in her drink or food. Maybe Victoria thought Gin had poisoned the box of candy. I shook off the thought. Beverly's death was way too fresh for me to be dwelling on the idea of murder.

Gin stood. "It's time for me to get to my shop, body or no body."

Her words were brave, but her posture and expression? Not so much.

Chapter Seven

What with body finding and breakfast at the bakery, I wasn't as prompt as usual—that is, early—opening Mac's Bikes. I'd hung out the OPEN flag a few minutes before nine o'clock when Orlean strolled up. She often arrived late, so I guessed we canceled each other out this morning.

"I oughta have Bev's bike done this morning, long's there aren't any fires to put out." Orlean bent to stash her lunch bag in our mini fridge. "Cleared the queue sooner than I expected yesterday."

I cringed inside. My mechanic was the only person I'd seen get along with Beverly Ruchart. The now-late Beverly Ruchart. Orlean wouldn't have heard the news, and I had to tell her before she learned about Beverly's death from someone else.

"I'm afraid I have some bad news about Bev," I said in a soft voice.

Orlean straightened slowly. "What bad news?"

"Beverly, um, passed away this morning." Or last night, I supposed. "Gin found her next to the clinic, the one by Salty Taffy's."

Orlean's eyes widened. She sank into one of three chairs in our tiny employee break room. "Are you kidding me? She can't be dead. She brought her bike in yesterday. Me and her, we were working on a project together." She planted her hands on her knees and wagged her head back and forth. "It can't be. Must be a mistake."

I laid my hand on her shoulder. "I'm really sorry, Orlean. I know you liked each other, and . . ." I let my voice trail off. I was about to say something about how nice Beverly had been to Orlean, but stopped when I realized it might sound condescending. Saying such a thing only made sense in contrast to how Beverly had treated nearly everyone else. And we didn't need to go into that. At all.

"I realize she rubbed a lot of people wrong," Orlean whispered. "But Bev was a decent human being when you got right down to it. I'm real sorry she's gone." Her voice wobbled on her last words, but she twisted away from my hand. She sniffed and squared her shoulders. "Want me to go ahead with her tune-up?"

True to character every time, Orlean was. I was the one who didn't know the answer.

"I don't really know. Why don't you wait until we hear more about the situation?"

Orlean jumped right back to her normal unemotional self. "The situation?" She lifted a shoulder and dropped it. "She's dead and that's the situation. We have plenty of other work. I'll leave her bike in the storage shed." She slipped into a repair apron and turned her back on me.

Even though her hands shook as Orlean tied the apron at her waist, I didn't offer any more physical comfort. It simply wasn't how she and I operated. I headed over to the cash register to finish the opening checklist. Nothing like checking an item off a list to make a woman feel like everything is right with the world. Everything was definitely not right with the world today, of course, but doing things in order comforted me.

News traveled fast when Main Street was half a mile long. And it wasn't only locals who stopped into my shop hoping for a bit of gossip. Four buff twenty-somethings in neon yellow and pink bike shirts clomped in at about nine thirty. One was a woman with curly dark hair, big brown eyes, and not an ounce of fat on her.

She approached the counter. "Miss, we heard a woman was found dead in town this morning. Is it true?"

"I'm afraid it is," I said.

"Everything happens for a loving reason," she offered, with a sweet, confident smile. "We're all on the blessed cycle of life."

Really? What did she know about Beverly and the reasons she died? I swallowed down my flare of ire. "Can I help you with something?" I asked, rather than querying her about where she got off thinking she knew the universal truths of life and death. *Down, Mac,* I cautioned myself. I was clearly still on edge from finding Beverly dead only a few hours earlier.

A light-haired man from the group approached and slung his arm around the pontificator's shoulders. "Yo, sis, take it easy." He had power thighs under his black shorts and a three-day rusty-colored beard that seemed popular among the twenty-something set. To me, an ancient thirty-six, it always looked like men forgot—or neglected—to shave.

Something about the two cyclists' eyes and their smiles made me think they were actually sister and brother, although their coloring was different. This new one seemed the older of the two.

"We're riding from Maine to Washington, DC, ma'am," Light Hair said with a smile. "Wondering if our bikes could get tune-ups today while we hit the beach."

I smiled back. "I'm pretty sure that's fine. Check with my mechanic in the repair side, okay?" I pointed the way.

The sister headed toward Orlean. Her brother lowered his voice. "Sorry if my sister's cycle-of-life beliefs got in the way of offering her sympathies. This is a small town. I'm sure you must have known the deceased. It can't be easy."

"Thank you. It isn't. I didn't know her well, but she wasn't elderly and I hope she went peacefully."

"I hope so, too. I'm sorry for your loss."

"Thank you so much."

He dipped his head and murmured something under his breath.

I didn't catch what he said but suspected it was a prayer of some kind.

Derrick hurried in for work just ahead of a family of six who made a beeline for the rental bikes.

"Excuse me," I said. "Duty calls."

Chapter Eight

It was one thing after another for the next hour. The foursome left their bikes for the day, saying they were catching an Uber. I sold a youth bicycle for a grandson's tenth birthday and fended off yet another inquiry about Beverly's death. Derrick handled a steady stream of rental customers. I peered into the repair side at around eleven to see Orlean wiping a tear from her eye before tightening a bolt. I wished I had some way to comfort her.

I'd finished taking a long-delayed restroom break when Florence Wolanski hurried in. She gestured toward the open back door. I checked the shop. No new customers chomped at the bit, so I followed her out.

"A body?" she asked. "You and Gin found a body? What has Westham become, Cabot Cove?"

Flo, head honcho of the Westham Public Library, was normally a matter-of-fact kind of person. Right now her excitement struck me as a little over the top. Her eyes were bright, her spiked white hair was extra spiky, and she nearly bounced on her heels.

"Chill, Flo. Beverly probably just had a heart attack."

"That's what you think? Then why is State Police Detective Lincoln Haskins over at Salty Taffy's questioning Gin?"

I groaned. "He is?"

"Yes, he's probably headed here next." She lowered her voice and her expression grew more serious. "So what did the body look like? Did you see a weapon? Was there blood?"

I pictured the sight of Beverly lying on the sidewalk. "She was just . . . dead. No weapon, no blood. I know she had heart issues. I'm positive that's all it was." Except I wasn't quite.

"I wouldn't be so sure. Listen, we need an emergency Cozy Capers meeting tonight."

"But it's only Monday. I haven't finished this week's book yet." Normally we met later in the week.

"No, silly. To talk about the suspicious death. I'll clear it with Derrick."

I shook my head. "Haskins isn't going to want our help. He didn't last time, either. And, anyway, it hasn't been identified as a homicide." *Yet?*

"We don't have to help. But we can at least talk about it." She paced out to the picnic table and back. "I'm going to send a group e-mail about a meeting. You don't have to come if you don't want to."

"Whatever." I saw Derrick stick his head out the door and wave to me. "Flo, I have to go. The shop is really busy this week."

"I have to run, too. I'll give Derrick a call later. If you

hear anything, let me know." She headed around the side of the building toward the street.

"I will," I murmured. With any luck, there wouldn't be anything to hear except a conclusion of a natural death.

And yet, as soon as I reentered the shop, I was greeted with the sight of Detective Lincoln Haskins. The big man wore his trademark flowered shirt untucked over light-colored khakis. It wasn't quite a loud Hawaiian garment, but it still projected a casual air. Very much the beach-detective style. I took another look. Lincoln had confided a couple of months ago his doctor had him on a heart-healthy diet, and in fact he had slimmed down noticeably.

"Good morning, Lincoln." I smiled and extended my hand. I'd eventually gotten on a first-name basis with him. I wasn't quite sure being so familiar with a state po-lice detective was a good thing, but informality suited me. "Let me guess. You're not here to buy a new bicy-cle."

His big, meaty hand could have held two of mine. "I'm afraid not, Mac. Would you have a few minutes to chat pri-vately?" His dark eyes gazed somberly down at me.

"Let me check." I headed over to Derrick. "I need a few more minutes off. You good?"

My half brother was also a big man, his six-two almost matching Haskins, who was about six foot three, although Derrick's coloring was light, where half-Wampanoag Has-kins's hair and eyes were dark.

Derrick frowned. "I'm good, but why is the detective here?"

Ouch. I hadn't had a chance to tell Derrick of Gin's and my early-morning find.

"I heard a customer talking about a body," Derrick

said. "Please don't tell me you're involved in another murder, Mac."

"I'm sorry. We've been so busy this morning I didn't find a free minute to tell you. I hope it's not murder, but Gin and I did find a body this morning. It was Beverly Ruchart."

His eyes widened. "She brings her bike in for tune-ups. Brought, I mean."

"Exactly. But it was probably a heart attack, not a homicide." I felt like a scratched CD, stuttering through the same phrase over and over.

"Right." He looked over my shoulder and murmured, "Lincoln Haskins doesn't investigate heart attacks." A couple holding hands approached. "Anyway, yeah, go," Derrick said. He turned to the couple. "Can I help you folks?"

"Follow me," I said to Haskins as I headed back outside and sat at the table. "Déjà vu, right?" We'd sat here and discussed Jake Lacey's murder only two months ago.

He sat across from me. "I've just spoken with Ms. Malloy about the discovery of Ms. Ruchart, but I'd like to hear your version of it, too. I'm the lead investigator again."

"We were both interviewed and signed statements, you know, Detective."

He sighed. "I know. But sometimes my chatting with a person can reveal bits of information someone else doesn't ask for."

"All right. Well, I went to meet Gin for our walk. She wasn't out front of Salty Taffy's, where we always meet up. I headed around to the far side to check out the clinic's flower garden. I saw Gin kneeling next to Beverly Ruchart's body on the walkway between her shop and the clinic."

"You were acquainted with the deceased?"

"A little. She brought her bike here for servicing. And on Saturday I was at my father's place when my niece's puppy got loose. Beverly brought him back and was rather upset about the little guy digging in her gardens."

His eyebrows went up. "I hadn't heard about that. Had you witnessed Ms. Ruchart being difficult about anything else?"

"Yes, she was unhappy about what she called the riff-raff who are our clientele at the soup kitchen and food pantry. She didn't have much sympathy for the many homeless and unemployed among us."

"I see."

Chickadees flitted and buzzed in the big swamp oak shading us. Three noisy motorcycles putted by out on the street. On the sidewalk a thin, dark-haired man stared intently at the detective. When the man saw me watching him, he hurried on.

"Det—I mean, Lincoln, I know Beverly had heart issues. She told me her cardiologist wanted her to get a lot of exercise, which was why she biked every day. Isn't it possible her death was from heart failure?"

"The autopsy won't be done until tomorrow morning first thing, but the medical examiner thought she detected something suspicious in the way the body looked. As to your question, yes, it's certainly possible the deceased's heart gave out. You must know we have to investigate the manner of death from all angles. Ms. Ruchart sounds like she might have made more than one enemy. And she was wealthy to boot, so someone will inherit a near fortune."

"Her grandson, Ron?"

"We have a call in to her lawyer. These are all pieces of the investigation. Can you think of anything else I need to know?"

I blinked, thinking. "No, not really."

"All right. You know to call me if something occurs to you or you learn anything." He extricated himself from the picnic table. "I need to move on. As I cautioned you earlier in the summer, please leave the detective work to the detectives. And inform your book group friends of same."

Exactly what I'd told Flo a few minutes earlier.

Lincoln's face looked heavy with the weight of solving an unattended and possibly suspicious death. He smiled, but it didn't go far.

Chapter Nine

Business slowed at about two o'clock that afternoon. "I'm going to the bank," I called to Derrick and Orlean in the two sides of the store, which joined in the middle. I needed to deposit the cash from the weekend.

Orlean merely raised a hand in acknowledgment.

"Good," Derrick said. "Don't be too long, okay? Remember, I have an appointment at Cokey's school at three."

"Right. Thanks for reminding me." Cokey had turned five in July and was entering kindergarten in a few weeks. Derrick was going to meet with somebody at school to make sure they knew he was a single dad and that my parents did a lot of Cokey's after-school care. I didn't know what else he wanted to discuss. Cokey was super bright and didn't have any behavioral issues, so I doubted she needed an individualized education plan. But she did sometimes have sad spells when she missed her French mother. Cokey had lived with her mom in France until last year, when Derrick's ex said she didn't want to raise her daughter any longer. We all did our best to surround the little girl with love and support. But her mom didn't even call Cokey or video chat with her, and she sent Derrick an e-mail to read to the little girl only every few months. Cokey was obviously hurt at having the bond with her mother cut. It wasn't easy to heal from, but my niece was pretty much the definition of the resilience that many kids had to muster.

I removed all the cash from the little safe in my office and counted it twice. I zipped it into a bank bag, slung on my EpiPen bag over my Mac's Bikes polo shirt, and headed out down the main drag otherwise known as Main Street. Westham was your classic walkable town. Sure, if you wanted to do a big grocery run, the supermarket was a little far to reach on foot, as was the big box hardware store two towns distant. For all my daily needs, nothing was more than a few blocks away. We had banks and a bookstore. A liquor store and an old-style drugstore. A locally owned hardware store and a library. Tim's bakery, of course, and Gin's candy shop. Even a small market surprisingly well stocked with fresh produce, good coffee, and organic dairy products.

Tourists obviously liked the town, too. Even in full August a sea breeze often cooled the sun-filled air, and this afternoon was no exception. Summer people in shorts and T-shirts strolled the sidewalks as they window-shopped, licked ice-cream cones, or carried bags of souvenirs back to their lodgings. Most stores flew colorful flags that rustled in the moving air. A gull cried from atop a lamppost.

But today the perfect weather didn't seem so ideal. I pictured tourists grimacing as they were forced to step around the police tape next to the taffy shop. How could a bigger-than-life personality like Beverly be alive one day and dead the next? And if someone had killed her, that someone could be any one of these pedestrians. The driver of a black car passing. A cyclist whirring by, head down. Even a store owner. I shivered despite the temperature.

As I neared the bank, I slowed in front of Game's Up, the game store where Gin had said Ron Ruchart worked. Surely he wouldn't be in today with his grandmother newly deceased, but there was a chance he'd be working. I'd never met him, never even been in the game store. A skinny man barely taller than I was emerged from the shop. He smiled at me, showing a silver tooth under a scraggly dark mustache. I stepped toward the entrance but instead of holding the door, he let it go and scurried away like a rat. *Nice.*

Inside was a game lover's paradise. Board games and card games filled the shelves. I spied vintage favorites like Clue, Risk, and Monopoly, but also boxes with names like Wise and Otherwise, Pictionary, Farkle, and Code Names. I proceeded farther in to find a table topped with a contoured landscape, right down to miniature trees, and lines of toy soldiers in blue and gray lined up opposite the other in what looked like a Civil War battle scene.

"Can I help you?" A young man in a Darth Vader T-shirt greeted me from behind the counter on the far wall. He looked back at the screen in front of him. Both arms were covered with colored ink that rippled as he thumbed a game controller. His straight dark hair lay lank on his head, and he had an oddly thin nose. On the counter next to his screen lay a light-gray cat in a Sphinx pose, eyes closed but clearly alert. Its ears stuck out to the sides.

"Good afternoon." I extended my hand to shake. "I'm Mac Almeida. I own Mac's Bikes down the street. I don't think we've met."

He set down the controller and stood to shake my hand. He was no taller than me. "Nice to meet you, Mac. I'm Ron Ruchart. Can I interest you in a game?"

Oops. I thought quickly. "My father's birthday is coming up. He's a big family man. What games can a group of all ages play?" What was Ron doing at work? He certainly wasn't acting sad.

Ron led me to the front of the store and pointed to a square box labeled Wise and Otherwise. "A lot of families like this. It has the beginnings of proverbs from around the world on the front of the cards. Everybody has to make up the end of the proverb except the person with the card, who has the real ending. Everybody writes down their endings and reads them out loud, and the players have to guess which the authentic one is."

I smiled. "Wise and Otherwise sounds perfect." I doubted Cokey could play yet, because she was still an early reader, but she'd be able to in a year or two.

He laid his hand on the box, but paused, gazing at it. "My mom and I used to play, back before . . ." His voice trailed off.

Before she died, certainly. Did he mean before she met Eli?

He almost imperceptibly shook himself and slid the box off the shelf. I followed him to the cash register.

"Is he the store cat?" I asked, keeping my distance from the animal. I was wildly allergic to most dogs and to a hundred percent of cats.

"Yeah." Ron grinned and stroked the cat. "His name's Yoda. Kinda looks like him, don't you think? I really dig cats. They're wicked smart and super independent. Aren't ya, Yo?" He raised his voice into a cartoony tone. "Smart am I."

"He does resemble Yoda." I swallowed. "Ron, I'm very sorry for the loss of your grandmother."

He jerked back as if I'd hit him. "How do you know about her?" His mouth turned down and he blinked hard.

"I'm so sorry if I upset you. I, um, was there when she was found this morning."

He stared at me for a moment. "You and Gin, the lady from the taffy shop. I met her for the first time last night. The cops came this morning and told me Grandma was found dead." He sniffed.

"Yes," I said. "She was a regular customer at my bike shop."

"Yeah, she loved riding her bike." His smile was a sad one.

"I'm surprised you're at work. Wouldn't they give you time off?"

He shrugged. "The boss is out of town and I'm the only employee. It's okay. Keeps my mind off the news." His gaze darted to the screen next to him, like he wanted to get back to his video game.

"What do I owe you? I'll let you get back to whatever you were doing."

"Thanks." He rang up the proverb game and handed me my change. "At least I won't have to be here much longer. Grandma left me everything."

"That's amazing." It was. Beverly's house and prop-erty must be worth well over a million dollars, and I expected she probably had some decent investments elsewhere, too. I did wonder how he knew he inherited. Maybe Beverly had told him.

He leaned closer. "I think my stepdad killed her. He hated my grandma when my mom was alive. I'm sure he poisoned Grandma to get back at her."

"Really?" Tim's friend Eli? Gin's new boyfriend? *Yikes*.

He straightened again. "Oh, yeah. No doubt. And I told the cop as much. Eli Tubin is one guy to, like, not let out of your sight."

Chapter Ten

I walked slowly to the bank. What an odd bird Ron was. He'd seemed broken up about his grandmother's death, and he'd ended by speculating about Eli. And about poison. By the time I pulled open the door, Ron had already returned to his game in progress. Had he been pretending his grief? I blew out a breath and straightened my shoulders. Speculating about someone I didn't know was futile.

After I made my deposit, I checked my watch, then hurried back along the sidewalk to Cape King Liquors, dodging strolling, taffy-eating tourists as I went. My friend Zane King ran the liquor store and the distillery behind it. He was a book group member, and since I wanted to buy a bottle of wine for the meeting, I could also give him a heads-up about tonight's unbook gathering. I still had twenty minutes to get back to my shop before Derrick needed to leave.

The door chimed a classic *ding-dong* when I pushed it open. "Hey, Zane." I greeted the tall, thin distiller, who was straightening bottles of his own Z&S bourbon on a shelf.

The air-conditioning in here was a cool contrast to the sunny afternoon outside. A half-dozen customers browsed the liquors and wines, and Zane's summer employee rang up a purchase.

"Mac, honey. Come give us a kiss." He hurried toward me and held out his arms. He wore a pink Oxford shirt, its sleeves carefully rolled up, tucked into tight jeans with cuffs. No socks with his boat shoes, as always.

Smiling, I shook my head at his characteristic over-the-top affection but bussed his cheek, anyway. "Looks like business is good."

"Been steady. You?"

"Same here. Some days we barely keep up. It's all good."

"Can I help you find something? My new batch of King's Bounty rum is on the shelves. It's a killer summer drink with pineapple juice, tonic water, and a touch of lime."

"I love pineapple juice. Sure, I'll get a bottle of the rum. Plus, I need some wine." I followed him to where he stocked rum and accepted the bottle he handed me.

"What kind of wine? Red or white?" he asked.

"I think a Pinot Gris. I'll have time to chill it before this evening." I wrapped my arms around myself. The initial cool of the AC was now too cold for my short-sleeved shirt and shorts.

"Good choice."

We went around the ends of two sections and, after some discussion, I ended up with a bottle of Oregon wine.

"Listen, did Flo tell you we're meeting tonight?" I asked.

He made an O with his lips, widened his eyes, and nodded. "Because of the, you know, what you and Gin found this morning."

"Exactly." I wrinkled my nose. "I think it's premature, but there's no stopping Flo. That woman's a force of nature."

"Premature because . . . ?"

"Well, they haven't—" I cut myself off and glanced around to make sure nobody was listening. I lowered my voice to a whisper. "Because they haven't determined how she died."

He whispered, too. "I know of one person who hated Beverly Ruchart."

"Who?"

"There's a waitress named Sofia who works at Jimmy's Harborside. She's a Russian girl, tall and blonde. Beverly was rude to her more than once. Right out in public." He shook his head. "It was ridiculous. Sofia hadn't done anything wrong, not that I saw."

"From what I've heard so far today, Beverly rubbed a lot of people the wrong way." I glanced at the back wall, where a stunning small quilt hung. It pictured bottles of wine, whiskey, and rum in vibrant colors—burgundy, gold, amber, green—with a vase of flowers in the same hues. "Is the hanging one of yours?" I asked him.

Zane beamed. "It's my newest quilt. Do you like it?"

"It's gorgeous. Really."

"Thanks." He bounced on his heels like a little boy. "It won Best of Show at the Bayberry Quilters annual show. That's the guild I belong to."

"Keep up the good work, my friend." I patted him on the arm.

"I will, of course. It's so calming to sit and stitch in the evenings."

"I don't even know how to sew on a button." I laughed. "I'd better pay and get back to my shop. See you tonight, then."

Chapter Eleven

By six o'clock I was on the little couch in my little house, feet up, sipping the drink Zane had recommended. It was definitely a perfect summer drink, with the rum, tonic water, and lime balancing out the sweetness of the pineapple juice. The only thing missing was a paper umbrella in my glass. I'd thrown together a smoked turkey and Brie sandwich on sourdough, with a thick slice of ripe farm tomato and a smear of basil pesto in place of mayonnaise for my dinner. I munched it as Belle sat on the back of the couch murmuring comments about snacks and what a good girl she was.

I loved this house. I'd moved in after I came back to Westham last year. My years working in finance in Boston had resulted in some excellent investments, and when I'd returned home from a few years abroad, I had the funds to buy the bike shop and the tiny house behind it. It was like living on a boat except it didn't rock underneath me. The builder had included clever storage options in every nook and cranny, essential for someone like me who needed my life tidy. The old adage "a place for everything and everything in its place" was pretty much my prime operating principle. The super-efficient kitchen at the other end of the space from the sitting area featured pullouts for storage and a clever hinged top for the stove. The top folded down over the stove for more workspace and folded open when I used the burners, which also added temporary counter space. It was perfect for someone like me who rarely actually cooked anything.

I had a comfortable sitting area with room for a bookshelf and a place for Belle's cage and roost. An efficient bathroom and shower were built into one wall, and above and behind my head was the sleeping loft, with steps leading up to it. What more could a woman want?

I yawned between bites.

"Time for bed, Mac," Belle said. "Time for bed."

She was so smart. I laughed. "No, it's not time for bed. But I had a really long day, and it's not over yet." I supposed I could skip the meeting at Flo's, but I was curious about what the group members might know about Beverly and her various dinner guests. Beverly. The memory of her lifeless face on the path haunted me. Not literally, of course. I was far too logical of a person to believe in dead people's souls floating around bothering people. Still, her image kept popping up unbidden.

I swallowed the last morsel of sandwich and reached for my iPad. Maybe by now Lincoln Haskins and his investigators had figured out what killed Beverly. No, he'd said the autopsy wouldn't be done until tomorrow. I clicked through to the local news station, anyway. Bingo—video of a press conference from an hour ago, with the detective at the microphones. Victoria stood to one side and the lead town selectman to the other. Westham didn't have a mayor but governed with selectmen—two of whom were women—and town meetings.

"Yes, we are following up all leads," Lincoln said in response to a question. "We have reason to believe the death was a suspicious one, and I can't share any details beyond that." He stepped back and Victoria replaced him at the lectern.

"We welcome any information relating to the deceased. If you saw something out of the ordinary or witnessed a suspicious act, please call our hotline." She rattled off the number and it also appeared on the screen. A reporter called out a question, but Victoria held up a hand. "That's all we have for now. Thank you for your time." She and Lincoln walked offscreen.

Beverly's death was looking a lot more like a homicide. My phone vibrated on the end table at my elbow. I smiled to see Tim's name.

After we greeted each other, he said, "I wanted to hear how you're doing, you and Gin. It must have been such a shock to come across a dead woman this morning."

"Definitely."

"And it was the second time for you. How are you, hon?"

"Right now I'm beat, and I can't stop thinking about poor Beverly. Flo called a book group meeting for tonight to talk through the suspects."

"The suspects? Was it murder?"

"I caught a press conference online where Lincoln Haskins said they have reason to believe the death was a suspicious one. So, yeah, it's looking like they're going to call it a homicide."

"Homicide," Belle said. "Homicide. Cheese it, call the cops!"

"Was that Belle?" Tim asked, a laugh in his voice.

"Who else?"

"Hi, handsome!" Belle wolf-whistled. "Homicide, homicide, homicide," she muttered. "Cheese it. Call the cops!"

"I guess homicide is her new favorite word, unfortunately." I smiled at her, despite her scrambled command. The old shows had people saying, "Cheese it, here come the cops," didn't they?

"Two murders in one summer," he said. "Kind of freaky, no?"

"I'll say." It was freaky, for sure.

"Do you want company after book group? I'd be happy to come over and provide comfort."

"I would, and it's very sweet of you to offer, but I think I'm going to be beat by the time I get home. How about tomorrow night instead?"

He paused before answering. "Sounds good. I can cook, or we can go out to eat." His voice was no longer smiling.

I sighed inwardly. I'd disappointed him. "I'm sorry, Tim."

Belle perked up. "Hi, handsome!" she squawked at the phone. "Give Belle a kiss!" She followed the demand with a wolf whistle.

Tim laughed. "Tell her I'll give her a kiss tomorrow. And you too. Love you, Mac."

"Love you." I disconnected, my gaze on the phone in my hand. I was one fortunate woman. I had a guy who was smart and caring and healthy and totally handsome. And I knew he wanted more. He wanted to marry and live together. He wanted to start a family. So why did I have this reluctance to do the same?

Chapter Twelve

I trudged up the stairs inside the empty first floor of the cylindrical lighthouse at a few minutes before seven, chilled wine in hand. Derrick was the caretaker for the privately owned structure, a former beacon of safety but now a historical building. The book group almost always met here so Derrick could be part of the group and not have to hire a babysitter or leave Cokey at my parents' place. My niece was a good sleeper and was normally already in dreamland before the meetings started.

But this wasn't a normal meeting. We weren't here to discuss the week's cozy mystery. Flo had summoned us to hash through what we knew about Beverly's death, Lincoln's caution notwithstanding.

Halfway up the stairs I glanced behind me at the sound of the door opening. Flo hurried in, followed by Norland Gifford, our previous chief of police, now retired and a regular at book group. We greeted one another and made our way up and into Derrick's living room, where Gin, Zane, and Tulia, a congenial lobster shack owner, sat chatting. A flying bundle of pink threw herself at me.

"Titi Mac, tell Daddy I'm big enough to stay up. It's not nighttime yet."

I picked her up and hugged her before setting her down. She smelled deliciously of soap, toothpaste, and little girl. Derrick shook his head from across the room.

"Listen, Cokester," I began. "This is a grown-ups' meeting. Let's go read a book before you fall asleep, okay?"

She set her fists on her hips but cocked her head. "Which book?"

"*Blueberries for Sal*." I knew the story about a little girl picking wild blueberries in Maine with her mother was Cokey's favorite, with one small modification.

"It's Blueberries for Cokey," she protested.

"You got it. Now go say good night to Daddy." I set the bottle of wine I'd brought on the table. "I'll be back in a couple of minutes," I said to the room.

Better I get Cokey to sleep now and miss the start of the discussion than have her lingering and listening. We headed into her pink-and-white bedroom, where a lacy curtain flapped gently in the evening breeze. I shut the door to the quiet conversation behind me. By the end of the picture book, replacing the name of the girl in the book with Cokey every time, my niece's eyes were heavy. Her worn, soft, stuffed Dalmatian puppy was nestled next to her cheek.

"Nighty night, favorite niece." I kissed her forehead.

"Ni-night, favorite *titi*," she murmured, turning on her side.

I switched on the scallop-shell night-light in the corner, which gave off a pale-pink glow, and turned off her bedside lamp. I pulled the door almost shut behind me, giving a thumbs-up to Derrick. Gin, her face still pale, waved me to a spot on the couch between her and Tulia.

"Poured you a glass," Gin said, pointing to a full wineglass on the coffee table. Her finger shook as she gestured.

"Thanks." I picked up the drink and slid into the middle seat of the couch. The cool wine went down exactly right.

"You're still shook up, aren't you?" I murmured to Gin.

She nodded without speaking, staring at her own glass.

I rubbed her upper arm with mine. "We'll get through this, girlfriend."

"Shall we get started?" Flo addressed everyone.

I raised my hand. "First, I want to go on the record by saying we don't yet know for sure if it's a homicide or if Beverly died of natural causes," I began. "That said, Detective Haskins has interviewed both Gin and me. He's on the case, and he told me there are signs it might be a homicide. Before I came here I saw a news conference. Haskins said signs are leading to them treating it as a suspicious death. No idea what those signs are, of course."

"Right, right." Flo's tone was impatient.

"Hang on, Flo." I gestured for her to stop. "He also made it very clear he doesn't want this group getting involved in his investigation."

"And he's absolutely correct," Norland chimed in. "They can't have amateurs mucking around with witnesses and suspects."

"All we're doing is talking," Derrick said.

"Of course," Zane said. "But it doesn't hurt to know what's going on. We all have a stake in this town. If her death was murder, putting the bad guy behind bars has to be everyone's priority."

"You're right," Gin said. "Those of us with businesses have a financial interest in keeping the town safe. Plus Flo at the library, you, Derrick with Cokey, and Norland with your grandkids, everybody wants a town where we don't have to worry about a killer walking around free."

"Okay to go on?" Flo checked with each of us and waited until she'd gotten a unanimity of nods. "We all know Gin and Mac found Beverly Ruchart dead next to the clinic this morning, and I understand Gin was at a dinner party last night at Ms. Ruchart's house. Gin, why don't you tell us what went on at the dinner?"

I listened with one ear as Gin went over again what she'd told me this morning at the bakery about the dinner.

"You brought her chocolates?" Norland stroked his chin.

"Yes. I didn't see her open them, though."

"If it was a homicide, you can believe they're going to test those candies for poison," Norland said.

Gin grimaced but continued. After she mentioned Ron Ruchart, I raised an index finger.

She paused. "Yes, Mac?"

"I dropped by the gaming shop where he works this afternoon."

Tulia twisted her head to look at me. "He wasn't there, was he?"

"He was," I confirmed.

"The same day his grandmother was found dead? It must not have affected him much. When my grandma died, I was in mourning for weeks." Tulia, a member of the Mashpee Wampanoag Tribe, frowned and shook her head. "We revere our elders."

"He definitely didn't seem weepy or down," I said. "He told me his boss was out of town and somebody had to keep the store open. He was playing a video game when I walked in."

"Did you learn anything from him?" Flo looked up from the yellow legal pad where she was taking notes.

"He said he was the sole heir," I said. "And that he thought Eli Tubin poisoned his grandmother."

"What?" Gin twisted to look at me. "That's crazy!"

"Whoa," Norland said. "Who is Eli again?"

"He's actually Ron's stepfather," Gin said. "Eli married Ron's mother when he was in high school. She died several years ago. I'm, uh, dating Eli, which is why I was at the dinner." Gin blushed.

"Ron said Eli always hated his mother-in-law," I added.

"Has Eli said anything to you about Beverly to indicate he hated her?" Derrick asked Gin.

"No." She crossed her arms. "Shall I finish about the dinner?"

"Please," Flo said.

The microwave dinged from the kitchen. Derrick rose and brought back a bowl brimming with popcorn, plus a stack of small bowls. "Sorry the snacks aren't more elaborate. I ran out of time today."

I'd already helped myself to a slice of sharp cheddar and a cracker, and a bowl of grapes also sat on the round coffee table in front of us. "Hey, this is fine," I said. "Don't apologize."

He took a sip from his can of ginger ale. "I'm trying, Mac." He had a habit of over-apologizing, and I'd been working with him to change the habit.

"So Wes Farnham was there, too, and his daughter, Isadora," Gin went on. "I'm not really sure why she went, because she didn't seem to like Beverly much." Gin explained to the group about how Beverly had helped Wes find his birth son and said Isadora was upset about him doing so.

"Isadora," Norland said, stroking his chin again. "My wife used to talk about someone with that name. An Isadora works at the dress shop in Falmouth, where Maireth loved to shop." His eyes grew sad, and no wonder. His wife had died the previous year.

"Beverly also had some nasty things to say about somebody named Sofia, Ron's girlfriend," Gin added.

Ron's girlfriend?

Zane, who had been munching popcorn, raised his hand. He finished chewing and swallowed. "I was telling Mac earlier today I know a Sofia who waitresses at Jimmy's Harborside. Stephen and I go there a lot. Tall, blonde Russian girl."

"That might be her. Beverly referred to her as foreign trash or some other insult," Gin said.

"Where is Stephen, anyway?" I asked Zane. Stephen Duke, Zane's husband, was Westham's town clerk.

"At the Monday night selectman's meeting. He's out every Monday night."

Book group had been meeting on Thursday evenings recently, partly to accommodate Stephen.

"Anyway," Zane went on, "we heard Beverly insult Sofia in public more than once. I can go back and talk to her."

Flo gazed at her pad for a moment. She looked up and surveyed the room. "We have a hand's worth of people who might have wanted Beverly Ruchart dead." She ticked names and reasons off on her fingers. "Ron inherits."

"So he says, anyway," I pointed out. "He could be just assuming he gets Grandma's estate."

"Granted," Flo said. "Then there's Isadora with her anger about the potential of losing half her own inheritance."

"I've met an Isadora." Derrick gazed over my head out the window as if he was thinking. "She always seemed to wear expensive-looking things."

"Where did you meet her?" I asked.

"At an, uh . . ." Derrick drew out the hesitation like he'd just changed his mind about revealing where. "Around town," he finally finished. "It's not a very common name."

I looked at him. He might have met her at an Alcoholics Anonymous meeting and realized he shouldn't reveal it. He'd told me that the identities of those who attended AA meetings, as well as what they talked about, were supposed to be kept strictly confidential.

Flo went on. "We also have Eli, who might or might not have hated Beverly."

"I know he wouldn't kill anyone," Gin protested.

She glanced at me for backup, but I'd only met the guy once. I flipped my hands open. I couldn't help her.

"We're only brainstorming here, Gin," Flo said. "This Sofia is a possibility. She was publicly belittled by the victim and is dating Ron. Anybody else?"

Gin grimaced. "I'm afraid the detective thinks I might have killed her."

"What?" Tulia leaned around me to gaze at Gin. "Why?"

"I told him she was rude to me at the dinner. Eli and I left earlier than we'd planned. I can't tell you how much of a relief it was to get out of there."

"If everybody killed people who were rude to them, it would sure solve the overpopulation problem," Flo said in a sarcastic tone.

"As if Gin would ever kill someone." Tulia made a tsking sound.

"Gin, you also mentioned Beverly acted really drunk last night," I said, "and that she said she wasn't feeling well."

"Somebody at the dinner probably poisoned her with a substance mimicking being intoxicated," Derrick said.

"Maybe. But what substance?" I asked. "What poison can do that?"

My brother lifted a shoulder. "I used to be an expert on being intoxicated. But I'm happy I'm not anymore, and I've never been an expert on poisons."

Gin wrinkled her nose. "After dinner Ron insisted on doing the dishes. He hadn't helped with anything else, and Beverly looked really surprised when he offered. Then Isadora joined him in the kitchen, which seemed completely unlike what I saw of her during dinner."

"Ron did mention poison this afternoon," I said. "Maybe the two were getting rid of the evidence?"

Gin frowned. "It's possible, right?"

"So, what are our action items?" Flo asked, pen poised. "Zane, you're going to ask questions at the restaurant."

Action items. I hadn't heard the term since I'd worked in high-power finance. Flo was a born manager. And she did run a good-size library, after all. She'd have to be.

"I can try to talk to Eli about Beverly," Gin offered. "Just to confirm he's in the clear."

"I'll research which poisons can make a person seem drunk and then kill them." Flo raised one eyebrow. "Head librarians have search talents and databases available like you wouldn't believe."

"I believe it." I'd seen her in action. "I'll go pay Isadora a visit in Falmouth."

"Noted." Flo jotted it down. "Let's meet again on Thursday. We can do a summary and then talk about the book, too."

"Listen, everybody, go lightly, okay?" I said. "If there's a real-life killer out there, we have to stay safe and not get his or her suspicions up." That was the last thing any of us needed.

Chapter Thirteen

Gin and I walked briskly along the Shining Sea Trail the next morning at seven thirty, our arms swinging, our strides matching. The sky was the color of the historical society building's slate roof, and the air was full of moisture. The salty, seaweedy scent of the tidal ponds was extra strong this morning.

"You didn't hear any news about Beverly this morning, did you?" I asked. I knew Gin always watched the television news when she got up in the morning.

"Nope, nothing new, that is. Some reporter was standing outside the clinic this morning. The camera person was filming the crime scene tape—real exciting—and the reporter said there were no new developments. I don't know why they bothered." She finally had some color back in her face, and her voice was normal, too.

"Lincoln had said they were going to do the autopsy

first thing this morning. I hope they find out what killed her." I swiped sweat from my neck.

"So, you're on a first-name basis with him now?" She glanced over at me.

"Yeah, he suggested it a couple of months ago. Fine with me. I guess we're getting to be old pals by now."

"Pals. Isn't that what Nancy Drew and her girlfriend George called each other?" Gin giggled.

"I think so." We strode in silence for a minute or two as we approached the bridge leading over an inland salt pond. "But seriously, I wonder if the group is going to be able to learn anything useful? What do you think?"

"I hope so. The last thing I want is Detective Haskins considering me a person of interest."

"Totally." A movement in the sky caught my eye. "Look, an osprey." I stopped and pointed at the majestic fish hawk with its white coloring and black elbows on the wings. As we watched, it landed with talons extended into a huge nest built on a platform twenty-five feet off the ground. "I love ospreys. There's something special about them. I always feel like it's a good omen to see one."

"You know there's, like, three or four of them out at Chapoquoit Beach."

I smiled. "Convenient, isn't it? I can get a dose of good omens whenever I need one."

"Did we learn anything new at the meeting last night?" Gin asked.

"I guess the only news for me was about Beverly being rude to Sofia." I watched as a flashy male bufflehead dove underwater. "Frankly, the only person who seemed to like Beverly was my mechanic, Orlean."

Gin laughed. "They seem like an odd couple."

"For sure. It was only two days ago Beverly brought her bike in. She and Orlean were talking genealogy together. It surprised me."

"Orlean keeps a lot under the hood, doesn't she?"

"Understatement of the century," I said. "She's a good egg and a great mechanic, though. I don't need her to be my best friend, too."

"You've got me for a bestie." She held up her hand for a high five. "You know, I think I mentioned Wes Farnham seemed to like Beverly, too."

I glanced over at her. "Like like, or they simply got along fine?"

"I got the feeling it was like like. He acted quite the gallant gentleman. Pulled Beverly's chair out, brought her flowers, doted on her every word. She seemed pleased about it."

"So he's either divorced or a widower," I mused.

"Widowed, I think."

"He's not much of a suspect if he was courting Beverly. Unless it was all an act to make people think he couldn't have killed her. Did you tell Lincoln about Wes?"

"No, it didn't occur to me." Gin wrinkled her nose. "I mean, I said he was at the dinner, but I didn't describe his behavior. It didn't seem important. You think I should tell him?"

"Probably, yeah. He might have already checked Wes out. If you call him, also tell him about Ron and Isadora doing the cleanup. Maybe he already knows, and maybe he's already searched Beverly's kitchen and trash, but it doesn't hurt to fill him in."

"I'll call him as soon as I get home."

We arrived at the spur leading out to the beach. "Go?" I asked.

"Go."

We'd been walking at a good clip, but now we speed-walked the trail extension out to the point, as we did most mornings. The spur ended in a parking lot overlooking the Westham Point beach.

Panting, I stopped when the water was in sight. "This humidity is a killer." I leaned over and set my hands on my knees. "It's hard to get a deep breath. I feel like I'm breathing underwater." I straightened, freeing my T-shirt from where it was plastered to my torso, and fanned the shirt to get some air circulating on my skin.

"I know." Gin was breathing hard, too.

The parking lot was surrounded by a waist-high, thick wooden railing, beyond which grew a ring of magenta *Rosa rugosa*, the fragrant scrubby beach roses. I leaned over them to inhale their scent. My reward was a buzzing sound followed by a sharp sting to my cheek. I let loose a long string of expletives as I fumbled in my little bag for an EpiPen.

"Mac, what happened?" Gin's eyes were wide. "What can I do?" She pulled her phone out of her pocket.

I didn't have time to answer. My throat was already swelling. I tore off the blue cap on the six-inch-long device and jammed the orange cylinder into my right thigh below the hem of my shorts. The needle stung, but I left it there for a count of ten. I yanked it out and plopped down to sitting, taking the longest, deepest breath I could, and another.

Gin squatted next to me. "Did you get stung?"

I nodded, pointing to my cheek. My throat was gradu-

ally opening again. My heart raced from the shot of epi-
nephrine. At least I was alive. I dug out the tiny container
of Benadryl I also carried in my bag and popped two into
my mouth. I tossed back my head, swallowing them dry.
It wasn't easy, but I had to do it.

"Should I call an ambulance?" Gin asked, concern
painting her face.

"No." I blew out a long breath. "I haven't been stung
in a long time." I touched the swelling on my cheek.
"Sorry for the alarm."

"I was worried about you. You moved so fast."

"I have to. Not last time, but the time before when I
was stung was when I realized I was allergic. Luckily I
wasn't alone and my roommate called nine-one-one. See
why I carry my little bag every time I go out?"

"Absolutely."

"I've rehearsed jabbing myself a zillion times, too."

"The shot must work really fast."

"It had better." I breathed slowly and deeply. "They
used to say one should go to the hospital after using the
EpiPen, but my Benadryl chaser should do the trick. Who
has time to go to the emergency room?"

"Are you sure?"

"I'm sure." I had a shop to run.

Chapter Fourteen

Even three hours later I was still feeling both shaky and wired from the EpiPen injection and the antihistamines, but I'd managed to walk home, shower, and open the shop on time. Business on the rental side had been light so far this morning. Maybe the heavy air made tourists want to stay inside an air-conditioned movie theater instead of physically exerting themselves on bicycles. Orlean was handling the repair side while I managed the rest of the store until Derrick got back from picking up a few things we needed in Bourne.

Mom and Abo Reba, my father's mother, strolled in together, looking as unlike each other as two women could get. Mom, with her flyaway graying blonde hair and light green eyes, was five foot six and dressed in a pastel-hued gauzy skirt. My eighty-year-old grandmother was a tiny woman with sparkling brown eyes, pale-brown skin, a multicolored beret on her head, and her signature hot-pink track suit, sans jacket today. Her pink Red Sox T-shirt had to be a child's size large.

"Mackenzie, I hear you had you a bit of excitement yesterday," Abo Reba said.

"It wasn't excitement so much as a terribly sad discovery." I leaned down to kiss her cheek.

"I'm sorry you had to go through such an experience again." Mom held out her arms for a quick hug.

"Me too. I felt even worse for Gin."

Abo Reba glanced around before beckoning for me to lean closer to her. "It was murder, wasn't it?" she whispered.

I shook my head. "I don't think they know yet, Abo Ree. But Detective Haskins is handling the investigation again, so it probably is."

"That darling Lincoln," my mother said. "Such a nice man."

I'd been surprised to learn a while ago that my mom knew the detective and had even danced with him at some function.

"It wouldn't shock me to learn that someone knocked off Beverly Ruchart, may her soul rest in peace," Abo Reba said. "That woman could make a saint lift the cleaver. I've never seen someone rub so many people the wrong way. Aren't I right, Astra?"

"I would agree," Mom said.

"Was she rude to you?" I asked my grandmother.

"To me?" She laughed her tinkly laugh. "She wouldn't dare. No, we talked roses and such. She quite enjoyed her garden."

"As long as a puppy wasn't digging in it," Mom said

in a wry tone. She wandered off to the section of the store where we kept the new bicycles.

"Did she ever talk about Ron?" I asked. "Her grandson?"

My grandmother rolled her eyes. "She most certainly did. Said he had a lot of debt, and that he was very poor at managing money. She didn't approve in the least."

"But she let him live with her."

"Yes. She was fond of him, of course. He was her only living relative, I do believe."

"Did you ever see them arguing or anything?" I asked.

"I can't say I did. Why do you ask?"

"I stopped into the game store where he works yesterday. He was there—the same day his grandmother died—and he barely seemed sad."

"Young people these days. I don't understand it."

"He also said he was inheriting Beverly's entire estate."

Abo Reba's eyebrows went way up. "I very much doubt that's true, Mac. Beverly may have made provisions for him, but she never would have left him her properties and her money. No, she did not care for how his wastrel ways resulted in his impecunity."

Leave it to the former English teacher to casually drop words like *wastrel* and *impecunity* into the same sentence. I smiled at her.

"Mac, honey." My mom headed back our way. "Reba and I have decided to begin a fitness regimen together, and we want you to sell us bikes and helmets and all."

My grandmother chimed in. "The works."

"The works?" My jaw dropped open. "You do?"

"Yes," Abo Reba said. "We thought it would be fun to

tool along the trail on bicycles and chat as we go. Except I think I'd better have a three-wheeler. I'm not getting any younger." She laughed again.

"Sounds like a plan. Come with me, ladies."

"And I think I'd prefer a bike like the model you rent out," my mom said. "You know, with the big, cushy seat and sitting upright. I'm not getting any younger, either."

It was true, she was sixty-three, but she always seemed more youthful than that to me.

"And a basket and a bell, exactly like we had when I was a child," Mom added.

"This yellow one is a seven speed. How does it look?" I pointed to a new vintage-style ladies' cruiser.

Mom pushed her fingers into the seat. "Perfect."

"They'll see you coming a mile away," Abo Reba said.

"And, Abo Ree, I do have an adult tricycle." I led her to the red three-wheeler in the corner. "It even has a little backrest on the seat. But I'm going to have to find you a much smaller frame. Even with the seat all the way down your feet won't reach the pedals."

"I like the basket in the back," Abo Reba said. "Please do order one for me, and in fire-engine red like the one over there. I want to be easily spotted, too. Can you put a rush on it? We want to get started right away."

"I'll call around the other shops in the area. Somebody up in Hyannis might have one in stock."

"What about the stretchy shorts all the cyclists wear?" Mom asked.

I wrinkled my nose "They do help, because they cushion your, you know, lady parts. Would you both wear them?"

"Of course, dear. It's part of the uniform. Right, Astra?" Abo Reba checked with my mom.

"Absolutely."

They were both full of excitement for their plan, picking out color-coordinated helmets, water bottles, and padded gloves. I loved these women. If, or more rightly, *when* we lost Abo Reba, like Tulia I would be in mourning for a good long time. Not like cavalier Ron, who apparently was in for a rude shock when Beverly's will was read.

Chapter Fifteen

I finished my ham and cheese sandwich out at the picnic table. I'd been monitoring my body all morning, but I didn't detect any more reaction from being stung. *Good*. I didn't need a health problem in my life this week. Or any time, for that matter. Wes Farnham popped his head out the back door.

"Your mechanic said I'd find you here."

I wiped my mouth, stood, and headed toward him. "How are you, Mr. Farnham?" I extended my hand.

He shook it heartily. "Now, now. None of this Mr. Farnham stuff. I'm Wes." He beamed, his florid skin curving into smile lines, his small eyes nearly disappearing.

"What can I help you with, Wes?"

"I'm dusting off my old bike. Now I have the place in Pocasset, I want to start riding again." He patted a thick midsection. "Need to do a little slimming down. Doctor's orders."

He was the third person today to launch a new fitness plan. "Sounds like a good idea. The trail is right there and it's a nice, level ride. So you want your ride checked out, tuned up?"

"The works. I think it needs new tires, too."

"Why don't you show me the bike?" I followed him around the side of the building to the parking area. A man's bicycle leaned against a black Mercedes convertible. "You weren't kidding about the dust." I laughed.

The bike was an old Peugeot with a white frame barely visible under a layer of dust. The chain was rusted, and both tires were flatter than the Shining Sea Trail.

"When's the last time you rode this?" I asked.

"Has to be twenty-five, thirty years ago. Before my daughter was born, certainly." He gazed at the bike. "Or should I just buy a new one?"

"It's up to you. We can absolutely clean it up. It'll take a few days, though. My mechanic has all the bikes from a big touring group coming in tomorrow for service."

The jovial expression disappeared, replaced with a downturned mouth and sad eyes. "There's no rush. I'm too late to ride with my lady love as I'd planned." He swiped away a tear. "She was the lady who died Monday right here in Westham, Beverly Ruchart. We were just getting started, she and I, on a bit of a later-in-life romance. And now it's over."

"I'm so very sorry for your loss, Wes." I was going to say more but shut my mouth instead. I didn't want to disturb him by telling him I had seen her dead.

"Thank you. I appreciate the sympathy, Mac. I'm not

sure why I told you. I haven't been able to discuss my feelings with anyone. My daughter didn't like her, and her grandson doesn't seem too broken up about her death, either." He pulled out a blue checked handkerchief and blew his nose. "It's only, well, you know, I worked hard all my life and didn't leave much time for relationships. Now I'm older, I see I no longer have forever. It's time to stop postponing what's truly important in life."

Which must have been why he first hired Beverly to find his birth son and then fell in love with her. The poor man.

"Well, I'll leave you to your work. I have to get back and meet the electrician at my house." He squared his shoulders.

I lifted the crossbar onto my shoulder. "Hang on, we need to fill out a repair ticket. Can you come in for a minute?"

"Of course."

As we walked toward the shop, he said, "I think I told you earlier in the summer I'd found a modest house in Pocasset. I'm having it remodeled, putting on an addition, adding a deck. It means I'm living in a construction zone, but I don't mind. It's great to watch it all come together."

"Is the project going well?" I asked. I set the bike down outside the door.

"Yes, very much so."

"Good luck with it. Come on in." He followed me into the shop and I turned away to find the ticket book. As I turned back, I blinked. Orlean and Wes were in the middle of a hug. What alternate universe had I slid into? She patted his back before they pulled apart. I watched as they murmured to each other. When I cleared my throat, Wes whirled.

"You two know each other?" I asked.

Orlean nodded. "Beverly had us both over for a genealogy training session."

"But I didn't know Orlean worked here," Wes said. "I think we were the only two people who liked Beverly, may God rest her soul."

"You might be right about that," Orlean said.

And maybe they were the only two she had been nice to in return. Plus Abo Reba, I remembered. But if Wes was putting on an act about his affection for the late Beverly Ruchart, as Gin and I had mused, it was a performance worthy of Broadway.

Chapter Sixteen

I left the shop with Derrick and Orlean at about four. Derrick said he was good to close at six, and that Cokey was with our parents. I drove over to Falmouth in Miss M, my red convertible sports car. I lived a simple life without a lot of expenses, so I'd treated myself to an indulgence once I'd returned from my travels. Miss M—for Miata—was the car I'd always wanted. She had cream-colored leather seats and a hand-stitched steering wheel cover. Her transmission was manual and she was wicked fun to drive, especially in the summer with the top down.

I parked in the municipal lot and walked the main drag. It was a popular town with tourists, but I had to admit I liked Westham better. We were smaller but had better shops, in my not-so-humble opinion. Falmouth did have a bigger library, and I enjoyed eating at C Salt occasionally, a fine-dining restaurant down the road a little from the center.

What Westham didn't have, however, was an expensive dress shop. I paused in front of Maxine's. The mannequins and displays showed tasteful dresses, tops, and slacks primarily in aqua and white, the colors of a beach town in summer. I made a little grimace. I hadn't come up with a story so I could have a conversation with Isadora. But I'd better, because I was going to have trouble showing interest in this style of clothes. My summer wardrobe ran more to store polo shirts, cargo shorts, and Keen's sandals. Maybe I could say I was going to a wedding next month and needed something extra nice to wear.

The door chimed when I pushed it open. A woman who was dressed like she shopped here regularly was flipping through blouses on the wall. A younger woman behind the counter wrote on a receipt pad with her left hand and handed the receipt and a tasteful bag with handles to another shopper.

As I passed by the counter, I saw a book lying facedown, as if the clerk had been in the middle of reading when customers came in. I did a double take. It was one of Hallie Ephron's domestic suspense novels. They weren't cozy mysteries, but her writing and character development were compelling, and the suspense among the women in her books kept me turning the pages every time. I was a little surprised to see the shop clerk immersed in an Ephron novel instead of an urban thriller or a romance novel. Then again, I didn't know her at all. Why shouldn't she be a serious reader?

I moved on to the racks, browsing and gasping silently

at the prices. Who would pay ninety dollars for a pair of white Capris? And a few cents short of two hundred dollars for a sleeveless dress?

I returned to the young woman standing behind the counter. Isadora? I hoped so.

"Good afternoon, ma'am." Her hair, cut and styled to fall just below her chin, was light like Wesley Farnham's, and she was tall, but she had a slender build, where his was stocky. This had to be her, though. Her small eyes were almost identical to his. I sniffed. Her breath smelled of alcohol. *At work?*

"Can I help you?" she asked.

"I hope so," I said, mustering my cover story. "I'm going to an afternoon wedding over Labor Day and I don't have anything nice to wear."

"So you're thinking a tea-length dress?" She wore an outfit that appeared to have come from the store, aqua slacks and a crisp white shirt with a chunky turquoise and pink necklace. A matching bracelet adorned one wrist and an expensive-looking gold watch the other. "We have a nice selection."

"I guess." Not that I knew what tea length was. "Or maybe a pair of flowing pants and a nice top?" Why did I say that? I had to remind myself I wasn't actually going to buy anything.

She looked me up and down. I was in shorts, polo, and sandals, as usual. An outfit definitely not purchased here.

"It's possible," she said. "With your figure you'd look good in a sheath with a pair of strappy sandals." She turned away and sneezed, drawing a tissue out of her pocket. "Excuse me. My allergies are super bad this summer."

I didn't wear heels, except she didn't need to know

that. I had a naturally high metabolism, so I was lean. Still, a sheath dress sounded uncomfortable for sitting.

"My name is Mac, by the way."

"Nice to meet you, Mac. I'm Isadora."

Bingo. "How are you liking *You'll Never Know, Dear*?" I asked. "I loved that book. You know she lives in the Boston area."

"I think it's one of her best." She tapped the book with a perfectly lacquered nail. "I've always been a big reader. It, like, takes you out of your life, you know?"

"I know. I read almost exclusively mysteries, myself. Ephron has a new one out." I thought, trying to remember the title. "Is it—"

A thud came from the large window at the front of the store. We both jumped a little.

"What was that?" she said, hurrying to the door.

I followed as Isadora stepped onto the sidewalk. She gasped and brought her hand to her mouth. A large crow lay on the ground. She stepped back, bumping into me.

"It must have flown into the glass," I said. "Sometimes birds think their reflections are other birds." I glanced at her.

She had wrapped her arms around herself. Her nostrils were flared, her mouth turned down, her eyes wide, as if she stared at a monster, not a stunned bird.

"Are you all right?" I asked.

The bird lifted its head, rolled to standing, and waddled away a few steps.

"I hate big birds," she whispered. "They terrify me."

The crow cocked its head and regarded us with a yellow eye. It scratched out a caw, then lifted off with a rustle of wingbeats.

It's only a crow, I wanted to say, but we all had our different phobias. I kept the thought to myself and gestured inside. "Why don't you show me the dresses you had in mind?"

Inside she recovered her equilibrium within a minute. "I'm sorry," Isadora said with a wry smile, patting her chest. "Birds like that totally freak me out."

"No worries."

"Come over here." She headed toward a rack of dresses and flipped through the hangers until she came to my size. "Any of these would be appropriate." She gazed at my face and arms. "And with your skin you can wear strong, warm colors." She picked out a dress in a deep fuchsia and another in shades of orange and red. She held the second one up to my neck. "Yes, very nice."

I wanted to keep up the shopping talk for a little longer. I pointed to a black and white geometric patterned dress. "I like the black and white one, too."

"Excellent choice. It's a very smart dress." She lifted the patterned one off the rack.

A smart dress? Who used "smart" to describe a garment except fashion show announcers? "Isadora." I feigned thinking hard. "I think my friend Gin mentioned meeting you earlier this week at a dinner."

She paused the dress hunt and nodded slowly. "I did meet Gin. It's such a tragedy." She lowered her voice. "Our hostess was killed the very next morning."

"I know." I swallowed. "Gin and I found her body."

Her eyes went wide. "You did?" she whispered.

"Yes." Lincoln and Victoria must have kept our identities from the press, which was fine with me.

"What did she look like? Was it awful?"

Isadora's breath definitely smelled of alcohol. Did she have a flask under the desk? She seemed functional and her speech wasn't slurred, but I was surprised she could keep a job in a high-end shop like this one if she drank on the job.

"She looked, well, dead," I answered. "And yes, it was very upsetting."

"The news hasn't been reporting how she died. Could you tell?" Her gaze shifted back to the dresses.

"No, not at all. She was one of my customers, and I know she had heart issues, so it might have been something cardiac."

"You own a shop?"

"Yes, Mac's Bikes in Westham. Retail, repair, rental, we do all of it."

"I think my dad was going to take his bike there."

"If your father is Wesley Farnham, he brought it in earlier this afternoon."

"That's him. He was at the dinner, too."

"Do you live in Pocasset with him?"

"He's renovating an old house. She shook her head fast with an expression indicating I was nuts to even suggest such a thing. "Me, live in so much dust and mess? No way. I have a condo in Westham."

Which Daddy bought her, no doubt. "Did you know Beverly Ruchart well?"

"I didn't know her at all. I don't know why Daddy wanted to drag me to her house, either." Her tone dripped distaste. "She helped my father with a little project of his and they both seemed very happy about it. I wasn't, though."

"Maybe he invited you to make peace between you and her," I suggested.

"Probably. He paid her for the work, but he also seemed, like, wild about her. It was disgusting."

Now her speech sounded more like the young twenty-something she was.

"So they were dating?"

"If you can call it 'dating.'" She surrounded the word with finger quotes and gave a little shudder.

So Gin had been right about Wes and his feelings toward Beverly. "Did Beverly seem ill at the dinner?" I asked, casually flipping through more hangers myself.

Isadora shot me a sharp look. "Why do you care?"

I thought fast. "I didn't know her well, but I feel a weird connection since I was the second person to see her dead."

"I get it. Well, what Beverly seemed was drunk out of her gourd. Her son and I had to do the dishes. She wasn't going to be able to, that was for sure." She seemed to shake off the memory.

One of the two women who had been looking at blouses stood near the counter at the side where the cash register was. "Miss? I'm all set."

"I'll be right with you," Isadora called in return. To me, she said, "Why don't we get you in the dressing room with these and see which one you like? And I'll keep looking for more."

I felt like sighing, but I kept it in. Trying on dresses was not my idea of a fun late afternoon, but I'd gotten myself into this lie and I'd better see it through.

Chapter Seventeen

I was home, iced tea in hand and listening to classical music, by five o'clock. I'd successfully avoided buying even one of the dresses at Maxine's, saying none of them was exactly what I'd been looking for. Isadora had given me a funny look, but surely she was used to women not finding what they wanted in the store.

Now I stretched out on the couch, as far as I could, anyway. It was a two-seater, so I hooked my knees over the arm at the other end. Belle munched her carrots and chattered away under her breath.

A hurricane of thoughts swirled in my brain from today. Isadora's disdain for her father having a love life. The alcohol on her breath. The sight of Wes and Orlean embracing, Orlean being the least touchy-feely person I'd ever met. Wes's obvious grief at Beverly's death. Abo Reba's saying she and Beverly got along fine. What my grandmother had mentioned about Ron, and what Beverly had told her about how he dealt with money.

Did anything I'd learned rise to the level of being important enough to tell Lincoln? Maybe. I could relay what I knew about Ron and money, both Ron's impression he would be inheriting and what my grandmother had said about his poor financial management skills. Abo Reba wouldn't be on the detective's list of people to talk with and he might not hear it any other way. He'd said once no fact was too small, and sometimes it was a mosaic of the small things that formed a picture of the killer for an investigation.

I decided to text him instead of call. I needed a break from talking about death.

FYI: Ran into Ron R, who said he's inheriting all B's estate. Told me he thought E Tubin killed B. My grandma—Reba— doubts it. B told her Ron is bad with $ and she was leaving bulk to charities.

I hit Send. Having discharged my civic duty, I sipped my tea. And my phone rang. I groaned when I saw it was Lincoln, himself. Guess I was going to talk about death, after all.

"Telephone, Mac!" Belle cried. "Hello? Hello? Telephone!"

"Ssh. I got it, Belle. Alexa, stop playing music," I instructed my all-purpose cylindrical robot. I connected the call and greeted Lincoln.

"Mac, what were you doing talking to the victim's grandson?" He was clearly exasperated.

"I went into the store where he works yesterday afternoon. I didn't expect him to be there. His grandmother had died earlier in the morning. And I had to get a birthday present for my father."

The detective let out a long, deep sigh. "All right. I suppose you told him you found the body and the two of you naturally fell into a discussion about inheritance and murder."

"You might not want to believe me, but that's exactly what happened. He told me he thought Eli Tubin killed Beverly."

"Did he give you a reason?"

"He said Eli had always hated Beverly while his wife—Beverly's daughter and Ron's mother—was alive. He claimed Eli killed Beverly to get back at her."

Lincoln made a scoffing sound. "That's really reaching."

"I thought so, too. Gin said she didn't know why Beverly had even invited Eli."

"Yes, she told me as much. Now, as for the other matter you texted me about. Ms. Ruchart had told your grandmother about her will?" He didn't sound like he believed me.

"My grandma is old, but her mind is totally sharp. She and Beverly were friendly. They talked about roses and stuff. It's not so odd the two would talk about end-of-life issues, even though anyone would have thought my grandmother was a lot closer to the end of her life than Beverly."

"True enough." He cleared his throat. "Very well. Please give me Ms. Almeida's contact info. Ms. Reba Almeida, I mean."

I complied. "I don't know if this is important, but Wes Farnham came into the shop today. He and Beverly were dating, apparently, and he seems to be genuinely broken up about Beverly's death."

"So I understand. But why did he visit your shop? He doesn't strike me as the bicycle type."

I laughed. "True. But he said he's going to start riding and wanted us to give his old bike a tune-up." I was about to tell him about Isadora not being sad about Beverly's death, but shut my mouth. In fact, I'd gone to the dress shop looking for her. Lincoln wouldn't like that a bit. Instead I ventured, "Have you made much progress in the case so far?"

"Not at liberty to say, Mac."

Chapter Eighteen

Somehow Tim had snagged a window table for two at busy Jimmy's Harborside that evening. We sat looking out at the last light of the day illuminating swallows swooping for insects over the salt pond outside. A welcome wind had picked up a couple of hours ago and blown away the clouds and humidity. I sipped a cool Chardonnay, while Tim was halfway through a summer Pilsner. Conversation buzzed around us punctuated by the clinks of flatware on porcelain. Everyone at a table of six near us wore plastic bibs as they dug the meat out of lobster shells.

"How did your day go?" I asked.

He pointed to the warm, chewy rolls in front of us. "Busy, but busy is good."

"These are yours?"

His smile was broad and happy. "They're mine."

I buttered the other half of the roll on my small plate. "They're way too good."

"I signed a contract a couple days ago to supply the restaurant with fresh-baked rolls, and it's a big one. I'll need to hire on another baker, but this restaurant gig is steady, guaranteed income. I couldn't say no."

"Of course not." I savored the last bite of the chewy, slightly sour crumb, delicious on its own and also the perfect vehicle for butter. "Mmm."

"And your day, Mac?"

I rubbed my cheek. "Got stung by a bee when I was walking with Gin, but my EpiPen did the trick. It was scary for a minute."

He reached over the table to lay his hand on my cheek, worry filling his eyes. "I'll bet it was."

"I'm fine now." I laughed and told him about my mom and grandmother buying bikes. "Those two are funny."

"Your grandma is a town treasure." He took a sip of beer. "Anything happening about the woman's death?"

I bobbed my head. "It appears she was murdered." I kept my voice low. "And at book group people were speculating she was poisoned with something."

"How awful."

"Yes." I gazed over his shoulder. "Here come our dinners."

Our server had been a slim dark-haired man. The person carrying our plates was a tall woman in her twenties with high cheekbones in a wide face and straight blonde hair pulled back in a ponytail. Her name tag read SOFIA.

"Who has the grilled scallops?" she asked in an accented voice.

I raised my hand. She set down the plate in front of me and gave Tim his fish and chips.

"Thank you," I said. I racked my brain to figure out how I could talk about Beverly's death with her. It turned out I didn't have to.

"I'll bet everybody here has been talking about the woman's death this week," Tim said to her.

I glanced at him in surprise. I had not set him up to ask about Beverly's murder. How did he know I wanted to discuss it with the Russian server?

She set her hands on her black aproned waist. "Yes, they have. Beverly, she was not nice lady."

"You knew her?" I asked.

"I date her grandson. She doesn't like me. She comes in here and is rude to me for no reason. She is calling me Slavic trash." She pressed her lips together.

"You're not sorry she's gone," Tim murmured.

She shook her head once, fast. "No, I am not sorry. She tells me she is knowing I am undocumented. I am not! I have visa."

She would have to be here on a work visa, even if a temporary one, to be employed in such a public place. Or not, but I doubted she would say she was legal if she wasn't.

"I believe that woman burning in hell now." Sofia gave a grim but triumphant nod.

Our server approached.

"I must work," Sofia said. "Enjoy your meal."

I thanked her. I watched her move on to a recently vacated table and start stacking dirty dishes.

"Everything all right here?" our server asked.

"Yes, thanks," Tim said. He swirled a fry in ketchup and popped it into his mouth.

"Burning in hell?" I said after the server left. "That's harsh."

"I know. Did anybody like Beverly Ruchart?"

"Orlean did. Wes Farnham, apparently. And Abo Reba. Did Beverly ever come into the bakery?"

"Sometimes." He took a bite of crispy, battered fish and swallowed before going on. "She was all business, bought coffee and baguettes. I never saw her with friends, though, and she didn't stay and eat. She'd pay for her stuff and leave."

We spent a few minutes enjoying our dinners and not talking about a dead woman and who might have killed her. My scallops were fat, sweet, and to die for, and were nestled next to grilled asparagus and several crusty disks of Parmesan polenta.

"Mmm," I cooed.

"This fish is perfect, too." Tim forked in another bite.

A man in his forties was shown to the table behind Tim. He seemed to be alone. As he examined his menu, I studied him. He had a thin nose and a scraggly mustache and reminded me of someone. I couldn't place who. Tim noticed my gaze and twisted to see what I was looking at.

Facing me again, he whispered, "He was in the bakery today. Never seen him before."

"It is August, after all, when the Cape hits its annual population peak." Strangers galore filled the town, and it was how most of us made our living.

Chapter Nineteen

"Give us a kiss. Hello, handsome," Belle repeated for the third time, following up with her wolf whistle.

"Thank you, Belle." Tim blew her a kiss.

Tim and I sat on my couch with our feet up on the coffee table, two little glasses of cognac at hand. I cocked my head at the sound through the open windows. "It's raining."

"As predicted."

"Local farmers are going to be happy about rain. It's been so dry." I got up to close the two windows most of the way, leaving them open only a few inches at the top. I rejoined Tim.

"It's been so dry. It's been so dry." Belle perched on Tim's shoulder, bobbing her head every time she spoke.

He twisted to make a kissing sound at her. "There, you

got a second kiss, Belle. Now can you be quiet for a few minutes?" he asked, keeping his tone gentle.

"Belle's a good girl. Snacks, Mac," she said.

"All right." I headed for the fridge, the door of which was covered with Cokey's artwork, and put a half-dozen frozen grapes in her bowl. "You have to eat them over here, though."

The parrot hopped down and waddled over to the bowl. I joined Tim again. I yawned as I nestled in under his arm, loving the feeling of his firm torso, his strong, warm arm, even his scent, a vague mix of rainwater shampoo, yeast, and healthy man.

"Boring you, am I?" he asked.

"No, it's just been a long day. Yours was even longer, no?" My man was always up and gone to bake by four in the morning.

"It was. I was kidding you." He sipped his cognac. "I went for a run with Eli Tubin this afternoon."

"Was it a good one?"

"It was. We kept up a really fast pace. But he had a couple of interesting things to say. About the, um"—he glanced at Belle—"the death."

I was careful not to talk about subjects I didn't want Belle learning the words for, and I'd asked Tim to watch what he said, too. "Really?"

"He said he wouldn't be surprised if Ron had poisoned Beverly."

"Someone at book group said the same thing. And Ron told me he thinks he's inheriting all Beverly's money. But Abo Reba said Beverly never would have left her estate to Ron, who is terrible with money."

"Interesting. Eli told me Beverly was really surprised when Ron insisted on cleaning up after the dinner. It was apparently quite out of character for him. Eli thought Ron might have been getting rid of the evidence."

"I thought about that, too. Except Gin said Isadora Farnham helped clean up, too." I filled him in on what Gin had told me about the birth son and Isadora's inheritance being cut in half. Belle waddled back and made her way into my lap. I stroked her smooth head. "So she might have wanted to get back at Beverly for helping her father. It sounds crazy, but crazier things have happened."

Tim caressed my shoulder. He took a deep breath before speaking. "Mac, honey, when am I going to be able to convince you to have a birth son—or daughter—of our own? I love you." He smiled tenderly. "I want to get married and start a family with you. We're good together. We can make it work. I'll be an equal partner."

I closed my eyes for a moment. *Here we go again.* "I'm going to be honest with you." I turned half sideways so I could see his face. "I love you, too. I love being with you. My family adores you. But I'm . . ." I shut my mouth. How could I say I was scared? Scared of being pregnant. Scared of all the mess babies bring. Scared things would change between us.

He stood, blowing out a breath. "You always have a 'but.' I don't think you're ever going to change your mind."

I looked up at him in anguish. "Don't be mad, Tim." That was all I could say. I couldn't promise him something I didn't know if I'd ever be ready for. "Sit down? Let's talk. Please?"

"Talk? We've been talking for months, Mac."

And we had. He'd been infinitely patient with me.

"I don't think you're ever going to be ready." He gazed at me with watery eyes. "You like your tidy world, your tidy life. But there's no room for me in it. I want to live with you, wake up every morning with you. I want to be a father. I want children to love and play with and teach stuff to, with you as their mother. I want a family. And I wanted to make one with you." His voice broke. He took two strides to the door, then turned slowly. "I'm not going through life without having kids, Mac. I can't. It kills me to say this. But if I have to find someone else to create a family with, or if I have to adopt as a single parent, I will."

The door clicked shut behind him. I sank my head into my hands. What had I done?

Chapter Twenty

When colored light glimmered through the wide, stained-glass transom window in my sleeping loft the next morning, I sat up, both groggy and agitated. I'd barely slept all night. I had tossed and turned and tossed some more, hashing through all sides of what Tim had said. I did have a tidy life, and I loved it. I knew I was obsessed with neatness and order. Did I need counseling? Was it wrong to accept who I was? Was I too set in my ways to change? Or, as Mom claimed, if I was a double Virgo, could I even change? Did I want to throw away the love of a good and caring man?

Men like Tim were hard to come by. I'd had one amazing boyfriend at Harvard, and we'd been on the path to getting engaged when he'd died in a skiing accident. After my grief at his loss ebbed, I waded into the dating scene, but it proved almost too much work to land date after date with men I wasn't interested in. And talk about messy. So I threw myself into my work instead. It turned out I had quite a facility for numbers, and I did well at a Boston-area bank. I also made more than one prudent investment.

After I turned thirty I had a period of examining my life and decided I'd been too much about me. I extricated myself from banking and joined the Peace Corps, teaching sound financial practices to women entrepreneurs in Thailand for two years. When I traveled in Southeast Asia for a year after my stint was up, I fell in love with a high-energy Kiwi cyclist and rode the mountains of New Zealand with him—until he dropped me like a flat tire and I blew out my knee in the same week.

I returned home, bought the bike shop and the tiny house, and met the jewel that Tim was. Everything was going right for once. Until he threw kids into the mix. I didn't have anything against children. I loved my niece with a passion. I just . . . yes, I was scared.

I climbed out of bed and stood on the steps to pull up and smooth the covers and neaten the pillows. Downstairs I uncovered Belle's cage and opened the door to it.

"Good morning, Belle."

"Good morning, Mac. Good morning, Mac. Give Belle a kiss. Grapes?"

I smiled. My bird was better for my mental health than any psychologist. I made a kissing noise and headed to the coffee machine. After the coffee was brewing, I checked the grape supply and saw I was running low. I surveyed the rest of the refrigerator while I was at it.

"Alexa, please make a shopping list," I said.

The black cylinder replied, "What would you like to buy?"

"Grapes, milk, salad greens."

Belle piped up. "Peanuts."

I laughed. "Alexa, read back the shopping list." I could always use peanuts.

"Grapes, milk, salad greens, peanuts."

"Alexa, stop," I said.

Five minutes later, I sat in my sleeping shirt and a pair of shorts outside on the brick patio. Belle hopped up onto the table next to my coffee mug. She was better dressed than I was right now. The feathers on her torso were tiny scallops of light gray edged in white. Her wings were a more uniform dark gray. She wore what looked like white knee socks to match the white eyeliner around her intelligent yellow eyes, and her red tail was a spectacular accessory to the outfit.

"Ah-ah-ah," I scolded. "No birds on the table. You know the rules, Belle."

"Rules, Belle. Rules, Belle." She dutifully hopped down onto the other chair, shaking her head. "Belle's a bad girl. Ah-ah-ah."

I giggled. I pulled my knees up to my chest in the cool morning air. Six o'clock and the August sun was peeping over the tall trees to my left. The rain had stopped sometime in the night and now the world was washed clean. The *Rosa rugosa* leaves in the hedge to my right sparkled in the sunlight. A blue jay sat on a branch at the back of the small yard and bobbed its head in time to its metallic call.

"Belle, what do you think? Should we move in with Tim? Should I make a baby or two with him?"

She extended her curved black beak a couple of times. "Mac make a baby." She followed up the words with her wolf whistle. "Hello, handsome."

One vote for Tim. Maybe I simply wasn't imaginative enough to picture a life together. Imagination had never been my strong suit. He and I couldn't live together in this little house, for certain. His cottage on the hill behind Main Street had two bedrooms and space out back to add on if need be. It had a yard big enough for a play structure. And it was within walking distance from my shop and everywhere else in town.

My shop. Could I be a mom and run a business, too? I scoffed. Of course, I could. Lots of women did. I was sure my parents would help with childcare, and I had a good team at Mac's Bikes to keep things running. Tim's bakery was thriving, too.

So what was stopping me? I'd been going out with Tim for, let's see, a year plus. Perhaps that wasn't long enough, although I didn't know how more time could make a difference. I sipped my rich, dark coffee. Maybe I'd give Pa a call, see if he had time for me to talk through my angst. He'd counseled hundreds of people in his role as minister, and he was a great listener. I nodded to myself. That's what I'd do. At lunchtime.

I picked up my phone and shot a picture of Belle where she perched on the back of the other chair near my coffee mug. A minute later it was posted to Instagram with a caption of: "Belle enjoys morning coffee outside. #AfricanGraysofInstagram #CapeCod #WesthamRocks." I scrolled through a couple of e-mails, retweeted a few bike-related tweets, and checked my texts.

My eyes widened to see a long book group thread. I

hadn't checked since before dinner last night. We'd maintained a group thread after Jake had been murdered. Each of us had added what we learned as we learned it. I'd forgotten we'd agreed to start it up again at the end of our meeting the other night. I scrolled back to the beginning of this thread.

Gin had had dinner with Eli.

Eli said he didn't hate B. She'd never liked him much, but after his wife died he hadn't seen B very often.

So that negated what Ron had said, if Eli was telling the truth. The next text was from Zane, who wrote that Sofia seemed happy Beverly was dead. I added to his message.

Talked w/ Sofia last night, too. She said she wasn't sorry B was dead and that she was burning in hell now. B had called her Slavic trash, falsely accused her of being undocumented.

Flo had texted she'd found a few poisons, but antifreeze looked like the best bet. It was widely available and tasted sweet.

"Ooh." I raised my gaze to Belle. "Antifreeze?"

"Belle's a good girl. Snacks, Mac?"

I laughed. She knew I got her grapes out of the freezer. "You are a good girl, and a smart one, too. Just a sec, Belle."

I sipped my coffee before starting a new text.

Visited Isadora in Falmouth. She wanted to know how B died, and said B was dating I's father.

Was that all I'd learned from Isadora? I thought so. I could report in about Wes, too.

Talked to Wes Farnham. Very broken up about B's death. Grief seemed authentic.

It was all I had. It didn't seem like much.

I had one more message I wanted to send, but I hesitated. Was it too soon to try to make peace with Tim? And what would I say, anyway? I set down the phone. I'd wait until after I talked with Pa.

I stood. "Come on, Belle. Let's get ready for the day."

Chapter Twenty-one

Gin and I set out on the path to the walking and biking trail at a little after seven. Her face was pale again, not like her usual healthy complexion. She'd texted a few minutes ago that she was up for the walk, but I wasn't so sure she was. The morning was breezy, with white puffs of clouds sailing overhead.

The path ran next to the Friends Meetinghouse. Behind the simple white structure with its tall, wide windows was an old Quaker cemetery. Most of the gravestones were from the nineteenth century, when people wrote actual letters instead of texts.

"Did you see the group text thread this morning?" I asked.

"Yes. Doesn't seem like we have much to go on yet."

I stole a glance at her, then walked in silence for a moment. "What's the matter? Did something else happen?"

"Detective Haskins showed up last night after I got home from dinner. He had a search warrant for my garage and my shop."

Ah. Paleness explained. "He did? Why?"

"He got a tip from somebody, apparently."

"The police didn't find what they were looking for, did they?"

She walked in silence for a minute. "The officer in charge of me didn't let me watch. I had to stay in my apartment above the shop, but I heard one person on the team mention antifreeze."

"Yikes." I grabbed her arm and stopped. No wonder she was pale. "The sweet, toxic, readily available poison."

"Exactly." She glanced around, looking like she was afraid Lincoln was lurking, ready to arrest her. "The stuff Flo thought might have killed Beverly," she whispered.

"But everybody's garage has antifreeze. How could they possibly think it came from yours, if in fact antifreeze was the poison?"

"I don't know, Mac, but I'm scared. I told Detective Haskins I didn't have any. Last spring I did a major cleanout of the garage. I threw away or recycled a bunch of stuff, cleaned all the shelves where I keep gardening tools, painted the inside so it was brighter. I am positive there wasn't anything like antifreeze. I don't know a thing about mechanical stuff, and I don't work on my own car. Why would I have any?" Her voice shook like an aspen leaf.

"Do you lock your garage?"

"No, I shut the garage door and I lock my car, because I live on Main Street in a town that's full of strangers half the year. But all I have in the garage is gardening stuff, and the building isn't attached to the house. Why would I lock it? Am I naïve?" She hugged herself despite the already warming August air. "Plus, I brought Beverly candy. I wonder if they were looking for traces of the toxin in my candy kitchen."

"Listen." I took hold of her shoulders and looked her straight in the face. "You didn't kill Beverly. We're going to find out who did. Period. Okay?"

Gin took a deep breath in and let it out. "Okay. Thanks, friend. I know they won't find any poison in the store kitchen. I clean it within an inch of its life every afternoon after I'm done making the day's batch."

"Are they going to let you open today?"

"He didn't say I couldn't. And really, why would I poison my own candy? That would be a really quick way to lose customers."

We resumed walking.

"So it's my fault if they found antifreeze in my garage because I didn't lock the door to it." Gin shook her head.

"If this was one of the mysteries we read, the murderer would have planted it there to shift suspicion onto you."

"What a rotten thing to do."

"Do you think killers care about being rotten?"

She gave a soft laugh. "I guess you're right. Anyway, it's locked now."

We turned onto the actual trail, but this time headed north toward Pocasset. I didn't want to go anywhere near where I was stung yesterday and there were fewer things in bloom in this direction.

"Eli told me something else at dinner last night," Gin said after a few minutes. "He talked about Ron's birth father. The guy's name is Danny Rizzoli. He deserted Ron and his mother a month after the baby was born. Never paid child support or anything."

"His leaving had to be rough on the mom."

"For sure."

"So Ron never had any contact with his real father?" I asked.

"No. But you know what I was thinking?"

"What?"

"What if this Danny found Ron recently, and they plotted together to kill Beverly. If Ron thought he was inheriting everything, Danny might have wanted a share in the loot."

I elbowed her. "You're going to be writing the books next, girlfriend. That's a classic."

She shrugged. "It was only an idea."

"Did you try to find any information on Danny Rizzoli?"

She wrinkled her nose. "No, because as soon as I got home the detective showed up with his team."

"I'll do it once we get back." We passed the start of a walking trail leading through a patch of woods, which was sure to be rife with mosquitoes right now. Except for the presence of bees, I preferred the open path. "I'm curious about something. If antifreeze is so toxic, why do they keep selling it?"

"Good question," Gin said. "You said in the text this morning you'd talked to Sofia last night. Were you out with the hunk?"

I nodded without speaking. I'd never told Gin about my only conflict with Tim. Now might be the time. "Yes, but we had a big fight when we got back to my place."

"A fight? You're kidding me. What's there to fight about?" She held up a hand. "Wait. I take it back. I was married. There's always something to fight about if you choose to."

"This is a pretty fundamental thing. He wants to move in together, start having babies. With me."

She waited a few moments before saying, "And?"

"I don't know if I want to. I like my life the way it is now."

"And he's tired of waiting?"

"Apparently. Last night he left after he told me he doesn't want to go through life without having children. And if I don't want to, he's going to find someone else."

"Whoa. That's a switch. Usually it's the woman who wants babies and the man who has cold feet."

"I know."

"Don't you ever want to have kids? For me, having a kid was the best thing I ever did. Seriously."

I sighed. "Maybe. But aren't they the epitome of messy? And childbirth?" I shuddered. "You know me. I don't like stuff that isn't tidy, that's disorderly."

She reached over and squeezed my shoulders with one arm. "Mac, you should do what's right for you. You don't want to have kids, you don't have to." She dropped her arm. "But this is life you're talking about, and life's kind of messy." She smiled. "And believe it or not, women's bodies are built to make and birth babies, yours included. It seems just a little bit like a phobia, this neatness thing you have. You can get help for it. I'm not saying you have to, but you know I'm here for support. No matter what you decide."

I exhaled a breathy sigh. "I appreciate that, Gin. I'm just not sure I want to fulfill my so-called biological destiny. Isn't that what women in our moms' generation fought so hard for?" I cleared my throat. "So, how about them Red Sox?"

Chapter Twenty-two

I made it into my shop at eight thirty, half an hour before we opened. I wanted to read up on antifreeze, and on Danny Rizzoli while I was at it. I kept my laptop in my office at the shop instead of at home. Of course, I could Google at home, but I thought I might as well do it here. Before I unlocked the door to Mac's Bikes I peered wistfully down the street toward Greta's Grains. Part of me wanted to keep walking, pop in the back door to Tim's kitchen, and throw my arms around him. But a joyous reunion was going to have to wait. He'd made it pretty clear he wasn't interested in my arms or any of the rest of me if I wasn't interested in having a family. I let out a deep sigh and let myself into my own shop.

Huh. I stared at the laptop screen five minutes later. Ethylene glycol was the sweet poisonous stuff. But you could also buy several other types of coolant that used propylene glycol, among other ingredients, which was far safer for both pets and humans. The types were apparently color-coded, with the poisonous stuff sold in a bright green color. The other kinds were orange, yellow, and dark green, and sometimes pink, red, or blue. Who knew? You'd think it was Kool-Aid or something.

I sat back. If alternatives to the bright green kind were available, why did they keep selling the toxic one? Doing so seemed crazy—and dangerous. I dug deeper. *Oh*. Ethylene glycol was used mostly in older cars, and you weren't supposed to mix the two types. To change over you had to drain and clean the entire coolant system, which was a lot of work. So that was why the stuff was still sold by auto parts stores and hardware establishments.

I opened a new search and typed in "Daniel Rizzoli," assuming it was Ron's father's full name. All I got was the Facebook page of a dark-haired man in his forties who lived in Buenos Aires and liked to take pictures of pretty flowers. He also had a YouTube channel with some videos in Spanish. Somehow I didn't think he was the one I was looking for. I changed Daniel to Danny and tried again.

Now I was getting somewhere. A Danny Rizzoli had been convicted of petty larceny in Maine ten years ago. And a Danny Rizzoli was listed as part owner of a New York auto parts store that had gone bankrupt. I clicked the Images tab, but all I got was pictures of the television show *Rizzoli & Isles*. Oh well. I'd sic Flo on the search with her super-secret librarian search engines. I tapped out a quick text to the group about the colors and kinds of antifreeze, and asked Flo to find a picture of Danny Rizzoli.

It was time for my store-opening checklist. I knew it all by heart, but looking at the list was comforting to make sure I didn't leave anything out. I'd read they'd cut way down on surgery mistakes in hospitals by requiring checklists, so I knew I was onto something.

I worked through the list. Turn on the lights. Take the starting cash out of the safe and put it in the register. Showcase one of the best retail bikes, since I rotated which one was in the front of the display every day. Straighten the merchandise. I kept ticking off tasks until I got to the last two—hang out the OPEN flag and water the window boxes. I filled the watering can, propped open the door, and slid the flagpole into its holder.

I pushed my finger into the soil of the first window box. Last night's rain had ended too soon to give them a good soaking, plus they were under the overhang of the eaves. As I stood watering the bright red and pink geraniums in the yellow-painted boxes facing the sidewalk, my thoughts dragged me back to talking about kids with Gin. Everybody seemed to be of one mind—I needed help with my OCD. And I was nuts if I wasn't inclined to want children with Tim right now. *Sheesh*.

After our conversation this morning, Gin and I had skirted anything personal. We'd talked about prospects for the Sox getting into the postseason, the antics of the Westham city council, the latest stalemate in Congress, the upcoming Falmouth Road Race, and the perennial favorite of shopkeepers in a tourist town, the weather. Neither of us had finished reading the book group pick for the week, and I wasn't sure I would have time to before our meeting tomorrow night. On the other hand, if all my evenings were suddenly going to be spent solo, I'd have lots of time for reading.

After I put away the watering can, I called Pa. I still had ten minutes before we officially opened, and Orlean rarely arrived early for work.

"How's my favorite daughter?" he asked.

"I'm okay. But I need to talk with you."

He stayed silent for a beat. "What's up?"

"I don't want to say on the phone. I meant I need to talk to you in person and, well, in private. Can I come by around lunchtime?"

"Of course, *queridinha*. Nothing's wrong with Derrick, is there?"

We'd had this conversation before when something had definitely been amiss with my half brother. Mom was Derrick's mother, but his father had died when he was one. After my parents married, Pa had raised Derrick as his own son.

"No, he's fine as far as I know. This is about me."

"I'll see you in my church office at noon, and don't eat. I'll make us sandwiches."

My throat thickened with love. "Thanks," I whispered. Family was everything to me. So why was I so reluctant to make a new one?

Chapter Twenty-three

The morning went downhill fast, but at least I was too busy to dwell on my own dilemma. Orlean called to say she was sick. I phoned my weekend mechanic to see if he was free, but he wasn't. Derrick texted to say he was running late. Two impossibly fit German men walked in as I stashed my phone in the back pocket of my work shorts. They were looking for new inner tubes but ended up each buying a bright red and blue Mac's Bikes cycling shirt, too. Next, eight girls and the leader of their Girl Scouts troop showed up to rent bikes for the day. Two minutes later, a newly retired man brought in a bike he'd bought from me only a month ago. Another customer who couldn't read the sign, which clearly asked for bikes to stay outside.

"It's all jammed up." He frowned and pointed to the chain.

"I'll be with you shortly," I told him. "And please take the bike back outside." I smiled to soften the message.

The glare he aimed at me was unwarranted, so I turned my back and resumed my work with the girls, who looked about nine or ten. They were all different sizes, of course, and I had to fit each of them with a seat at the right height, not to mention a helmet. They all wore matching green backpacks and had metal water bottles labeled GSA in the bottle holder on the outside. Three girls were bubbly and excited, and two shy ones whispered to each other.

"You're a brave woman," I murmured to the leader after she'd signed the rental agreement.

She laughed, her round cheeks agleam. "I love it. And they're good kids. My co-leader got sick at the last minute and I didn't want to disappoint the troop."

"Are you going to be making any stops? I have locks I can provide."

"Definitely. We'll be going to the beach and for ice cream at a minimum."

I handed her several slender cables and keyed locks. "You can lock more than one bike together. It's a long cable."

"Thanks." She stuffed them into her own green pack. "I heard about the woman who died here a few days ago, and I read online she was murdered." She kept her voice soft. "Are you scared to be open to the public?"

"No, not at all. We have an excellent police force, and I'm sure they're close to an arrest."

"I hope so. The girls wanted to have an overnight here, but some of the parents objected." She smiled. "I'm not worried, either, but we're only in town for the day. Came down from Providence."

"I appreciate the business." I wished them a good ride and watched as the group rode off.

"Let's take a look at your bike, sir," I said to the impatient man, then carried the cycle into the repair area and set it on the stand. And gaped. The chain was encrusted with sand. No wonder it was jammed. I looked over at him. "Did you ride this on the beach?" I reined in my incredulity that someone could be so clueless.

"Sure." He lifted his chin. "The sand was hard packed. It's nice to ride down by the water."

"Sir, it's not a beach bike. Even hard sand throws up particles. You can get a bike with an enclosed chain, but this isn't one of them." In fact, it was one of the cheapest bikes I sold.

"Whatever. Can you clean it out?"

"Of course." The customer is always right. *Sort of.* "It will be a couple of days, though. My mechanic is out sick." I grabbed the repair book from the counter and jotted down the job. "I'll need your phone number so I can call when it's ready."

He told me the number. "My grandsons are coming down on Friday. I'll need it by then."

A pair of couples strolled in. The women, in their forties, looked like they were twins. "You have the cutest shop," one said in a Southern accent. "I just love the window boxes and those pretty flowers."

"Thanks so much. I'll be with you in a minute." I smiled at my sand-rider. "I'll do my best to have it ready before the weekend. But if it isn't done, you can always rent one."

He twisted his mouth but had the decency not to complain. He pushed by the newly arrived group and hurried out the door.

I greeted the newcomers. "What can I help you with?"

"We're wanting to rent some tandem bikes?" the other sister said with a drawn-out upturn at the end. The way she pronounced "bikes" was so broad and open it almost sounded like "backs."

"Renting is what I'm here for." I smiled. I loved all the different kinds of people who stopped in. From European cyclists to cheerful Southerners to clueless cranky retirees to Girl Scouts. Okay, maybe I didn't love the cranky ones, but I had a bike for everybody.

Next, two women ushered in a sullen teen girl and two younger boys. Norland Gifford from book group was right behind them. He stood in the open doorway holding a pint-size pink bike with streamers on the handlebars. I asked everyone to please wait and led the Southerners around the side to the rentals. I spied Lincoln Haskins ambling down the sidewalk and coming straight for me. Why was he back? Anyway, he was going to have to take a number. Where in the heck was my brother? At this rate I wouldn't be able to leave at noon to talk with my father.

The Southerners rode off on their bicycles built for two. Haskins waited at the door to the shop, leaning against the jamb with folded arms.

"It's not a good time, Detective. I'm solo today."

"I can wait."

I didn't know how he kept his calm, but I'd never seen him impatient or rattled. Solving homicides must put him under a lot of pressure, and he seemed to have some way to stay above it. Meditation? Yoga? An intrinsic inner peace? I had no idea.

It turned out the family had their own bikes, but they wanted trail maps, and one of the women bought Mac's Bikes water bottles for each of the kids. The teen grabbed a black headband and added it to the purchase. I thanked them and turned to Norland, who had left his grand-daughter's bike outside.

"No employees today, Mac?" he asked.

"Orlean is sick and Derrick is late. You need a tune-up for Pinky?"

He nodded. "It has a flat tire, too. Do you want me to help out until Derrick arrives?"

Norland had come to my rescue on other occasions when I was understaffed, picking up the basics of running retail and rental in minutes.

"I have a couple hours free," he added.

"Help would be more awesome than you know." I lowered my voice. "Detective Haskins is out there wait-ing to talk with me."

"I saw him." He raised one eyebrow in his lined face. Ever since Norland had retired from the police force, he'd let his formerly close-cropped silver hair grow longer. It now curled over his ears in a much softer look. "Any news?"

"Not that I know of. You saw the text thread?"

"Yes. I might have learned something through the grapevine. I'll tell you if we get a minute to ourselves."

Three college-aged men arrived and started browsing the retail shelves.

"I've got this," Norland said. "Go talk to Lincoln."

Huh. Of course he would be on a first-name basis with a detective he'd worked closely with in the past. "Thanks. We'll be out back. Give me a shout if it gets nutso in here." I headed out the front door.

"Got a minute now?" Lincoln asked.

"Barely. Want to sit at the table in the back?"

"Yes, thank you."

A minute later we sat opposite each other, the oak providing dappled shade.

"I expect you heard from Ms. Malloy we searched her property yesterday." He tented his fingers under his chin.

"She told me. Did you find anything?"

He gazed above my head at the thick tree trunk behind me. "Have you known Ms. Malloy to own an older vehicle? Perhaps she garages it elsewhere?"

"No, she has a little Prius c and that's it. It was new two years ago. Look, she told me she heard the word *antifreeze*. And I know the bright green kind is really poisonous."

"And how do you know this?"

"I read a news story about a dog dying after licking up some that had been spilled," I said. "And I looked into the stuff."

"It is highly toxic. And yes, some was located in Ms. Malloy's garage. We have reason to believe it was the substance that killed Ms. Ruchart."

"Well, it wasn't Gin's substance. She cleaned out her garage. She knows she didn't have any. If you found it there, somebody planted it." I folded my arms.

"We are considering the possibility."

"Gin met Beverly for the first time the night before she died. You can't believe she would kill someone she'd never met before."

He nodded.

I hoped the nod meant he agreed with me.

"I wondered if you have heard in the last day or two any gossip about others who disliked the victim," Lincoln asked.

"The grandson, Ron, is dating a server named Sofia. We were talking with her last night at Jimmy's Harborside and she seemed happy Beverly was dead. Sofia said Beverly was burning in hell right now."

"I am aware of Ms. Burtseva, yes. I assume you did not go looking for her." His deep brown eyes broadcast a message of, "You'd better not have."

I crossed my fingers under the table. "I simply went out to dinner with my boyfriend." My possibly ex-boyfriend. "And she brought our meals."

"Anyone else?"

"I've heard Isadora Farnham wasn't too happy about Beverly helping her father find his birth son."

"And that she wasn't pleased her father was smitten with Ms. Ruchart?"

"That, too," I said.

"How did you learn her views?"

"I was shopping in Falmouth and ended up in a shop where she works. It was well before five o'clock and she smelled like alcohol. She was the only person running the shop, too."

"Interesting." He rose. "Thank you, Mac."

I stood, too. "Wait. I heard something else from my boyfriend, Tim Brunelle, who goes running with Eli Tubin. Ron's birth father is named Danny Rizzoli. You might check him out. I thought maybe he found Ron and the two of them decided to kill Beverly to get the inheritance."

"You have a vivid imagination." He pushed up his glasses.

Me? He had it all wrong. My brain operated along lines of logic, not fantasy. My suggestion came from plausibility. No flights of fancy for me.

Lincoln smiled. "But I will follow up on the information. I appreciate the tip." He headed at his usual amble out to the sidewalk.

I stopped before I entered the back door when I saw Derrick approach on his bike. He paused to greet Lincoln.

A moment later he walked the bike toward me. "Mac, I'm so sorry. I had to put out a fire at home."

What? "Something caught fire? Are you okay?"

He laughed and unclicked his helmet. "No, a figurative fire. What did the detective want, anyway?"

I gazed in the direction Lincoln had gone. "I'm not sure."

Chapter Twenty-four

I'd emerged from the restroom at around eleven when
Sofia appeared in the open front doorway. Derrick and
Norland were both busy with customers, so I gave Sofia a
wave and headed toward her.

"You are Mac, yes?" she asked. She was not in her
server uniform of white shirt and black pants today, but
rather wore a green Provincetown T-shirt and a swingy
short skirt with black canvas sneakers. She looked even
more Slavic, with her blonde hair plaited into two braids.

"I am." I smiled at her.

"I am Sofia. We talked at the restaurant." Her gaze
darted around the store as she worried the strap of her
slender backpack.

She seemed nervous. Had she come here with a bike
problem or to talk about the murder? I waited for her to
go on.

"I have the flat wheel on my bike. You can fix it while I wait?"

"Of course we can." And we could, the rush finally having ebbed to a dull roar. "Is it outside?"

"Yes." She led the way out. The bike leaned against the bench in front of the store, an older model that had seen better days and had a collapsed front tire.

"Did you ride it like that?" I asked. She could have bent the rim.

"No, my friend gives me a ride here."

"Good." I wheeled it into the repair room and hoisted it onto the stand. I spun the wheel to see if the rim was bent. "This will only take a few minutes. Do you want to have a seat out front?"

"No, I wait here." She leaned against the doorjamb and watched me work.

The wheel was bent. I removed it from the bike and laid it on the bench. Using the flat end of two tire levers, I worked the inner tube out. It was in such bad shape I laid it aside. I inspected the tire itself, running my fingers along the inside, and shook my head.

"I'm afraid the whole wheel is shot. The rim is bent and the rubber has all these cracks, see? I could patch the tube and put it back in, but it'll be flat again in no time."

"How much is it costing, a new wheel?" She folded her arms, frowning.

I cited her the amount and watched her wince. "But I have a lightly used one I think is the right size. It'll only cost a few dollars."

"A few dollars is better. Thank you."

I picked the used wheel off the pile on a high shelf and checked the size. It was perfect and the tire was in reasonably good shape, too.

"I hear you are detective," Sofia said. "You help police with this murder case."

I glanced at her and laughed. "I'm not a detective at all. I run a bike shop. You must have me mixed up with someone else."

"No, my friend tells me." She lowered her voice. "I don't like police. I have papers, but police can be bad. But I am worrying about something." She definitely looked worried, with her wide brow furrowed and her mouth drawn down.

"What are you worried about?" I asked.

"If I tell you, you tell police? But not with my name?"

Ah. "You want me to pass along information anonymously."

Her expression brightened. "Would you?"

"Why don't you tell me what it is and I'll decide if I can or not." The used wheel didn't have an inner tube in it, so I worked one in. I inflated it about halfway and checked all around to be sure the tube wasn't pinched by the tire before fully inflating it. "The detective on the case doesn't like secrets."

She laid her hand over her mouth and gazed at the floor as if thinking. She looked up with resolve in her eyes. "I tell you. Ron, the grandson, he is my boyfriend. But he is acting odd these days, this week. Different. Like he hides something from me."

"Do you have any idea what he's hiding?"

"No, I ask and he doesn't say. He has phone call and goes outside to answer."

"And you think it might have to do with his grandmother's murder?" I kept an eye on her even as I set the wheel back into the fork blades and snapped closed the lever to secure it.

"Maybe."

I lifted the bike off the rack and set it on the floor. "Do you think he killed her?"

She stared at me, her blue eyes wide. "Maybe."

Chapter Twenty-five

"I'll stick around until one o'clock," Norland offered, when I told him I had to be somewhere at noon. "You're an angel." I grabbed my EpiPen bag and hurried toward the big white UU church at a few minutes before twelve, my heart racing. I had requested the meeting with Pa, but suddenly I was nervous about it.

Or maybe I was simply hungry. My granola and buttermilk with a cut-up local peach seemed like a long time ago. The conversation with Sofia had unsettled me, too. I'd finally reassured her I wouldn't be able to tell Lincoln what she said without identifying her, but she shouldn't worry. After she rode off on her repaired bike, I'd texted Lincoln with her concern and added it to the group thread, too.

Now I pulled open the big, heavy door to the white church and let myself into the sanctuary, a room as familiar to me as my own face in the mirror. I'd grown up in this beautiful old church with its tall windows, second-floor gallery running around three walls, and antique pew boxes. My heart rate slowed and I walked at a meditative pace, making my way to the front and through the door on the left to the church offices. I could have entered from the outside, but this lovely sanctuary when empty was as peaceful a place as I'd ever been.

Pa's office door was open, but he was on the phone. He held up a finger and I nodded. I moved about the edges of the comfortable room, with two walls of bookcases holding family photos as well as books. I picked up one of my favorite pictures. I was about Cokey's age, already wearing glasses, and Derrick was ten or so. My parents stood behind, all four of us dressed in Easter finery. I was holding Derrick's hand and looking up as he gazed down at me, laughing with me. We'd gotten along well as kids, both of us ignoring the "half" part of being siblings. He'd protected me, but we'd also rough-housed and played ball sports together. He'd almost never said, "Go away, bratty little sister." Family. That's what I was here to talk about.

I turned back to my father when I heard him say good-bye, and went over to kiss his cheek. He stood, enveloping me in a hug for a welcome and reassuring moment.

"How's my girl?" He sank into one of the armchairs in front of the desk and opened a small cooler sitting on the floor.

I sat opposite him. "I need your counsel, Pa."

"I heard a need in your voice this morning." He handed me a sandwich, a napkin, and a bottle of water. "Let us have a moment of silent grace and gratitude before we eat." He closed his eyes.

I did the same. It was a practice I'd grown up with, one a Quaker friend had said her family followed, too. It usually brought solace. Not so much today. When my stomach growled, I opened my eyes to the sight of him laughing.

"Dig in, *querida*."

"Bon appétit." I took a bite of the tuna salad sandwich, savoring the crunch of celery, the salty bite of capers, the fresh taste of a leaf of lettuce mixing with the fish. The bread was thick slices of a delicious multi-grain. "Mmm. Perfect sandwich."

"Bread's from your man's bakery," Pa said.

"I thought so. And he's the reason I'm here." I took another bite and set my sandwich on the desk.

Pa chewed and waited.

"Pa, he wants to have children with me. Marry, move in together, start a family." I gazed at my father, the epitome of a family man.

"And?"

"And I'm not sure." I folded my hands in my lap and regarded them before looking up. "To tell you the truth, I'm afraid. I'm afraid to lose control over my life."

He nodded as if he already knew what I was going to say. "As a child you were always so tidy. You kept your room clean, your school backpack in order, and your toys all lined up like a regiment. In that way you were very different from Derrick, and your mother and I thought it was an admirable trait, at least in a child. What do you think of those habits now?"

"It's the way I am." I lifted a shoulder. "Mess bothers me, throws me off-kilter. Right now my life is exactly how I like it."

"You're thirty-six. Do you want to have children?"

"I think so. Our family means everything to me. I kind of want the same."

"Do you love Tim? Admire his values? Like him?"

"Of course!" When my eyes filled with tears, I swiped at them. "I do. Last night he as much as said he will leave me if I don't agree to get the family ball rolling. And I don't want to lose him," I murmured.

"He seems an extraordinarily decent man to me, and I've seen how much he cares for you."

I had, too, over and over.

"Has he discussed marriage?"

"A little. It's family that's more important to him, though. And whether we were married or not, I know he would be committed to me and to our children." *Our children.* I'd never said those words before. I blinked. It sounded nice. It felt round, unifying, a comfort. The image of tall, strong Tim holding a baby in one arm and a toddler by the hand rose up in my mind. My throat thickened with emotion.

"Have you and he talked about a living arrangement, the details of daily life?"

"No." I swallowed. "Although I've thought about it a little. His house would work for a small family."

"Having those conversations together might make the possibility seem more real, honey, if you are inclined. I would hate to see you unhappy either from losing this love you cherish—which is not always easy to find—or from entangling yourself in a living situation you can't deal with. I hope you will sit with these thoughts and pray on them, if you are so inclined. I have every confidence you will come to the right decision."

I smiled. Pa saying "I have every confidence you will . . ."

had been one of his mantras as I grew up. I might have come wailing to him that my friend was being mean, that the kite string was impossible to untangle, or later that I couldn't solve a particular trig-onometry problem. Sending me back to work it out on my own had been a wise parenting practice and solution that fostered my ingenuity and independence. I noticed he hadn't given me a single word of advice in our conversation just now, but had listened and asked questions. No wonder he was such a good counselor. He gave people with troubles the space to counsel themselves.

"Thank you, Pa." I let out a deep breath.

"Now, catch me up on poor Ms. Ruchart's demise. Do you know if the police are close to apprehending the killer? Certain members of the congregation are becoming increasingly agitated and nervous about the situation." He took a bite of sandwich.

I sipped my water. "I don't think the police are close. Lincoln Haskins has dropped by to ask questions a few times, but he doesn't tell me anything in return. They apparently searched Gin's garage and shop yesterday, and antifreeze appears to be the poison that killed Beverly."

"We lost a dog in that way when I was a child." He grimaced. "A car had leaked some of the fluid and he licked it up off the driveway.

"Pa, that's so sad. I never heard you talk about that before."

"These things happen. But in the current case, surely the authorities must have one or two persons of interest, as they put it."

"Gin is one, although it's a preposterous suggestion. If they found the antifreeze on her property, somebody planted it there. Beverly's son Ron is a possibility. He's

kind of sketchy and thinks he's inheriting her entire estate. His girlfriend, a waitress locally, also seems to have
hated Beverly. And do you know an Isadora Farnham?"

Pa's eyebrows went up. "Actually, I do. She, ah, at-
tends a meeting here from time to time." He frowned.

The same answer Derrick had offered. The church
hosted an AA meeting a couple of times a week. But Pa
would keep Isadora's confidentiality sacred. It wasn't any
use asking him.

He cocked his head. "Why do you ask?"

"She didn't like Beverly much, either."

A yip and the sound of four small feet tapping along
came from the hall.

"To the point of killing her?" Pa asked.

Mom appeared in the doorway, Tucker's leash in hand.
When she let go of the strap, he ran to Pa, who scooped
him up and got a chinful of wriggling doggie smooches in
return.

"Killing who?" my mother asked.

"Beverly Ruchart," I said, accepting a kiss on the
cheek.

"Mercury was retrograde when she was killed. Mis-
communication can be disastrous in those periods."

Being murdered had definitely been a disaster for Beverly.

Chapter Twenty-six

"Mac, got a minute?" Victoria called out. She stood behind the open driver's side door of her cruiser, which was parked at the curb in front of the church when I emerged a few minutes after my mom and Tucker had arrived.

Was Victoria following me? I shook off the thought. "Only a few. I have to get back to the shop."

She waved me toward her before sliding in behind the wheel. When I got to the car, I leaned my forearms on the passenger window's opening.

"What's happening?" I asked. "Does Lincoln have the local force on the case?"

She nodded slowly. "As usual, the staties can use all the help they can get. Them and the BCI."

"What's the BCI?"

"Bureau of Criminal Investigation," she explained. "Barnstable County crime scene squad. It's several agencies joining forces to look into homicides and a lot more on the Cape and the islands."

I wondered why I hadn't heard about the BCI during the last case. Probably because I was a civilian, not a law enforcement official, and I planned to keep it that way.

"So you're following responsible citizen-witnesses around town to see if they were telling the truth?" As soon as I said the words, I wished I could erase them. Abo Ree would scold me up one side and down the next for such a rude response.

She reared back in her seat. "What makes you think so? I stopped by the bike shop to ask you a question, and your brother told me you were here at the church."

Ouch. "Sorry. I'm a little on edge this week. What did you want to know?"

"We're all a little on edge." She cleared her throat. "Get in for a minute so we can talk?" She pointed to the passenger seat.

I sighed to myself but opened the door and slid in. "What's up?"

"Lincoln asked us to follow up on a couple of things. You're aware Sofia Burtseva and Ron Ruchart are a couple?"

"I've heard that, yes."

"Do you think they worked together to kill Ron's grandmother?" Victoria asked.

"I have no idea." I was pretty sure she was asking so she could trip me up about something. In the past she hadn't cared about my considered opinion. "How would I know?"

"Also, you told Lincoln about Ron Ruchart's birth father." She checked a small notebook on the dashboard. "One Danny Rizzoli."

"It's what my boyfriend said Eli Tubin told him."

"Got it. Lincoln neglected to note the chain of information." She checked the notebook again. "Tubin is Ron's stepfather, correct?"

"Right."

"Do you know where he works, where he lives?"

"He works at the Oceanographic Institute, and I think Gin said he lives in Woods Hole, too."

Victoria pulled a pen out of her breast pocket and jotted in the notebook. "Gin Malloy?"

"Yes, she's been dating Eli."

The chief paused her pen and turned her head to narrow her eyes at me. "Aha. Does Lincoln know this?"

"I think so. I don't remember if he asked me, and I don't know if Gin told him. Does it matter?" I was getting a bad feeling about this line of questioning.

"It could. Two people who were at the dinner. Two who had a connection to the victim—and to each other. It definitely could matter."

"You have to be kidding," I protested. "Gin had no reason in the world to hurt Beverly. You saw her right after she found the body. Gin was in shock."

"Or she's a good actress." Victoria lifted one eyebrow. "I'm not kidding, Mac."

I shook my head, exasperated. "Are we done?"

"Not quite. What's your boyfriend's name?"

I squinted at her out of one eye. What was she trying to pull? "You know who it is. Tim Brunelle. He owns Greta's bakery, which is next door to the police station."

She knew very well who he was. What she didn't need to know was he might not be my boyfriend much longer.

"Thanks for your time, Mac. I have to get going."

"Right." I climbed out, closed the door, and bent over to speak through the open window. "Have a good day."

Victoria didn't meet my gaze as she tapped her pen on the notebook. "What's today's date?"

I thought. "It's the fifteenth."

"Yeah, it is. Hope Brunelle is able to bounce back after you drop him." She started the cruiser and drove off.

August fifteenth. I groaned aloud as I watched her taillights disappear around the bend. Twenty years to the day when I'd broken up with her older brother. Twenty years since Vince Laitinen killed himself.

Chapter Twenty-seven

I trudged back to the shop, my feet lumps of concrete. Victoria clearly still blamed me for her brother's suicide. I had gone out with him for only a few months. A year older than Victoria and me, we'd dated one summer when I was home from college. The memory was bittersweet. While Victoria was petite, Vince had been nearly six feet tall, his pale hair long on top but short on the sides so it was always falling in his eyes. He was the first boy who had showed interest in me, a skinny, geeky girl with glasses. He'd flashed his wicked grin at me and stolen my heart.

But as I got to know him during that summer, I understood Vince was troubled in some way I couldn't help him with. His moods were all over the place: one day all energy and love, the next day dark and stormy. Victoria and I weren't friends—on the contrary, she'd never liked me and had treated me like an adversary for years—so I wasn't able to ask her what his issue was. Finally, I couldn't handle the drama any longer and told him I couldn't be his girlfriend.

As an adult I realized Vince was probably bipolar or had some other mental illness. But the Laitinen parents were followers of Christian Science, and their kids had never seen a conventional doctor. When I learned the next morning he'd hung himself, I felt awful for a long time. I didn't go near a boy again until my last year of college. And Victoria? Her grief only intensified her treating me like the enemy. After I returned to Westham last year and settled into being a shopkeeper, we'd achieved a wary détente. Her comment a few minutes ago indicated she still harbored a grudge.

I arrived at my cheery shop. The yellow window boxes overflowing with flowers were lovely against the blue-painted exterior walls. The OPEN flag flapped in a sea breeze, and the giant-wheeled vintage bicycle in front added a note of whimsy. Too bad I didn't feel so cheery. Before I went in, I took a deep breath and exhaled it, intending for the tension of the current death and the dark, sad memory of Vince's to go out with my breath.

Inside Derrick was perched on the stool behind the counter. I didn't see Norland anywhere.

My brother glanced up. "He just left. We were wicked busy until about a quarter of one. Suddenly we had a lull and I told him he could head out."

"Thanks, Derr."

"Sure. How was your meeting with Pa?" He tilted his head.

"Fine. You know how he is. Never tells you what to do, but somehow you end up knowing what the right path is." *Mostly*.

"I do know." He didn't ask what the talk had been about.

I stashed my bag in my office. "I would have been back sooner, but Victoria grabbed me, wanted to ask a few questions about various people associated with Beverly's death."

"She's on Haskins's payroll now?"

"Or whatever. It makes sense different law enforcement agencies would work together." I picked at a thread on the hem of my shorts.

"You okay, sis? You seem, I don't know, less energized than usual." He slid off the stool, slung his arm around my shoulders, and squeezed.

I let out a sigh. "Did you know Vince Laitinen at school?" Derrick was five years older than me, so he might not have. And Vince and I hadn't really gotten to the dinner-with-the-family stage of dating in our few months together.

"A little bit from cross-country. When I was a senior he was such a fast runner they let him train with the high school squad even though he was only in eighth grade."

"Today's the twenty-year mark of when he committed suicide. The same night I broke up with him."

Derrick faced me, nodding slowly. "And Victoria was kind enough to remind you of his death anniversary?"

"She was. She still blames me. I guess you never get over a sibling's death, but I wish I had some way of making peace with her."

"Hang in there, kid." He laid a smooth palm on my cheek. "You're both adults. You'll figure it out. And you know his death wasn't your fault, right?" He leaned over a little to peer straight into my eyes. "It was his life. He was the only one responsible."

"I know. But . . ." But I still felt partly to blame.

"No buts, Mackie. No buts."

I nodded in slow motion, as if it would convince me. "Thanks, bro." I gazed at his face, which I knew as well as my own. "I sure hope neither of us has to lose the other, not until we're way old."

"You and me both, sis."

Chapter Twenty-eight

With Derrick holding down the fort at the shop later that afternoon, I drove Miss M to pick up Cokey at the parsonage, where Mom was taking care of her. My niece was super excited about the Family Fun Run coming up the day before the road race, and she'd asked me to take her running so she could practice. I belted her in the passenger seat and didn't lower the top. Seating her in the front wasn't quite kosher because of how little she was, but I didn't have a back seat and we weren't going far. Derrick had given his permission, so off we went.

"Titi Mac, are you going to run, too?" she asked.

"No, honey, I can't run. I have a bad knee."

"What did your knee do? Did you put it in a time-out?"

I laughed. "That wouldn't have helped. A bad knee means I hurt it a few years ago and it never got better."

"That's too bad." She shook her head, her face solemn. "But I'll watch you, okay?"

"Goody." She brightened. "When I run you have to timer me."

I smiled to myself. "Yes, I'll time you."

After we'd set foot on the long, flat beach, I had a pang, remembering my breakfast here with Tim only a few days ago. Watching him run into the water to cool off. Our companionship, our sharing. I shook off the memory. For now.

Cokey switched her pink Red Sox cap around so the bill was in the back. Her angel hair was in two braids today, and she wore a little sleeveless jersey, pink stretch shorts, and sneakers. "I have to lean against you to stretch."

"You do?"

All serious, she bobbed her head like a little grown-up. "Tio Tim teached me to stretch. Before and after I extracise."

"Then you'd better do what he said." I braced my legs and watched as she planted her tiny hands on my thigh and stretched first one hamstring, then the other.

She let go of me, balanced on one foot, and reached her hand around to pull her other foot up toward her rear end, but she lost her balance and plopped onto the sand.

"Oopthie," she lisped. "Okay, I'm ready now. Timer me, Titi Mac."

"Draw a line in the sand with your foot. It'll be your starting line."

She dragged her heel until the line was a yard long, then crouched in a starting position behind it, one foot back, one forward, hands splayed on the bent front knee. I checked up and down the beach. A number of sun lovers and families were to our left, but it was mostly clear to our right.

I'd hung a whistle on a string around my neck and pointed to the right. "Run that way until I blow my whistle and then turn around and run back." I whipped out my phone and set a timer. "On your mark, get set, go!"

She sprinted away from me and I speed-walked after her, but she was going way faster than I was. My niece was going to sleep well tonight. As I walked, I gazed for a moment out at the sparkling water, at a white sail puffed out with wind, at a sandpiper hurrying away from me along the water line.

When the timer read two minutes, I blew the whistle and stopped walking. I peered after her. *Uh-oh.* A figure crouched next to her. A man jogged in place next to him. Where had they come from? Cokey had stopped running and it looked like she was talking with the person who was squatting. What an idiot I was, to let her go off alone on a public beach. What was I thinking? I broke into a run toward her, despite the pain in my left knee. I slowed when the figure stood and I saw it was Tim. He, Cokey, and the other person started jogging toward me.

The relief of seeing someone familiar weakened my knees. The love I felt for both him and Cokey filled my heart. Then, because of how he'd left last night, an attack of nerves turned my palms clammy and my heart into a jackhammer. And who was the other guy? Maybe Tim's running friend, Eli. I dropped to sit on the sand and wait.

They sprinted the last few yards until they reached me, with Tim and the other guy—it was Eli Tubin, I now saw—staying a pace behind Cokey.

"Titi Mac, I won the race!" Pink-cheeked Cokey beamed. "I beat Tio Tim and Mr. Eli."

"Nice job, Coke." I held up my hand for a high five. "You're really fast."

Shirtless Tim stayed standing, backlit by the sun. He didn't speak. Eli, about five-nine and lean, jogged in place again.

"Hi, there." I extended a hand to Tim. "Help me up?"

He obliged but dropped my hand as soon as I was on my feet. *Ouch*. His feelings were still raw about our future. And would they ever not be? Cokey darted off to chase after a sandpiper at the water's edge.

Eli raised a hand in greeting. "Hi, Mac." He smiled. "Great niece you got there." Looking his age, his sandy hair had receded up to the top of his head, and his high brow gleamed with sweat.

"She's awesome, isn't she? It's good to see you again, Eli. I've heard a lot about you from this guy since our double date."

"I'm in trouble now." He grinned. "Hey, man," he said to Tim. "I'm going to run on, keep my heart rate up. Meet you at the end?"

"Cool," Tim said.

We both watched Eli continue on his run.

"I don't know what kind of message you think you're sending me, Mac." Tim's voice was soft, hurt. "But having her run to me was a low blow." His chest moved with his breath, or maybe it was with sorrow.

What? "I didn't have her run to you, Tim. I didn't even know you were out here. Cokey wanted to practice for the kids' race."

"I don't believe you. You want to see me but on your terms. Eat your cake and have it, too."

"That's not how it was." I took a step toward him.

He stepped back and folded his arms. "You didn't

think it was dangerous sending her off jogging alone? I could have been any man." He sounded angry, but he blinked and sniffed, like he was barely holding back emotion.

"I had her in sight the whole time. Tim, please . . ." *Please what?* What was I asking him? He'd said he didn't want to talk any more. I searched his face with my eyes, but he wouldn't meet my gaze.

He pressed his lips together and shook his head. He stepped around me. "Excuse me. I have to finish my run."

"But I—"

He took two long strides to Cokey and scooped her up for a hug before setting off down the beach after Eli.

I watched him, elbows swinging, feet coming up cleanly behind, head high, until he became a speck. The jackhammer in my chest morphed into a motionless lead anchor. My man was angry with me, and he was hurt. We'd been talking for weeks about his wanting to have children, but we'd never actually fought about anything before. I wasn't sure I could stand it. My emotions were a mess.

"Look, Titi Mac, I built a house." Cokey pointed to wobbly walls of damp sand in a square, with pebbles and seashells adorning the top.

I tried to shake off my heavy mood. "I love it, sweetie. Do you want to run some more?"

"No, I runned enough. Will you play with me?"

"Sure." I knelt next to her.

"Let's pretend this stick is the mommy fish and this one is the little-girl fish," she lisped, holding up two small pieces of driftwood.

Twenty minutes of play later, we'd built little beds in the house, for "the fishes to sleep on," Cokey had said, and had lined a tiny front porch with pebbles. Apparently play was the medicine I'd needed, or at least a welcome distraction. Pretending with Cokey had definitely lightened my mood.

"I'm hungry," my niece announced.

"Then it's time to go. I have a snack for you in the car."

She slipped her sandy hand into mine with simple trust and connection.

As we neared the top of the wooden stairs leading up the dune to the parking area, a beat-up old Jeep blocked the view. A soft-top model, now sans roof, the car had been backed into the spot directly in front of the steps. Ron Ruchart sat in the driver's seat talking with a woman in the passenger seat, her ear-length blonde hair blowing in the wind—Isadora. They knew each other? Gin had said they'd both been at the dinner, of course. They'd both lost their mothers, so maybe they later connected about their mutual loss. Isadora held up a metal flask and drank from it.

Cokey pulled on my hand to stop. She squatted to smell a beach rose.

"Watch out for bees, now," I cautioned. Meanwhile I listened for what Ron and Isadora were saying, staying as far away from the flowers as I could. The breeze was offshore and coming straight at me. I was still two steps down from the landing at the top, so only my head and torso were visible, and Ron and Isadora didn't seem to see me.

". . . met my father." Ron's words arrived on the wind.

"You never knew him?" Isadora asked.

"No, but he's . . ."

The wind shifted and his voice went elsewhere. *He's*

what? So my musing had been right about Ron's father. What I wouldn't give to hear the part of the conversation I was missing.

"That bike shop lady was in the game store asking me all kinds of questions." Ron's voice was back.

"She came into Maxine's, too," Isadora said. "Did you know she was involved in a murder a couple of months ago?"

"I heard. Crazy . . ." Ron's voice blew away again.

They were talking about me. *Great.*

Ron started the engine and the Jeep drove off, Isadora drinking again from her flask.

Cokey tugged at my arm. "I have to go peepee."

"Race you to the restrooms," I smiled at her. "But stay on the walkway. Don't go through the parking lot, okay?"

"You got it." She clambered up to the top and dashed around the perimeter walk to the building on the far side, which was way closer than the end of the beach I'd let her run to a little while ago. I walked as fast as I could after her. I wished I was a sand flea with excellent hearing in the Jeep, instead.

Chapter Twenty-nine

I'd told Derrick I would close, so I took Cokey back to the shop.

"No big rushes, no fires to extinguish?" I asked my brother after we'd greeted each other.

"No. We still have a couple rentals out that are due back today. Oh, and Orlean called to say she'll be in to-morrow. She apparently ate a few oysters last night that didn't agree with her."

"That's no fun, but I'm glad she'll be in."

"Daddy, I beat Tio Tim in a race on the beach." Cokey bounced on her heels.

"That's my girl." He beamed down at her.

I waved as she rode off in the child's seat on the back of her father's bicycle, her braids flying out from under her pink helmet. Now that I was alone, the lead returned to my feet and my heart. Once again I pictured Tim beaming down at a child, but one of ours, not Cokey. I thought of him riding away with a toddler on the back of his bike. But I also saw the hurt on his face this afternoon, hurt emerging as near anger. Why wouldn't he be both hurt and mad? So far I'd been choosing me over us. On the other hand, he had, too, except his "me" included an expanded "us."

I checked the clock. Five thirty was early to start my closing checklist. Since we had rentals due, I'd need to stay here until six, but I could start the closing routine now. I began with closing out the cash register. I wouldn't need it, because rentals prepaid by credit. I didn't actually bill until the bikes were returned, but if I had to charge additional days, I already had their payment information. Once the till was in the safe, I wheeled in the couple of display bikes we put out front and grabbed the OPEN flag from its holder.

As I furled it, I caught movement behind me and turned to see ruddy-cheeked Tulia in the doorway. Her Lobstah Shack was only a few doors down Main Street. I stashed the flag behind the counter and walked to the door.

"Hey, Tulia."

She extended a thick paper bag. "Brought you some cod cakes." She was wearing one of her dozen variations on a lobster T-shirt. This one read, GOT BUTTER? under a picture of a lobster.

"You did? What's the occasion?"

She chuckled. "Didn't sell 'em all today. They don't keep so great."

"Looks like I have dinner, then. Thanks. You closed early?"

"Not by much. Have to get over to a meeting at the cultural center in Mashpee." She frowned. "Mac, you haven't been checking your texts."

"No, I was at the beach with my niece. Did something happen?"

"The detective took Gin in for questioning 'bout an hour ago."

No. "He did? He didn't arrest her, did he?"

"No," Tulia said. "She was able to send a quick text."

"I can't believe he would think she could have killed Beverly."

"I know, right?"

Was there some way I could help Gin? "I don't suppose there's anything we can do for her."

Tulia shook her head. "Doubt it. She'll probably be home before too long. She said she knew she didn't have any antifreeze in her garage."

"I'm thinking it had to be a plant, not that anybody's said so."

"She said she didn't have any, and I believe her." She shrugged. "Hey, gotta run. Enjoy your supper."

"Thanks again. See you tomorrow night?"

"You bet." She headed down the sidewalk.

I slid the bag of fish cakes into the little fridge, perched on the stool behind the counter, and checked the text thread. It was exactly as Tulia had said. *Darn.* I scrolled through but didn't find anything I didn't already know. I'd asked Flo to dig up a picture of Danny Rizzoli. She must not have had time yet. I added a text about overhearing Ron saying he'd met his father. While I was at it, I should share the information with Lincoln.

FYI, saw Isadora Farnham and Ron Ruchart at beach. Overheard Ron tell her he'd met his father.

There. My civic duty was done. I tapped out another text to Gin.

Tulia said you're at station. Call me after?

I worried that whoever left the antifreeze in Gin's garage also left some other kind of evidence that would point to my friend as the killer. I knew she was innocent, and I hated the thought of her having to endure being a suspect. My phone dinged with a text. It was from Flo on the group thread.

Learned they found Beverly's car parked behind Gin's place.

Another ding, this time from Zane.

Will they think B was coming to visit G? G poisoned her and dragged her body to the clinic?

I sucked air in through my teeth. His suggestion didn't sound good. But wait. The municipal lot was behind Gin's store, and where we'd found the body was on the path cutting through between Salty Taffy's and the clinic. I added a text.

Lot also near clinic. Maybe B called clinic to get hours or something. Have to prove she drove herself there for med help.

Lincoln had to be looking at Beverly's phone records. And probably at Gin's, too. Gin wouldn't have any reason to call Beverly after the dinner. Another text came in, from Gin to me.

Heading home now, will call later.

She'd been released. What a relief. I was dying to know what had transpired, but I was going to have to wait. I slid off the stool and paced to the door and back. My rentals had exactly five minutes to return the bikes or they faced a high daily charge for every day they didn't return them. For someone who liked things neat, my life was a big, stinking mess right now. Uncooperative customers weren't my favorites, although dealing with them was part of running a business. What was worse was my best friend being under suspicion, as well as my love life being in shambles. I tidied the merchandise at the end of the counter—the lip moisturizers, headlamps, and energy bars. I straightened the pens in their tray next to the register and wiped a speck of dust off the top. None of it tidied the jumble in my mind.

I whirled at a noise behind me. One, two, three rental bikes were wheeled in by three sun-kissed and wind-blown college women. At least something was going right. I had to trust the rest of it would, too.

Chapter Thirty

I ate my to-die-for cod cakes along with some sweet-potato oven fries I whipped up. When the fries were nearly done, I'd added the cod cakes to the oven so the heat crisped up the crusts. When I dug in, the meat was tender and full of flavor, seasoned with fresh dill. I tasted exactly the right amount of garlic, too. I topped one of them with a spicy peach salsa I had in the fridge, but the plain one was equally delicious.

"Belle, what should I do about Tim?" I asked after swallowing the last bite.

"Handsome!" She broke into her wolf whistle.

Big help, bird.

My phone buzzed, revealing a call from Gin, who asked for a ride to Eli's place in Woods Hole.

"I'm too shaky from my police interview to drive. Would you mind taking me, say, in half an hour?"

"I'm not doing anything else. Of course I'll drive you over there."

"Thanks, Mac. You're the best."

"See you in thirty."

"How are you?" I asked after she climbed into Miss M.

"I've been better," Gin responded. "Lots better." She gazed at the inside of my car. "Mac, how can you keep your car so clean? It looks brand new."

It was true. I never let trash or clutter accumulate in the car, the same as in my house. Even my cloth shopping bags were neatly folded into the passenger door side pocket.

I laughed. "I like it that way. And I don't drive her very often."

"The inside of my car is suitcase, delivery vehicle, and wastebasket all in one. I don't think I've vacuumed it once since I bought it." Gin shook her head.

To each her own. "Anyway, I heard Lincoln took you in for questioning." I was curious about a million things, but I wanted to let her tell me at her own pace.

"I didn't know what else to tell him. I don't use anti-freeze. What they found wasn't mine. I didn't know where it came from. Period."

"So they did find it in your garage?"

"Yes, unfortunately. And he asked me about it five different ways. I always had the same answer." She let out a sigh. "Thanks for the ride. I had a stiff drink when I got home and between that and my nerves, I just wasn't up to getting behind the wheel."

Gin had a fondness for her namesake alcohol and often enjoyed a gin drink. "G and tonic or gin rickey?

"I had a Paradise."

"What's in it?"

"Gin, apricot brandy, and orange juice." She smiled. "It's good, like dessert in a glass. And think of all the vitamin C, too."

I laughed. "I'd have to cut the drink with seltzer or something. It sounds way too sweet for me."

She extended a flat hand. "I even had seconds on the drink, but I'm still shaking."

I glanced at her hand. "You are. You know I'm happy to drive."

"I appreciate it, Mac. Detective Haskins also said they found Beverly's car behind my building."

"In the municipal lot by the path leading to the clinic?"

"Exactly. Why would the cops think she'd driven to my shop so I could conveniently kill her right there? Geez. It's like they're living in an alternate universe, Mac."

"They should be focusing on phone records, alibis, real evidence, right?"

"Of course!"

"Anyway, did you see the thread after you got home?" I asked.

"Yes. Interesting that Danny Rizzoli might be around."

"At the dinner, did Isadora and Ron seem like they knew each other before then?"

"No, I don't think so." She shook her head.

"It seemed odd to me they were in a car at the beach together." Traffic moved slowly as we wound through a hilly, wooded area. The two-lane road was the primary route to access the scenic peninsula and the ferry to Martha's Vineyard, so it was heavily traveled in the summer, even now in the evening.

"Isadora's mother died when she was young, and Ron lost his, too," Gin said. "Maybe they're bonding over both of them losing moms."

"I thought about that, too. They both seem a little messed up, you know what I mean?" I knew if my mother had died when I was at any age it would have devastated me. Astra was quirky, but I had never once doubted her unconditional love for me. Even though Cokey's mother was alive, she wasn't around for her, not even virtually. All of us in the family tried to make up for that lack. "I can only guess at what losing a mom when you're young would do to a kid's emotional state."

"Maybe it's the reason Isadora seems like she wants a lot of material things, to make up for not having a mom. And why she's upset about Wesley finding his birth son."

"Yeah, although you'd think Beverly filling in for Ron's mom would have meant something to him."

"Right? He sure didn't seem very upset about her death."

I slowed for a pedestrian crossing near where the ferry was docked. A young woman in a skirt and helmet walked her bike across. I was glad to see lights on the cycle's front and rear already illuminated, plus one flashing on her headgear. Riding at dusk was wicked dangerous without good lights. "I do know neither of us is a shrink, and we probably shouldn't go overboard with psychobabble."

"No kidding." Gin yawned, then laughed. "Sorry. I'm beat." She glanced around. "Oh, turn right there," she instructed, pointing at the next corner.

"There?" I screeched. I barely had time to make the tight turn, but Miss M grips the road like nobody's business, so we made it. Gin directed me half a block down to a silver-shingled home with a detached garage to the side and behind.

"Park on the street," she said. "Eli rents the converted garage, and the owners don't like his guests using the driveway."

I pulled over and waited for her to get out.

The passenger door shut with a thunk. Gin took two steps and twisted to look back at me. "Well, aren't you going to come in? I want you to say hello to Eli."

"Oh? I saw him briefly on the beach this afternoon," I said. But why shouldn't I go in? I didn't have any plans other than reading tonight, what with things up in the air between Tim and me. "Sure, but only for a few minutes." I had to admit I was curious about Eli, given what Ron had said. Plus his relationship with Beverly intrigued me.

At the side door to the garage, Gin knocked twice. "It's me," she called before pulling open the screen door. The inside door stood ajar.

Eli stood with his back to us at the stove in a kitchen nook to the left. The large former garage was fragrant with the delectable scents of aromatic vegetables sautéing—onions and garlic, at a minimum—plus nutty sesame oil, soy sauce, and a hint of hot pepper. It was a good thing I'd eaten or I might have invited myself to dinner. It was also warm inside. Eli wore an apron but was shirtless under it, and his shorts were minimal running wear, showing off the same firm runner's butt Tim had, except sized proportionally to someone half a foot shorter. He stirred the vegetables in the wok with eighteen-inch chopsticks. A ray of the nearly setting sun slanted in through a western window and turned his sandy hair to a rust color.

Without looking, he said, "Hey, kid."

"Mac's here, too," Gin began.

Eli whirled. His hand jerked and a shred of onion flew through the air, landing on Gin's bare arm. She cried out in pain from the hot oil.

"What's sh—" He bit off the question but left his mouth open, lips drawn down. His face had alarm written all over it for a split second. Just as suddenly it transformed into the smiling runner's face I'd seen this afternoon.

Huh? It was as if I'd caught him at something. But what? All he appeared to be doing was making stir-fry for his new lady friend. Had I seen alarm on his face, or something worse?

Gin rubbed her arm as she bounced her gaze back and forth between the two of us in bewilderment. "She drove me over and I wanted her to have the chance to say hi, see your place. That's okay, right?"

"Good to see you again so soon, Eli," I said. "But I don't need to stick around. I thought I was only going to drop Gin off."

"Nonsense." He spread his hands, beaming. "Of course you'll stay. We'll have a glass of wine."

Should I? It wouldn't hurt and I might learn something. "A small one," I said. "I have to get home."

"Sit down," he directed, waving toward the right. "Let me take the food off the heat and I'll get us all a glass of something. Sauvignon blanc all right?"

I glanced at Gin. She nodded. I followed her to a small sitting area with a futon couch and two chairs, where two empty wineglasses sat on a low table along with an array of cheese and crackers. A gauzy curtain hung at the end of the space, not hiding the wide bed it separated from us. A door near the kitchen nook must lead to a bathroom. Next to the couch was a low bookcase with framed pictures on top. I peered at them. Several portrayed a family of five, with one boy and two girls, likely Eli with his siblings and parents. Another was of a slightly younger Eli, his arm around a short woman who smiled up at him. His late wife, Beverly's daughter? What was glaringly missing were any pictures of stepson Ron. *Why?* I took a chair, leaving the couple the couch.

Moments later, Eli, having shed the apron and now wearing a Falmouth Road Race T-shirt, approached holding a third glass and a frosty open wine bottle. He poured for all of us with the widest, stubbiest fingers I'd ever seen.

"Cheers," Gin said, raising her glass.

We all clinked and returned the toast.

Eli laid his arm along Gin's shoulders. "Pretty rough interrogation, was it?"

"Not rough per se." She wrinkled her nose. "But I don't want to talk about it right now."

We chatted about news and the upcoming road race for a few minutes. I was dying to ask him about Beverly and what Ron had said about our host hating her. I cleared my throat.

"You must be pretty broken up about your former mother-in-law's death, Eli." I kept my tone casual.

Gin squeezed one eye shut and squinted at me out of the other. She knew me well enough to realize I was digging for information.

He shot me another odd look. "I'm deeply sorry she has passed, of course." Eli reclaimed his arm and folded his hands in his lap, a gesture losing some of its piousness by how scant his shorts were. "That said, we weren't close, not even when my late wife was alive." He gazed at the photograph of him with the short woman. "So, no. Beverly's death did not break my heart."

Chapter Thirty-one

By eight thirty I was back in my house with my feet up, my too-busy brain happily reading about the quirky fictional town of Frog Ledge, Connecticut. As happy as I could be, that is, with the prospect of losing Tim lurking behind my heart. I'd cleaned my kitchen and made my lunch for tomorrow before Gin had called for a ride. With my driving favor accomplished, I didn't have anything to do or anywhere to be except right here.

On my way home from dropping off Gin, I'd kept thinking about the look Eli gave me, and how he didn't meet my eyes when he'd said he wasn't really sorry Beverly was dead. Something was off about his behavior, but I couldn't figure out what.

Now, even though a murder investigation was underway, nothing stopped book group on Thursday nights, and I wanted to finish *The Icing on the Corpse* before the discussion. Despite it being early August, the author's writing had me believing there were piles of snow on the ground outside and a doggie wedding going on. Belle snoozed on the arm of the couch.

I was immersed in a tale including a ghost hunter, a medium, and a murder, of course, and jumped when my cell rang. Belle woke up and knocked the phone from the arm of my chair to the floor.

"Get the phone!" she squawked. "Get the phone, Mac." She hopped onto the coffee table and bobbed her head as she hummed the tune of "Hit the Road Jack."

"I will. Calm down, Belle." I shook my head at my nutso pet and grabbed the phone from the floor, ever grateful for the military grade pink case and bumper. I dropped my phone a lot.

I connected and greeted my mother. "How'd those bikes work out?" I'd been able to snag a small adult three-wheeler from Hyannis and they'd delivered it, too. It was even fire-engine red.

"Your grandmother and I had the loveliest ride. We're starting slow, naturally."

"Wise move."

"We only rode up to the estuary and back. We caught an oyster catcher, too."

I thought about the name. "I can't figure out what you just said, Mom. You caught someone digging oysters? What do you mean?"

She snorted. "It's a bird, silly. We saw one. They have striking black-and-white plumage, a long, red pointy beak, and pink legs, like they're wearing tuxes with pink knee socks."

I giggled at the image.

"But I called because your Pluto is transiting in aspect

to your sun right now. The effect will be intensified by your Virgo moon. Please be careful in the next few days."

I rolled my eyes. "I will, I promise." I had other reasons to be careful this week.

"I'm serious. Pluto has its dark side. Not something to mess with."

"Yes, Mother. But back to the bikes. Abo Ree did fine with her tricycle?"

"She did. She loaded up the basket with a picnic, so we had a nice lunch break at the halfway point."

I smiled at the image. "I hope her legs won't be sore."

"Hello!" Belle hopped up to the open window in my kitchen, the one next to the door on the side of the house. "Hello, there! Hello, there."

"What's Belle going on about?" my mom asked.

"I don't know. Belle, is someone there?"

"Hello! Belle's a good girl. Snacks, Mac? Hello!"

Belle was smart, but she wasn't Einstein.

"Hang on, Mom." I rose and flipped on the outside light. I peered out the window, but I didn't see anybody. I set Belle on the floor, and closed and locked the sash just in case. "Sorry for the interruption. What were we talking about?"

"Our bicycle ride. We decided to go out again tomorrow afternoon if it's not too hot."

"Sounds like a plan."

"You take care now." A voice sounded in the background. "What'd you say, Joseph?" she asked away from the phone. "Your father sends his love."

"Send mine back to him. And thanks for calling." We said our goodbyes and I disconnected. I pulled out a few frozen carrot chunks and gave them to Belle to eat in her cage. When she was done I latched the door. "Sweet dreams, Bellinha."

"Sweet dreams. Belle's a good girl."

"Belle's a very good girl." I pulled the cover over the cage. African grays needed more than ten hours of sleep and this was already past her bedtime.

I settled back in to read for another hour. By nine thirty I had only a few chapters left to the end. I was at least as tired as my parrot, and hoped I could finish the book in bed before I fell asleep.

I rose and wandered over to the open window facing north. Beyond a low hedge was the path to my shop. There was a streetlight at the front of the shop, but what I could see of the back of the building was in shadow. It was a new moon and the night was dark. Crickets buzzed in the cool air, and somewhere an owl called. I even spied a few fireflies dancing above the hedge. When I was a child I'd thought the winged beetles were fairies, and Mom hadn't disabused me of the notion. I'd been embarrassed in the third grade to learn *Lampyridae* were insects, and I'd come home complaining bitterly she'd let me make a fool of myself.

I narrowed my eyes. Did I see movement behind my shop? I'd been planning to put a motion-detector light out there and hadn't gotten around to it. The hair on my arms stood up and it wasn't from the temperature. I spied more motion. Someone was definitely behind my shop. Beverly's murderer was still at large, and I'd been asking questions around this town and the next. Or maybe it was a teen vandal. Either way, I grabbed my phone, my heart racing faster than the lead runner in the road race.

Crash. The sound of breaking glass was unmistakable. I hit the 911 icon.

Chapter Thirty-two

Dispatch told me to stay inside and not to disconnect. "Don't worry, I'm not going out in the dark alone," I told her. "I'll be right here." I closed and locked the remaining open window.

"An officer will be there shortly."

I hoped so. I hoped the bad guy wasn't inside my shop doing further damage. I hoped he or she wasn't lurking outside my windows here, about to break one. My hand shook, so the phone did, too. I sat abruptly, my knees threatening to collapse. I was getting a motion-detector light installed tomorrow. And maybe a security cam, too.

I listened as she kept talking. "Yes, my house is directly behind Mac's Bikes on Main Street, and yes, my door is locked and the windows, too." I hated to close windows in the summer unless we had a driving rain. In this case? No-brainer.

I stood, my fear turning to anger. I paced the length of my house and back, which resulted in lots of very short round trips. How dare someone—anyone—vandalize my bike shop? I worked hard to make it a thriving business and a welcoming place for tourists and locals alike. My pacing slowed. If the murderer broke the window because they wanted to stop me from investigating, why hadn't they broken a window of my house? That would be a much more personal attack. Maybe Belle had scared off the intruder. A stress giggle bubbled up at the thought of a guard bird.

Relief flooded me when I heard sirens roar up to the shop. I peered out the now-closed window and saw blue and red lights strobing. *Whew*. A fire engine rumbled into the store parking lot, too. A bright searchlight on top of a cruiser flared into life. The light flooded the back of the shop as two officers with flashlights disappeared around the corner.

A minute later, someone knocked at the door. "Mackenzie Almeida? Westham Police responding to your call."

I parted the curtain covering the glass in the top of the door, glad I'd left the outside light on. "They're here," I told the dispatcher. "I'm going to disconnect." I hit the red icon before I unlocked and opened the door to the bike officer standing on my small, covered porch, the same dude who had interviewed me after Beverly's death.

"Thank you for coming, Officer Jenkins. I'm so glad you're here. I assume others are over at the store? What's going on? Is my shop okay?" The words poured out in a gush.

"My colleagues are checking out your establishment, ma'am."

Ma'am. *Really?* "Please call me Mac. When can I see the damage?" I tried to get a glimpse over his shoulder.

"I'm here to assure your safety." He clasped his hands behind his back, elbows out. "Please remain in your residence until I'm notified your place of business has been cleared and is safe to enter."

Did I have to? I supposed I did. All I wanted was to rush over there. But if I had to wait, I would.

"Do you want to come in?" I asked him.

"Thank you, no, ma'am. I'll stay right here."

My phone rang in my hand. I glanced at it to see my mother's picture.

"Okay to answer?" I asked.

At his nod, I connected. "Mom?"

"What's going on over there? We heard sirens and can see the lights from here."

Of course they could. They were less than a quarter mile down Main Street.

"Are you all right?" she went on.

"Yes, I'm fine. I think someone broke a window at the back of my store and I don't know what else they damaged."

"My goodness, that's terrible. If you want to spend the night here, honey, you know we always have a bed for you."

I turned away from Officer Jenkins's eyes because my own were suddenly full. "I know. Thank you. I'll call after I know more, okay?"

"Love you."

My dad's voice chimed in, too. "Love you, *querida*."

"Love you both," I whispered before disconnecting. I sniffed and took another moment to text the group.

Break-in at the shop. I'm fine, was at home with door locked. Will text more when I have info.

Should I text Tim, too? No. I set the phone down, my heart awash with sadness. He wouldn't want to hear from me.

I swallowed and turned back to Jenkins. "At about nine or so, my pet parrot got agitated and started saying hello out that window right there." I pointed to the one next to the door. "It was open at the time. I wonder if the vandal was trying to get in here." I glanced at Belle's cage, grateful that, once she was covered and asleep, nothing woke her.

"Thank you." He turned his back and murmured into the radio thing near his shoulder, then listened to it squawk. He faced me again. "A window is broken at the back of the store. You didn't see anyone prior to the vandalism?"

"Maybe. Right before I heard the crash of glass breaking, I thought I saw a movement in the shadows behind the shop but I didn't get a clear look."

"Have you received any threatening communications?" He pulled out his phone, a large, industrial-looking model, no doubt police issue, and tapped into it. "A note, an anonymous phone call, an e-mail?"

"No." I thought again. "No, I haven't."

"I'm aware you were active in the investigation of the homicide in June. Have you been conducting your own inquiries into the current one?"

"Of course not. I have sent several messages to Detective Haskins since the murder, but only about a few pieces of information I happened to overhear." I crossed my fingers behind my back for my little white lie. I knew I was guilty of seeking out information. It was just as well I was out of sight of the church I'd grown up going to.

I checked the shop again. The fire truck had moved, and the floodlight revealed a jagged hole that marred the window next to the closed back door. Had someone gone inside? Had the vandal reached in, unlocked the door, and entered? But why? Money was in the safe. I didn't carry any super-valuable merchandise, not like a jewelry store. I certainly didn't have any secret letters or whatever. Some of our tools had been expensive to acquire, but unless you were a bike mechanic, you wouldn't know which.

Chief Laitinen—Victoria—hurried toward us. Jenkins stepped aside.

"Mac, can you give us the key to the shop's door?" she asked.

"Sure." I grabbed my keys from the hook next to the door and sorted out two. "This one is for the lock on either door, and this one is to the storage container."

"Thanks. I can't believe you keep getting involved in criminal activities."

"What?" My worry slid away and I set fists on hips. "I'm involved when somebody vandalizes my store? In what universe?"

"Look, Mac, you and I both know you've been bringing this on yourself, you and your mystery group." Victoria glanced over at Jenkins, who studiously surveyed the goings-on at the back of my store, his hands behind his back. She lowered her voice and looked more concerned than put out. "You have to cut it out. Really. One of these days you're going to get hurt. And"—she swallowed—"I'd hate to see that happen."

My mouth dropped open wide enough to let mosquitoes in. I wrested back control from my shock at her caring. "When can I—"

Victoria shook her head, turned, and hurried across to the shop. I glanced at Jenkins. "I really need to go see the damage for myself."

"Sorry, ma'am." He shook his head. "You need to wait here until they've cleared and secured the building."

Patience was not my superpower. I liked to do, not wait. In this case, doing was following police procedure, which apparently was keeping the owner from the vandalized premises until it was safe. I straightened the magazines on my coffee table. I wiped down the sink, which didn't need it. I smoothed a wrinkle in the throw on the back of the couch. And I waited.

Chapter Thirty-three

I finished checking the shop, Victoria at my side, half an
hour later. She'd come back to the house to get me at
about ten twenty. We both pretended she hadn't acted out
of character a little while ago.

"I don't see anything out of place or missing," I said,
still glancing around. "Except the glass." I pointed to the
floor under the broken window.

"And you don't keep cash here?" Victoria asked.

I gestured toward the open empty drawer of the small
cash register. "I put it in the safe each night." I went into
my office and squatted to press the six-digit code that
opened the reassuringly heavy door of the safe. I drew
out the cash envelope and the drawer liner with its coin
compartments and sections for ones, fives, and twenties. I
counted the bills in the envelope and compared the sum
with the slip I'd already filled out.

"It's all here." I replaced it all, closed the safe's door, and pressed the lock code. When I straightened, Lincoln stood in the doorway leaning against the jamb, except he had to tilt his head to avoid bumping the top of the door-frame.

"Hi, Lincoln," I said. I was drawing the top brass tonight. "What are you doing here?"

Victoria pulled her mouth like she'd tasted moldy bread. "I could ask the same thing."

What beef did she have with him? Surely as a police chief she knew about the division of labor, that the staties investigated homicides except in the commonwealth's three largest cities. Westham was not one of them. Not that tonight was a homicide, unless the break-in was re-lated to Beverly's.

"Evening, ladies," Lincoln said, ever calm, ever under-stated. "Somebody attacked your store, Mac, I hear."

"You heard right," I said. "I don't know why, though."

He lifted a single dark eyebrow but didn't offer a rea-son. "Did they make it inside?" he asked Victoria.

"Not sure. Both doors were locked, but they could have exited through the front before we arrived on the scene." She lifted one pale eyebrow. "It's that kind of lock which, Mac, is not a good way to secure your premises."

True. It was a button in the doorknob that you could depress to lock the door and then pull it closed. "I know." I wrinkled my nose. "I've been meaning to get dead bolts installed. I'll call a locksmith tomorrow." And an electri-cian. And a glass person.

"Let's move out here." Lincoln stepped back. "I'm getting a stiff neck."

Victoria and I followed him out into the retail area. An

officer was working with powder at the front door, and Officer Jenkins did the same at the back door.

"We're dusting for prints," Victoria said. "Mac says nothing appears to be missing or harmed."

"Right," I said. "Cash, merchandise, tools. Everything is where I left it, except for the glass in the window."

"Made any new enemies lately, Mac?" Lincoln asked.

"Enemies?" I widened my eyes at him. "Who would be *my* enemy?"

"Persons of interest in a homicide case, maybe?"

So that was why he'd shown up.

"Of whom you've been asking too many questions, possibly?" Victoria pressed, her annoyance once again taking the lead.

Lincoln gave a little nod, like he approved of her backing him up.

"But I haven't." I heard my voice rising in indignation and told myself to cool it.

"You've been texting me pieces of information you 'happen' to have overheard." Lincoln used finger quotes and exaggerated his pronunciation of "happen." "While I appreciate alert citizens doing their civic duty, it's a little too convenient, isn't it?" He peered at me over the top of his dark-rimmed glasses.

Victoria had been following our exchange, gazing back and forth at each of us. Now she threw up her hands and shook her head. "I can't believe it, Mac. After the kind of trouble you and Ms. Malloy got yourselves into a couple months ago? Now you're doing it again?"

"I've got this, Chief," Lincoln said in his low voice.

Ouch.

She handed me my key ring. "Here." Victoria shot

Lincoln a dagger-filled look before turning on her heel and heading out the back door.

"I swear, Lincoln," I said. "I was at the beach today with my niece. We were heading home and nearly at the top of the steps to the parking lot. She stopped to smell a flower. Ron and Isadora were in an open Jeep right in front of me but facing away. I had to wait for Cokey and I happened to hear what they were saying. They didn't even see me. I absolutely did not go looking for them."

"Today, maybe. But coincidence you happened to stop into both the game store and a dress shop in Falmouth? I think not."

I folded my arms. "Believe what you'd like." Even though what he believed was true. Neither visit had actually been from serendipity. "Aren't you glad I'm sharing information?"

"Yes, of course." He stifled a yawn. "Sorry, long day."

I blew out a breath. His yawn had humanized him again. "I know what you mean."

"Do you have something to board up your window with?"

"Like plywood? I don't think so." I was a mechanic, not a carpenter. The shop had been in good shape when I'd bought it. All I'd had to do was have it painted to my liking and fill it with bikes, biking merchandise, tools, and a few specialized pieces of equipment in the repair area.

He ambled to the broken window, which was next to a six-foot-tall heavy metal filing cabinet. I'd found it at the dump and had cleaned it and painted it bright blue.

"Officer, you finished with these shards?" Lincoln asked Jenkins.

"Yes, sir. We bagged some of the bigger pieces in case we can locate evidence on them."

"Good. Mac, if you have a broom, we can clear the mess and move this cabinet in front of the window for now."

"Good idea." I got the broom and dustpan from the restroom closet and started to sweep up the glass.

"Let me do it, ma'am," Jenkins said. "You don't have gloves on. I wouldn't want you to cut your hand."

What a nice guy. "Thanks," I said, happy to turn over the task.

A minute later, the floor was swept clear of glass and the two men had wrestled the cabinet in front of the window.

"What do you have in here?" Lincoln asked. "This thing's heavier than a sumo wrestler."

I laughed, glad for a touch of levity on this scary night. "We keep spare bike parts in it, which includes metal things like chains, bearings, and derailleurs." As the labels on the drawers indicated.

The detective surveyed the shop. "I think you and I are done here, Mac. As always, you think of something related to the break-in, drop me a text or call."

"I will."

"Officer Jenkins will close up when they're done with the premises, correct, Jenkins?" Lincoln asked.

"Yes, sir. I will, ma'am."

Lincoln gestured for me to precede him out the back door. The strobe lights were off, but the searchlight was still a beacon in the darkness. Cicadas buzzed on and off, and a salty breeze made me shiver and hug myself.

"Do you feel safe staying in your home tonight?" He gazed down at me with concern.

I looked beyond him at my very tidy house, with light pushing out from its double-paned, lockable windows.

"Yes, I have a dead bolt on the door, and my windows lock. I'll be fine."

"All right. We'll have an officer on patrol loop through your parking area every hour. And, Mac?"

"I know. Stop asking questions about the murder. I will, Lincoln. I promise. I don't suppose you'd tell me about any progress you've made? Anything the team has learned?"

"You suppose correctly." He shook his head with an amused expression.

My phone buzzed in my pocket. I pulled it out to see Tim's face. "We're done, right?" At Lincoln's nod, I said, "Good night. And thank you." I hurried toward my house and connected the call when I got inside.

"Mac, are you all right? I saw a news flash your shop was broken into."

I heard the caring in his voice and it about did me in. "I'm all right." My eyes pricked with tears and I swallowed down the fullness of emotion. "Somebody broke a back window of the shop. I didn't see who did it, and they had gone by the time the police showed up."

"You must have been scared."

"Absolutely."

"Do you want company? Because . . ." His voice trailed off. "I'm sorry for last night and this afternoon. I hope you'll forgive me. I would die if anything happened to you. I can come over right now."

Did I want the company of a big, strong man I adored? You bet I did. "Please."

Chapter Thirty-four

I tossed and turned and tossed some more in the darkness of the wee hours. Tim and I had had a sweet reunion, leaving talking about anything important to another time, but we hadn't actually slept until midnight. He'd left at four for the bakery and now I couldn't sleep. The sound of glass breaking played on a Möbius strip in my brain. It was accompanied by Belle's frantic recognition that someone had lurked outside my house.

Lincoln had warned me the day of Beverly's death not to get involved in the investigation. I'd ignored his caution, even though I thought I wasn't taking any real risks. If my intruder hadn't been some random teen vandal, he—or she—had to be Beverly's killer. I lay there berating myself over and over. Why was I asking questions? Why did I let the group proceed with a parallel investigation? If we didn't all cease and desist, one of us could experience an attack a lot worse than a broken window.

Taking slow, regular breaths, I tried counting backward from a thousand. It didn't work. I tried visualizing myself floating carefree in the warm, salty water of an Aegean cove on a Greek island. My thoughts still raced. I let my body go limp, feeling heavy, relaxing each muscle from my big toes to my forehead. But I kept worrying each intrusive thought. What if Belle had been harmed? What if the window-breaker had broken the window of my tiny house? I would have been trapped inside with my beloved pet. I pictured myself stroking her smooth feathers and felt myself calming. I noticed, in the odd half-dream state of falling asleep, that I was seeing faces on the inside of my eyelids.

I struggled to pry my eyes open after light pressed in through the window, which meant it was after six. I didn't know how Tim functioned on such little sleep, but he'd always said he simply didn't need more than six hours, and he often grabbed a nap in the afternoons after the bakery closed. I, on the other hand, was at my best with eight hours of slumber or more. Mornings like this were tough, especially with my hour of wakeful angst subtracting from the total.

My phone dinged with a text. I grabbed it and peered through sandpaper lids. It was from Gin.

You okay? You didn't text group back last night. Still walking?

I winced. I hadn't texted the group, or called my mom back, either. And I definitely hadn't finished the book. I tapped an answer.

I'm fine. Sorry. See you at 7.

I groaned. Time to rise and shine, as Pa had said every weekday when he woke Derrick and me for school. I swung out of bed and onto the steps. When my bed was tidy, it was time for coffee. I'd had a friend at Harvard who used to say, "I'll do it ASAC"—as soon as coffee.

The window in the kitchen, though, was also the one looking out onto my broken shop window. My groggy mood turned into a darker state of mind when I saw the jagged edges stark against the blue of the file cabinet blocking the hole. How were the police going to figure out who did it? If the window was broken from something heavy having been hurled at it, wouldn't the object have been found inside or on the ground outside? And if the vandal had stood in front of the window striking it with a hammer, he or she might have gotten hit with shards of flying glass. Maybe they'd used a long pry bar or a pike pole, like sport fishermen employed to snag a big fish and wrestle it on board. That way the attacker wouldn't have risked getting cut.

The air was musty in here from the closed windows. I unlocked and slid up the one next to the door. I opened the outer door, letting the cool morning air into the house. I had to put thoughts of the window-breaker out of my mind or I'd never get anything done. Still, as I brewed my extra dark roast, as I lifted Belle's cage cover and opened her door, as I dosed the coffee with light cream, I couldn't help myself from thinking about it. If the police didn't figure out who vandalized my shop, the person might come back tonight. I'd rarely felt unsafe in my town. This morning I did. I was taking my coffee inside today, not out on the patio.

"Good morning, Mac!" Belle, ever chipper, cocked her head. "Hello, handsome," was next, followed by the wolf whistle she used for Tim.

I cocked my own head. Had she heard his voice in her dreams? Did parrots even dream?

She prattled on. "Give us a kiss. Belle's a good girl. Snacks, Mac?"

I kissed her smooth head. "You're a very good girl. I think you scared away a bad person last night." I drew out her container of cooked brown rice and beans, and heated it for a minute in the microwave. I stirred and tested it to make sure it wasn't too hot, then set it down for her. It was one of her favorite breakfasts.

"Belle's a good girl." She hopped over to her bowl.

I settled on the couch in my sleep shirt, bare feet up, coffee at my elbow, and texted the book group. It was time to put the cease and desist plan into action. But first I needed to reassure anybody who had heard the news.

Am fine. Broken shop window only damage. Could have been teen vandal. Am worried it was B killer. Plan to ease up on asking questions. See you all tonight.

Last night had been so crazy I hadn't taken time to dwell on Eli's somewhat odd behavior at his place. Gin, of course, insisted he would never have killed Beverly. But she hadn't spent the night of Beverly's death with him, or the afternoon before. I knew people's emotional leanings can easily overpower their memories of facts, and Gin was definitely leaning toward this romance with Eli.

To me, something felt off about him. For one, why was a forty-year-old scientist renting a converted garage for his residence? Not that there was anything wrong with a bachelor apartment. From what I'd seen, it had more square footage than my house. I grabbed my iPad off the end table, where I'd left it charging.

"Let's see what Mr. Google says about Mr. Tubin," I said aloud.

I poked around the Internet a bit, rejecting an animal-control officer in Pennsylvania and a guy in Ohio obviously proud, judging from the crazy grin in his photograph, that he'd killed a mature stag with a full rack of antlers. Those two might or might not be the same person, but neither was Gin's Eli.

I added Woods Hole to my search and, bingo, I found Gin's new guy. I'd never asked her where he'd lived before he moved to the Cape. Maybe she didn't know, either. I wished I'd asked Tim last night. Eli's Oceanographic Institute profile said his full name was Elijah. Following that Internet rabbit hole got me to his wife's death notice in *The Boston Globe*, his mother Iris's obituary before that, and his doctorate in oceanography and atmospheric science from Princeton University only four years ago. So where had he been prior to that time, and what had been his occupation? Clearly he was intelligent. So why the garage rental? It seemed kind of low-rent for someone with a doctorate. I shook my head. Hey, I lived in a small place, too, and I was happy.

Continuing with my own version of the hunt, I finally came across one small mention. It tickled my virtual antennae. A decade and a half ago, Eli had gone through foreclosure on a dry cleaning business bearing his name. Three hits later, I discovered his loan had been paid by Beverly Ruchart. So he must have already been married to her daughter, who I supposed was still alive at that time. And a little further back in time he'd had been arrested for dealing drugs. I couldn't find either a conviction or a dismissal of the charges. He must have gotten off, but what if Beverly knew about the arrest? What if she'd been blackmailing him, threatening to derail his graduate degree and employment prospects? She wouldn't have needed the money. It could have been that she wanted to exert some kind of psychological control over her son-in-law.

I might never find out, but it was worth mentioning to Lincoln next time I saw him. Of course, this was all information accessible to anyone. Still, I'd had to travel several twists and turns in my search. Not everyone might make the same connections. I wouldn't let the group know, though, not without something more damning about Eli. It would hurt Gin deeply to learn I even considered the possibility he'd committed murder.

I drained my coffee. It was six thirty by now and time to get moving, angst or no angst, a murderer lurking or not. I cleaned Belle's cage and lined it with fresh paper, earning me a wolf whistle from her. I called my early-riser father, who did not text.

"We were worried when you didn't call back, Mac," he said after we'd greeted each other. "But it seemed too late to telephone."

"I'm sorry. Tim came over to keep me company and I forgot."

He was silent for a beat. "I'm happy to hear you were able to have his solace, honey."

"We didn't talk about anything serious, but he did apologize for getting upset with me. I think there's hope for us." I did. Tim seemed to sense I couldn't be rushed in my decision. If anything, his not pushing me led me closer to a yes.

"Nothing would make me happier than to see you happy, my dear. Please stay safe and—"

I cut him off. "And don't poke my nose in police business?"

He laughed. "Something like that."

"I'm cooling it, believe me. Have a good day, Pa."

"You too, *querida*."

I smiled at the phone in my hand after I hung up. I knew many people my age who did not have close relationships with their families, either by choice because of past hurts and present tensions, or because of geography. Me, I was lucky to experience none of those issues. Of course I'd had the usual teen fights with my folks, but by the time I'd finished college we were all close again. For both Pa and Mom to like and approve of Tim was more important than almost anything. Their disapproval would have been a deal breaker for me.

Chapter Thirty-five

"**W**eren't you scared?" Gin asked as we set out on our walk at seven.

It was a cool morning, with an onshore breeze making cottony clouds scud overhead. I was glad I'd worn a long-sleeved T-shirt with my shorts. A marsh hawk circled on a kettle of rising air, its flat wings seesawing, the white patch at the base of its tail brilliant when the sun caught it. I'd filled Gin in on the details of the vandalism while we stretched in front of Salty Taffy's.

"I was terrified, of course. I happened to be looking out the window when I saw movement in the shadow behind my shop. I grabbed my phone, and after another movement came the big crash."

"Do you think it was Beverly's killer?" Her eyes were wide.

I shook my head as we set out. "No way of knowing

unless the police figure out who did it. They didn't even find what the window was broken with. I don't think the vandal got inside. Certainly nothing was missing." I thought about Belle's excitement earlier in the evening. "A while earlier Belle had been looking out the same window while I was on the phone with my mom. She got all agitated and kept saying hello. After the crash, I wondered if the same person had been outside earlier and had gotten scared off by Belle."

"Belle's scary?" Gin laughed out loud.

I smiled at the thought. "Hey, anything's possible. Haskins showed up last night, too."

"Why?"

"I think he thought I might have been attacked because I've been looking into Beverly's murder. I asked him if he'd talk about the case, but of course he wouldn't. And I got the usual warning not to involve myself looking for a murderer. Believe me, I'm obeying orders this time."

We walked, arms swinging, in silence for a few minutes.

"I'm not sure anyone else is," she said.

"Oh? Did someone find out something new?"

"Flo said she was going to research Danny Rizzoli, and despite his earlier caution to us, Norland thought he had a line on some information about Sofia."

I hadn't checked the thread since I'd texted the group at six thirty. I stepped around a branch on the path. "They need to be really careful. We're dealing with a person who already crossed the line once, Gin."

"Do you mean crossing the line of committing murder?"

"Exactly." I stopped and looked at her. "You know, if

you or I really hated someone, we still wouldn't actually end their life. Hardly anyone would. But once a person kills, they must feel so desperate not to be caught they probably wouldn't stop at doing it again."

She nodded without speaking. Two cyclists approached and I waited until they passed to speak again.

"You remember what happened last time." I hugged myself. "The murderer thought we were getting close and planned for us to be victim numbers two and three. I'm not messing with that again, Gin. Not after what happened last night."

"You have a point." Her phone dinged and she dragged it out of her shorts pocket. "What would I do without Google Calendar? I almost forgot I have food pantry this afternoon. Will you be there, too?"

"No, I told them I couldn't come this week." Gin and I almost always did a Thursday stint together, stocking shelves and whatever else the organizers needed to have done. "I feel bad, but I have too much going on. I've kind of been neglecting the shop as it is."

"I hear you." She hunched her head into her shoulders and shivered. "Can we get walking again? I'm getting chilled standing here with this wind."

She was right. The breeze, in fact, had turned to wind. "Sure." We set off again, arms pumping.

"Back to the murder, it seems like it can't hurt to do online searches and such," Gin said.

"I guess not. I'm certainly not going around asking any more questions, though." I absolutely wasn't, I thought, as I filled my lungs with fresh sea air. No way. And I also wasn't telling her what I'd discovered about Eli.

She snapped her fingers. "I just remembered. I talked

to my daughter last night. Lucy said she knew Ron in high school."

"So they're near the same age?"

"They're both twenty-five. Lu told me Ron's mom died when they were juniors, and it really hit him hard. She said he was really smart and he'd been in the Coders Club. You know, programming apps and stuff."

"He was playing a video game on the computer when I went into the gaming store. I wonder if he writes them, too."

"Maybe," Gin said. "But after he lost his mom, he got pretty messed up. He was busted for shoplifting a beer, got in fights, that kind of thing."

I shook my head. "Poor guy. It couldn't have been easy, especially living with a stepdad you don't like. Has Eli talked to you about that period?"

"He said it was tough. He'd been dating Ron's mom for several years but had only married her the year before she died. He told me Ron really resented him no matter what he did. Ron barely managed to graduate from high school the next year, and he's lived with Beverly since."

"No wonder there weren't any pictures of Ron in Eli's apartment." We walked with our own thoughts for a few minutes. I still wondered why Eli lived in such a low-rent place, but it didn't feel like the right time to ask my friend about it.

"Lucy also told me Beverly wasn't particularly kind to Ron despite taking him in."

"That must have been hard for him, too. Tough love, maybe?"

"Maybe. So Cozy Capers is meeting tonight," Gin said. "Did you finish the book?"

I shook myself back into the present. "I thought I was going to last evening. It all changed when my shop was vandalized. "

"At least your house didn't get attacked, Mac."

"I'm wicked relieved about that. I'd hate to think of Belle being assaulted along with me," I said. "Did you get to the end of the book?"

"Yes, and I loved the story."

I smiled to myself remembering what happened in my house in lieu of reading. "Tim came over last night after Lincoln let me go."

"He did? Fight's over? Did you tell him yes?"

I shook my head. "We made our peace, and we didn't talk about anything serious." My cheeks heated up with the thought of what we'd done instead of talking. "And, even though I haven't quite made up my mind, at least he's not shutting me out."

"He's such a jewel, Mac." She elbowed me.

"I know he is."

"Don't you dare let him go."

"I'll take it under advisement." I skirted an untrimmed branch sticking out into the path. "How was your own night? You seem a lot calmer this morning."

"Eli has that effect on me." It was her turn to blush.

"I couldn't talk about it last night because Eli was there, but did you catch the look he gave me when he realized I'd come in with you?" I asked. "It was like he was alarmed I was there."

"I didn't see. He was probably just surprised, since he expected me to be alone."

Maybe. Or maybe something else was going on with him.

The scenery opened up at the salt pond. As we strode across the bridge, a tern hovered and beat its wings, somehow staying in one place despite the wind. I watched as it dive-bombed the pool and came up with a wriggling fish in its beak. If only it were so simple to catch human prey.

Chapter Thirty-six

By ten o'clock the shop was bustling. Both of my employees had arrived on time, for which I was grateful. Despite the cool wind, which hadn't abated, we had a steady stream of locals and tourists wanting our services. Flat tires and requests for tune-ups occupied Orlean on the repair side. Derrick was renting out bikes as fast as he could. I'd made a number of sales of shirts, tubes, and helmets. It was like everyone realized summer would be over in several weeks and they wanted to pack in the experiences—on a bicycle. My bottom line was going to be happy this week.

I'd described the window assault to Derrick and Orlean. Both had looked concerned.

"The vandal didn't appear to have made it inside," I'd added. "I'm going to call for new locks today. It's time to beef up our security."

"I'll check all the tools, just in case," Orlean offered.

"Good idea."

"Do you think it was the killer coming after you, Mac?" Derrick asked.

I shook my head. "I have no idea."

I'd managed to find time to schedule an electrician to come and install motion-detector lights. He couldn't make it until next week, unfortunately. And someone from Cape Window Woman would be here any minute now to install new glass in the broken window. The business was a woman-owned shop employing almost exclusively women. They not only did repairs like mine but also restored antique sashes and installed new energy-efficient windows, and I'd heard only good things about them.

At a brief lull in customers I looked up locksmiths and succeeded in finding one who could be here this afternoon to make my shop doors a lot more secure. Abo Reba strolled in the front as I pressed End on the call. She held up a white paper bag with the Greta's Grains logo on the outside.

"Pastries for all of you." She grinned.

"You're the best, Abo Ree." I leaned down to buss her soft, papery cheek. I took the bag and peeked inside, spying four of my favorite pastries, bear claws. The yeasted delicacy was light, sweet, and buttery. It was usually made with almond paste, but Tim's version had cinnamon and ground pecans inside, and chopped pecans and sugar on top. "Died and gone to heaven."

"I thought, what with your night last night, you might need a lift."

She'd already heard about the break-in. I might as well

live in a rural village, news traveled so fast. "Thank you. Talk out back?" I drew out two bear claws and two napkins, which were also tucked into the bag, then took it to Derrick's rental counter. "When you have a minute, and the other one's for Orlean," I murmured.

"Thanks, Abo Reba," he said.

"My pleasure, dear." She blew him a kiss.

"We're going out back for a minute," I told him. "Call me if you need me."

When he nodded, our grandmother and I headed for the picnic table. Once outside, she took a detour to the broken window.

"It's a crying shame, it is. To go and break perfectly good glass like that." She shook her head before joining me at the picnic table. "Now, Mackenzie, you weren't in any danger last night, were you?"

"I might have been. I was talking to Mom on the phone and Belle got all wound up saying hello out the window. I think she scared off the person from trying to attack my house. So he—or she—went for the store instead."

She leaned closer and lowered her voice to a conspiratorial tone. "Do you think it was the murderer?"

"I don't know." I had the feeling I was going to be asked the question repeatedly today. "I never thought I'd say this, but I hope it was some misguided teenager trying to stir up trouble. It's a lot more innocent than thinking the person who killed Beverly is now coming after me." I shivered.

My grandmother stroked my arm in a comforting move. "Beverly, may God rest her soul. Why, for all her rude ways, the woman had a big heart."

I cocked my head. "She did? How?" Big heart and Beverly Ruchart somehow didn't seem to fit in the same breath.

"Yes, indeed. She was a major donor to the free health clinic." Abo Reba raised her eyebrows. "The one local residents frequent, the ones who can't afford health insurance."

"I had no idea." I wrinkled my nose. "Do you know what she called the clients at the food pantry and soup kitchen?"

She shook her head.

"Riffraff. She called them riffraff," I said. "I expect many of them also use the free clinic."

"We don't know what was in her past, Mackie. Perhaps a loved one died for lack of medical treatment. Let us always carry charitable thoughts in our hearts."

I was duly chastised. Just because I'd only ever seen Beverly's bad side didn't mean she didn't have a good one.

"In fact," Abo Reba went on, "she said she had changed her will to leave the majority of her estate to the clinic. That's how much she believed in them."

"Really? Her grandson is going to be surprised by this news. He told me he was inheriting all of it." The irony of Beverly dying outside the beneficiary of her will did not escape me.

"It never pays to count your eggs before you put them in the basket."

I covered a smile. My grandmother was famous in the family for scrambling her aphorisms.

She took a big bite of her bear claw. "My stars, this is tasty."

I smiled at her. "How in the world can you be so tiny and eat so much? You must weigh all of ninety-eight pounds soaking wet."

"Ninety-seven. Now, dear, you know we've had this conversation before. You're the same as me, only a deal taller. We both have fast metabolisms. Or maybe it's our inefficient digestive systems, which let a lot of calories pass through untapped." She smiled.

It was true. I could wear the same clothes I had in high school. If I wanted to, which I didn't. But they would still fit. I could eat pretty much all I wanted and had always been that way. "I thank you for those genes. Mom said you and she had a nice ride out to the estuary. I hope your legs aren't sore."

"No, dear. You know I do other kinds of exercise, like my ladies' water aerobics and such. I have good, strong legs, always have." She snapped her fingers. "I remembered why I came by." Her nearly perennial smile slid off her face. "I do believe I saw someone skulking about your store last night with a flashlight."

"You did? You were out that late?"

"No, but I was up. You know, anymore I don't sleep much. And what with my spyglass, I see a lot."

It was true. Her senior apartment was across the street and down the block from my shop with a good line of sight if you had a little telescope like the one we'd given her as a joke one Christmas. She'd taken it seriously, and now said she was responsible for the safety of our end of town. She'd accurately called in suspicious behavior to the police more than once and possibly prevented break-ins. Victoria had instructed her department not to treat Reba Almeida as a loony old lady but to pay attention to her reports instead.

"Did you recognize who it was?" I asked before popping in my last bite of pastry.

"No, the person was in black. Not a heavy build is all I could make out."

"Hair color?"

"Hair the color of a black watch cap. He or she stuck to the shadows but took a look in your shop's front windows when nobody was walking by. The person ducked in beside the store when anyone approached."

"What time was it?"

She pursed her lips and thought. "Seems to me it was nine thirty, ten o'clock. Around then."

"Why didn't you call me?"

"I thought it was too late. I thought you'd be asleep. You get up so early, honey. I didn't phone the police, either. Now that I think of it, I wish I had."

I wished she had, too, but that tide had passed under the bridge long ago.

Chapter Thirty-seven

After Abo Reba left, I stayed at the picnic table and started to text the group about Beverly's leaving her estate, or most of it, to the Westham Free Clinic. I lifted my thumbs from the phone. What was I doing? Hadn't I resolved not to go forward with looking for the murderer, and urged the group to do the same? On the other hand, the daylight and my routine made my fears from the wee hours of the night seem less dire. And it couldn't hurt to simply let the group know.

I finished the text and hit Send. Flo returned a text almost immediately.

I might be getting close to digging something up about Danny Rizzoli.

Which was good and not good. The danger of poking around on the web didn't seem like much of a threat, though. I wouldn't dissuade her from her hunt. I added a reply.

Let us know what you find out.

I took a minute to scroll back through the thread to see if I'd missed anything. I paused at a message from Norland. He'd been hinting for a couple of days about being on the track of something. And Gin had said this morning it was about Sofia. Sure enough.

Appears to be some irregularity in Sofia Burtseva's work visa. Tracking it down now. Motive to help Ron? Maybe Ron promised to marry her to provide permanent status but needs Ruchart's money to do so? Have communicated details with Haskins.

No text shortcuts for Norland. So Sofia wasn't exactly telling the truth about her legal status. She wouldn't be the first temp worker to fudge permission to stay. At least I didn't have to be the one telling Lincoln. Norland had accomplished that himself.

I was back in the shop ringing up a purchase when Flo hurried in the door at a few minutes past noon.

"Mac, got a minute?"

"Let me finish helping this customer."

"Sure." Flo headed over to browse the merchandise.

"Thank you, sir," I said to a lean, tanned silver-haired man who had bought a shirt, shorts, shoes, and gloves. I handed him his bag and his receipt.

"Thanks." He beamed. "I'll be wearing all of it on a tour of the Dalmatian Coast in Croatia next month."

Lucky guy. "I've heard it's a great place to ride. Beautiful, with enough hills to not be boring without being the Alps."

"I heard the same. I'm going with a tour, of course."

"Of course. Do you live on the Cape?"

"I summer in Hyannis. They have a bike shop there, but your store has an excellent reputation so I thought I'd check it out."

"I appreciate the business." I smiled at him. "Please come back, and enjoy your trip." Nothing like an unsolicited compliment to raise a girl's spirits.

He bustled out, and I surveyed the store. Nobody else was waiting to make a purchase.

"I've got a few minutes, Flo. What's up?"

She pulled her phone out of her bag and brought up a photograph. "Danny Rizzoli in the flesh. I wanted to show you first." She kept her voice low.

I peered at the close-up of his face. It looked like a mug shot. He was staring straight into the camera, and had a thin nose, a scraggly dark mustache, and sparse dark hair down to his collar. "His mug shot?" I spoke quietly, too.

"Exactly. He's been arrested more than once."

"I think I shared that someone named Danny Rizzoli did time for petty larceny about ten years ago."

"This is the mug shot from that incident."

I looked at him again. "I saw him in Jimmy's Harborside the other night. And Tim said he'd been in the bakery, too. Now I see why I thought he looked a little familiar. Ron Ruchart has exactly the same nose."

She rubbed her hands together. "He does?"

"You bet. And come to think of it, I think I saw this dude coming out of the game shop the afternoon Beverly was killed."

"So he has to be Ron's father. And he's a former criminal. And he came here to help Ron knock off his grandma and split the inheritance with him."

"But, according to my grandmother, Ron isn't the heir," I said.

"And the plot thickens," Flo whispered as if she were narrating a bad mystery movie. She waggled her eyebrows in a Groucho Marx imitation.

"I guess. But how will the book end? That's the question." I tapped the counter. "Sofia told me Ron had been acting strangely this week, taking phone calls outside and seeming to hide something from her. Maybe it was all about his father."

A burly man carrying a tool chest appeared at the front door. He paused a minute to inspect the doorknob. "Bobby's Locks. Is there a Mackenzie Almeida here?"

"Hang on a sec, Flo." I waved at the man. "I'm Mackenzie, but call me Mac." I walked over to him and held out my hand.

He shook. "Nice to meet you. I'm Bobby. I understand you want some decent locks?" His green polo shirt bore a Bobby's Locks patch. "You realize the ones you have are basically worthless, I hope."

"I'm afraid I do. And yes, please, I want to increase the store's security." I led him to the back door. "I'd like dead bolts for here and the front door." I cringed inwardly at the name, which I'd never thought about. Why use the word *dead* for a type of lock? Maybe because once it's in one position it stays there. Kind of like a dead person.

"No problem. Different keys for both or the same one?"

"The same would be great. Is there any downside to doing it that way?"

"For a business? Sometimes the owner wants one lock only he or she can open."

I hadn't thought about it. "I guess it might be a good idea. Sure, let's go with two keys. I'll color-code them or something."

"Easily done," he said. "I'll start on the rear door. Which one do you want to be keyed only for you?"

"The back door, I think. Thanks." I left him to his work and returned to Flo. "Where were we?"

"You mentioned how the imaginary book would end, which of course we don't know."

"Yeah, and the detective won't tell me a thing."

Flo slapped her forehead. "Look at me. I didn't even ask you about the break-in. Do you think—"

"Do I think the murderer did it? I don't know. One might tend to surmise that, right?"

"Yes. Have we followed up on all the ideas we had? I mean, we the group?"

"I don't know." I thought back, but my brain was simply too full.

She took her phone back. "Rats. Twelve thirty already? I have to run. See you tonight?"

"Of course. Thanks for showing me the photo, Flo. Text it to the group, okay?" I watched her hurry out. It didn't seem like we were getting anyplace. Which was exactly how Lincoln wanted it.

Chapter Thirty-eight

We had a bit of a break around three o'clock. "I'm going to the bank," I told Derrick and Orlean. "I won't be long."

Orlean, head down working on a derailleur, nodded.

"We got it." Derrick waved me away.

I emptied the till of big bills and extracted the zippered cash envelope from the safe. I took a minute to count it all and make out a second deposit slip for today's intake. EpiPen bag on, envelope in a cloth bag, I headed out. I passed Pa's church and parsonage, which were on the corner of a side street, Beach Plum Road. I glanced down it and paused. Beverly's home with its lovely gardens was down there. What would happen to her house and land? If the clinic inherited her estate, they would probably sell the properties—this one and whatever she owned in New York—and have an endowment to tap into for years. Would Ron contest the will? Not if he was convicted of murder, he wouldn't. Had it been him breaking my window last night? Or his mysterious father?

On a whim, I turned down the street. An eight-foot-high hedge bordered the parsonage house and backyard. When I reached the end of the hedge, the scenery opened up to gently curving edged beds, immaculate ground cover under the trees, and a discreet black wrought-iron fence separating the back gardens from the front. Along the right side of her property ran another hedge, the one abutting my parents' yard. The house itself was a classic Cape Cod cottage with dormered windows set into the front slope of the roof like eyes watching the street. The natural cedar shingles had silvered with age. The cottage had been added onto. I glimpsed a glassed-in sun porch full of flowering plants on the right and an addition to the back.

I thought of Beverly living here, tending her gardens—with the help of professional landscapers, of course. Doing her genealogy work. Writing checks to the clinic. Dealing with her grandson. And at least once carrying an errant puppy back to its owners. I didn't care if she'd been difficult. It was immeasurably sad someone had snuffed out her life with a dose of poison.

I took a few more steps, gazing at the house. On the driveway to the left, a man emerged from the back. He was whistling, hands in the pockets of baggy jeans. The gardener? I did a double take. It was Danny Rizzoli. *Speak of the devil*.

I thought fast. "Excuse me, sir?" I raised a hand as I called to him. "I'm not from around here and I'm trying to find the Shining Sea Trail. Can you help?" I sure hoped my made-up tale didn't come back to bite me.

"Not a chance." He strolled toward me. "Sorry, I barely know my way around town, myself." This was definitely Rizzoli. Same nose as Ron's. Same straggly mustache as in the mug shot. Same dude I'd seen coming out of the gaming shop and sitting behind Tim at Jimmy's Harborside. He had a thin, wiry build buzzing with nervous energy. Small dark eyes regarded me with the magnanimity of one who thinks he's in a comfortable spot.

"I thought . . ." I let my voice trail off as I gestured toward the driveway.

"It's my son's place. Pretty nice digs, aren't they?" He turned and regarded the property as if he were an earl surveying his estate.

Not so fast, buddy. "Very. Where are you visiting from?"

"Here and there. I might be moving into this very house after a bit." He faced me again. "I was sadly estranged from my boy for some time. His grandmother kept him away from me. But now the old bird's dead, and Ron and me, we've patched up our differences." Danny definitely had a New York accent, the way he said "bird" and "Ron."

The old bird? *Nice.* And she kept Ron away? Not likely. "Being together again must be nice for you. I'm sorry his grandmother passed away."

He turned his head and spat on the ground. "Don't be. She was a mean, selfish lady. No two ways about it. And somebody killed her for it."

I pretended to gasp. "Really?" A skipping cloud paused over the sun, making the wind almost too chilly for comfort. I wrapped my arms around myself.

"Yes, indeed." He bobbed his head once. "You don't watch the news or nothing? Happened right down the road here. This may be a fancy tourist town, but ya can't escape murder. It's everywhere."

Chapter Thirty-nine

By six I was home and changed into loose patterned pants and a light sweater. I perched on the couch with my phone and opened the text thread to see that Flo had posted Danny's picture. I added my news.

Ran into Danny Rizzoli at B's house. I pretended I was a lost tourist. He acted like he already owned the property, said he might be moving in with his son soon. Said B had kept Ron away from him but now they'd patched things up. He said B was mean and selfish.

I ignored the small, scolding voice deep inside reminding me of my vow from much earlier in the day.

I'd invited Tim to stop by for a drink before I went to book group. I'd been thinking about him all day and was thirsty for a drink of his face, his laugh, his embrace. I'd said I would bring an appetizer to book group, so I drew out six eggs I'd boiled earlier and began to shell them. I hadn't gotten far when Tim knocked on the screen door.

"Anybody home?" he asked.

"Belle's home," she announced, followed by her signature wolf whistle. "Hello, handsome. Belle's home."

I laughed and unlatched the door for him. He stepped in and bent over to unbuckle his sandals, honoring my no-shoes house policy. A long, hot kiss later, I pulled back and stroked his freshly shaven cheek. "You're a welcome sight." His hair, which he usually pulled back into a low ponytail, was clean and loose on his shoulders. He wore an unbleached Greta's Grains T-shirt and summery drawstring pants.

"As are you, darlin'." He set a bottle of chilled pinot gris on the counter and foraged for the wine opener. "Did you survive the day?"

"Yes." I returned to my shelling. Once done, I sliced each egg carefully in half lengthwise and laid the whites on a clever deviled egg plate, with indentations so the eggs didn't go sliding around. "But if one more person asks me if I think my vandal was the killer, I might run screaming into the Atlantic."

"Had a lot of that, did you?" He handed me a full glass and clinked his with mine. "Here's to no more vandals, no more homicides."

"No more of either."

Belle strutted around the floor muttering, "No more homicides. No more vandals. No more homicides. No more vandals."

"Oops," Tim said. "Might have taught her a new word. Sorry, Mac."

"It's okay." I halved a ripe avocado and scooped the flesh of both halves into the bowl with the egg yolks, mashing them together with lime juice, a spoonful of drained and chopped capers, and salt and pepper.

He picked up one of the avocado skins, which still had some of the flesh in it. "Can Belle have this?"

"Snacks, handsome?" Belle hopped over to Tim.

"No!" I gazed at the skin in alarm. "Please don't. Avocados are poisonous to parrots."

"Wow." He held the skin away from Belle. "I'm sorry. Had no idea." He set the skin back next to me on the counter.

"It's okay. A few foods are really toxic to her." I minced some cilantro and added it to the egg mixture, and knocked in a few drops of hot sauce for good measure. "Taste test?" I scooped out a small spoonful and offered it to Tim.

"Mmm. The complete opposite of toxic for humans. It's delicious. Maybe a touch more lime juice?"

I tasted the mixture, too. "Agree." I squeezed in another quarter lime and stirred.

He picked up a spoon and helped me fill the cavities in the egg-white halves. Standing close to him, working together, having my world restored filled me with rosy contentment. After we finished, I covered the egg plate and stashed it in the fridge. I cleaned up before joining Tim on the couch, wine in hand.

"Did you learn anything new about the homicide today?" he asked.

"I met Ron Ruchart's father."

He frowned. "Don't tell me you went looking for him."

"Of course not. After last night? No, it was a complete accident."

"Good. I mean, I'm not telling you what to do. You know that." He waited until I nodded before going on. "I just don't want to see you hurt, sweetheart." He stroked my back.

"I know. And I appreciate it more than I can say." I'd had guys tell me what to do in the past and it hadn't been pretty. "The thing is, I was walking to the bank this afternoon and took a little detour past Beverly's house. No matter how difficult she was, she didn't deserve to be killed. And Danny Rizzoli came out from behind the house, acting like he already owned the property."

"How did you know it was him?"

I had my mouth open to answer when Belle spoke first.

"Alexa, read the shopping list," Belle said. The blue circle on top of Alexa lit up.

Tim looked at me in surprise. "She knows how to use Alexa?"

"This is news to me."

"The most recent five items on your shopping list are . . ." the surprisingly realistic mechanical voice began. "Grapes. Grapes. Tim. Hello. Grapes."

I grinned at Tim. "Huh? I love you, but I didn't put you on my shopping list."

"Do you want me to read the next five items?" the black cylinder said.

"Yes, please, Alexa," Belle answered.

"The next five items on your list are grape. Grapes. Belle's a good girl. Peanuts. Snacks. Do you want me to read the next five items?"

I dissolved in laughter but managed to squeak out, "Yes, please, Alexa."

Tim hooted in amusement.

"The last five items on your list are grapes. Milk. Salad greens. Peanuts. Hello."

"Thank you, Alexa," I said before Belle started dictating more grapes. "Alexa, stop." I shook my head and snickered some more. "Belle, you're something. No more talking to Alexa, now." Although I couldn't control what she did when I wasn't here unless I powered down Alexa before I left the house.

"Who knew a parrot and a robot could have a meaningful relationship?" Tim asked.

"Belle, why did you make a shopping list?" I asked between giggles.

"Belle likes Alexa. Belle likes to shop. Belle's a good girl."

Chapter Forty

The usual suspects gathered in Gin's upstairs living room at seven o'clock. Gin, of course, Flo, Norland, Tulia, Zane, Stephen, and Derrick. It was a large room, although since Gin lived alone we had to supplement her couch and easy chair with several folding chairs to seat everybody. Her walls were covered with artistic photographs of the kinds of candy she made, all photos taken by Gin herself. A whimsical close-up of brightly colored saltwater taffy made my mouth water, and a black-and-white shot of a child gazing at a giant, spiral-striped lollipop was timeless. Another photo showed a plate with a half-eaten piece of fudge, a cookie with glistening sugar on top, and a coffee mug reading: LIFE IS SHORT, MAKE IT SWEET.

"Cokey with the folks?" I asked my brother.

"Yes," he said. "She's all excited to have a sleepover with Tucker. What could possibly go wrong?" He grinned.

I smiled back. "Tomorrow's headline will read, PRE-SCHOOLER SQUEEZES PUPPY TO DEATH."

Gin's coffee table held my deviled eggs, a plate of carrot muffins, and a bowl of bone-shaped cookies, plus small plates and napkins. This odd assortment was dinner for me, so I helped myself to one of each. I set my glass of wine on the table and held up the bone.

"These are really edible for humans?" I asked.

"It's one of the recipes in *The Icing on the Corpse*," Gin said. They're called Breakfast Bones and I rather like them. Flo, you have a dog. Take some home for her, too."

"I will," Flo said.

Zane's husband, Stephen, spoke up. "I noticed the recipe in the book. Warning, they have bacon in them." He glanced around the room. "Except I guess I'm the only vegetarian in the group."

Being a vegetarian clearly wasn't a weight-loss plan. Stephen was a stocky man no taller than me with more than a little gut. He was also super congenial and a fabulous cook.

"My granddaughter loved the cover," Norland said, holding up the book. On the front sat a tall dog in a top hat and necktie, a long-haired dog wearing a pink hair ribbon, plus two other dogs and two cats gathered around a pink tiered wedding cake. An arch decorated with pink flowers and greenery completed the scene. "Now she wants a wedding for her pets. Including cake. I'm never going to hear the end of it." He laughed.

"Who made the muffins?" I asked.

Derrick raised his hand. "I know I'm jumping the gun,

but they're from *Murder Most Fowl*, next week's book, which takes place in March. I wasn't sure if any of the *Icing* recipes were edible for people. The carrot muffins are fabulous, and easy, too."

"It has another killer cover." Flo grabbed her copy of the book from the end table and held it up. On the yellow dust jacket, a fox gazed in through a glass door at a box of fluffy baby chicks.

"Uh-oh," Gin said. "Why do I think some of those chicks aren't going to make it?"

Zane tasted one of my deviled eggs. "Mac, these are splendid. What a brilliant idea to add avocado to the yolks."

I smiled at him. "Thanks. I saw it mentioned online and had to try it. You know I'm not much of a cook, but I can boil eggs, contrary to popular belief. And if all I have to is mash stuff, even I can handle that. Plus, the avocado is so rich you don't need to add mayo."

"All right, everybody," Marshall Flo said, clapping her hands to get our attention. "Let's talk about the book, but I want to leave time to discuss the case, too."

I nibbled on the bone cookie, which was a bit dry but surprisingly tasty, its sweetness mixing with the salty bacon. Gin read the cover blurb aloud. It was how we always started. I sipped wine, worked my way through a couple of eggs and a muffin, and listened as various people chimed in on the suspects, the suspense, the setting. I commented on a couple of things, but my brain was over-full of the ideas and facts about the murder right here in Westham. I found it hard to focus on the book discussion. I felt compelled to sort out the facts of the case and had really come for the second part of the meeting. I knew Lincoln wouldn't approve, but as long as we didn't put

ourselves in harm's way, what could a bit of remote research hurt?

Lincoln. *Shoot.* I should have texted him about what
Rizzoli had said. I took out my phone and copied the text
I'd sent to the group earlier.

Ran into Danny Rizzoli at B's house. I pretended I
was a lost tourist. He acted like he already owned the
property, said he might be moving in with his son soon.
Said B had kept Ron away from him but now they'd
patched things up and that B was mean and selfish.

I hit Send. I knew he wouldn't believe I had simply
run into Ron's father, but it was the truth. When I looked
up, everybody had set down their books or e-readers.

"Earth to Mac," Flo said. "Do you want to fill us in on
what happened last night?" Her pen was poised above the
yellow legal pad where she tracked the investigation.

"As long as nobody asks if I think it was the murderer
who broke a window in my shop." I smiled. "For the
record, I suppose it was, but I can't be sure unless the police find whoever did it. And I don't know how they're
going to do that."

"Did the person get into your shop?" Norland asked.

"The police dusted for prints everywhere, but I doubt
the vandal got in. It all happened pretty fast and the WPD
arrived promptly." I frowned. "My grandmother said she
saw someone snooping around my shop."

"With her spyglass?" Zane asked. "Your grandma is a
hit."

Several heads nodded. Who didn't love Reba Almeida?

"Yes, with her spyglass. But the person was wearing
all black, including a black watch cap. All she could say

is they didn't have a heavy build." I blew out a breath. "Not actually very helpful."

"Let's see," Flo began. "Neither Ron nor Eli is heavy. Isadora isn't heavy. Sofia isn't, either."

Gin flinched at the mention of Eli, but she didn't object.

"And neither is Danny Rizzoli, for that matter," I said.

"No one saw a person all in black with a black cap around town last night?" Flo surveyed the room. All she got were heads shaking and a few responses of "Not me" and "No."

"All they'd have to do is take off the cap and the black jacket and you would have no idea it was the same person," Norland pointed out.

"Exactly," I said.

"Mac, is there anything you can add about meeting Rizzoli today?" Gin asked.

I thought more about seeing him. "I said in the text I pretended I was a tourist so he wouldn't know who I was. I hope it doesn't backfire, like if he's with Ron around town and Ron sees me. But, anyway, he basically said good riddance to Beverly. It was pretty blatant. He claimed she'd kept Ron away from him."

"Eli said something completely different," Gin chimed in. "He told me Rizzoli abandoned Ron and his mother when Ron was an infant. Eli said they never heard from him, never got any child support."

"I know," I said. "I thought the same thing when Rizzoli said Beverly had been the reason he hadn't seen Ron all these years."

"He sounds like a gold digger to me," Tulia said. "An opportunist. Maybe he's not even Ron's real father."

"They sure look alike," I reminded her.

"Gin, has Haskins contacted you further?" Flo asked.

"No, thank goodness," Gin said. "He must have decided I was telling the truth."

Flo checked her pad. "One thing one of us could do would be to see if any of the suspects have made a recent purchase of antifreeze."

Norland shook his head. "It might work, but do you know many people keep old antifreeze in their garage or shed? Most of which aren't locked?"

Flo lifted her chin at the challenge. "If it might work, we should do it. It's our civic duty to help catch this murderer. None of us is safe until he is apprehended."

"How are we going to stay safe catching a killer?" Stephen frowned. "Take pictures of four or five people in the auto parts store and ask if any of them bought the toxic kind of antifreeze lately? Asking questions so publicly is getting way too close to the detective's job, isn't it?" He was our town clerk and as such probably felt an obligation to stay out of the way of the police.

"I tend to agree," Norland said.

Former police chief. Same way of thinking.

Make that three of us. "I really think we need to stay online with whatever we do." I gazed at each of them in turn. "It's way too dangerous to be seen asking questions around town."

"Very well," Flo said, tapping the pad with her pen. She didn't look happy at being challenged. "Is there anything we can be proactive with?"

"Did we ever learn about alibis?" Tulia asked. "Who was where that night after the dinner?"

"Haskins kept bugging me about who I was with," Gin

offered. "I told him Eli dropped me at home after the dinner. I live alone, and he does, too. I don't have any Airbnb guests this week. Eli and I both have zip for alibis."

I frowned. "I wonder if Ron stayed in Beverly's house after the dinner or spent the night with Sofia. Is there any way we can find out?"

"Does anyone know where she lives?" Flo asked. "Maybe we could ask the neighbors."

Zane raised his hand. "One time when we were eating at Jimmy's it came up. She said she shares a two-bedroom with three other Russian girls in the apartment building over near the supermarket."

A decidedly low-rent apartment building. But she was probably saving a lot of money by sharing living quarters.

"My cousin lives there," Tulia said. "I'll go see what I can find out."

"Good," Flo said.

"Wait a sec," I said. "I thought we were only going to do online searching."

"I agree with Mac," Norland said. It's the purview of the authorities to ask questions in person.

Tulia shrugged, then sipped her drink.

Flo rolled her eyes. "What about Danny Rizzoli? We should find out if he came to town before the murder, and where he's staying."

"Tim and I saw him at Jimmy's, but it was on Tuesday, the day after Beverly died," I said. "Did anybody see him before Monday?" Again a unanimous negative response.

"Simply because we didn't see him doesn't mean he wasn't here, of course," Norland pointed out. "But, again, only the detective and his team should be checking into it, not us."

"How about Isadora?" Gin asked. "Where does she live?"

I raised a finger. "She told me she lives in a condo in Westham, but I don't know where."

Derrick looked at Flo. "Can you find the address?"

"I imagine so." Flo jotted down something. "And once we have the address, we can ask neighbors if she went out again after the dinner."

"Flo, I don't think asking neighbors about anything is a good idea." I shook my head. "What if the lady next door tells Isadora one of us was snooping around about her comings and goings? If she's the killer, whoever asks could be the next victim." I finished my wine. "Questioning neighbors is Haskins's job, or his team's."

"Absolutely," Norland said. "Querying neighbors takes us over the line from safe to dangerous, in my opinion."

"Should I not ask my cousin about Sofia and Ron?" Tulia asked.

"Do you trust her not to tell them you inquired?" I asked.

Tulia scoffed. "Yes, I trust her. We grew up together. We're like sisters. If I tell her not to talk about it, she won't."

"That should be all right," Flo said in a hurry before Norland could tell Tulia to desist.

"Norland, did you get any more information about Sofia's immigration status?" I tapped the side of my wineglass.

"Unfortunately, no." He frowned. "Flo has her top-secret librarian databases, and I still have access to the law enforcement ones because I've been doing some consulting for the BCI."

"BCI?" Gin asked.

"Bureau of Criminal Investigation," Norland explained what I'd learned from Victoria the day before. "It assists the fifteen Barnstable County communities here on the Cape, as well as Nantucket and Martha's Vineyard, in crime scene investigation and a lot more. But, anyway, I wasn't able to dig any deeper about Ms. Burtseva. And her status is only pertinent insofar as it would give Ron Ruchart a motive to kill his grandmother."

"Such motive being money so he could marry Sofia," I murmured.

Norland nodded.

"What about what you texted us, Mac?" Flo asked. "Where Sofia said she thought Ron was hiding something from her. Do we know anything more about that?"

I glanced around at a few heads shaking no. Nobody spoke up, either. "I don't," I said.

"Maybe she was imagining it," Gin finally said. "You know how easy it is to read stuff into somebody's behavior—somebody you're involved with, I mean—that just isn't there."

"Like the cartoon where the woman makes up this whole relationship-ending story about what her silent guy is thinking?" Tulia asked with a delighted grin.

"And his thought bubble has him wondering if it's time to change the oil in his car?" Flo finished the story.

"Exactly," Gin said.

I smiled, except it turned into a yawn. I tried to suppress it but didn't quite succeed. "Are we done?" I asked. "I had a long day and should get home."

"I think we've pretty much exhausted all the ideas for tonight," Flo said. "I, for one, am going to follow up on antifreeze. Everybody else, keep your eyes out for clues, and, Tulia, you add to the thread if you learn something about Sofia and Ron."

"Or even if you don't," I said, "that'd be good to know, too."

"You got it." Tulia set down her can of seltzer and stood.

Derrick stood, too. "I'll walk you home, sis. We should all be extra careful."

"Thanks, bro." After last night, I wouldn't mind the company. Even though I'd only be walking the length of Main Street and nine o'clock wasn't very late, it was nighttime with a murderer at large. Having a big brother— in both senses of the phrase—escort me wasn't a bad idea at all.

Chapter Forty-one

"You know it's been four days since we found Beverly dead," Gin said the next morning, ten minutes into our walk.

"I know." I cast a look behind us as we passed through a particularly dense, dark stretch of thick undergrowth amid taller trees. "I feel like somebody could dash out and attack at every turn."

"Don't say that." She scrunched her shoulders. "It gives me the creeps."

"Sorry. I'm feeling jumpy."

"Don't they say the more time passes after a homicide, the less likely it is the police will catch the killer?" Gin asked.

I wrinkled my nose. "I've heard that, but only in books and on shows. Do you think it's really true?"

"I have no idea." A shiver rippled through her like a

malicious rock disturbing the calm of a salt pond on a windless day. "You could ask your detective buddy."

"He might interpret the question as criticism."

"Huh. It sort of is, right?"

"Or I could ask my BFF, Victoria."

"As if. Have you ever told me why you have a problem with her?"

I waited a half dozen steps before answering. "Probably not. It's from a long time ago. She was super competitive in high school and she didn't really like that I was as good as her or better on both debate team and at volleyball."

Gin stared at me. "That's it?"

"Yeah, pretty much." I could tell Gin about Vince's suicide, about Victoria blaming me. Gin would understand. But I didn't feel like talking about it. And it was over now, or at least it was for me.

The telltale whir of a bike approached from behind us as we crossed the bridge over the marsh. I glanced over my shoulder.

Isadora slowed as she rode up next to us. She wore jeans with frayed knees, but they were the kind you buy with holes, not because she'd worn out the knees doing actual work. Her hot-pink T-shirt clung to her body and her head was helmet free.

"Hey, girls," Isadora said.

"Beautiful morning, isn't it?" I asked. And it was. Yesterday's chilly breeze had gone wherever chilly breezes go in the summer, and the weather had reverted to a normal, sunny, starting-to-warm-up August morning.

"Kind of comes with the territory when you live in paradise, dontcha think?" Isadora squinted at Gin. "How's it going?"

I'd been about to introduce the two when I remembered they'd met at the fateful dinner party. At least for now the younger woman's breath didn't reek of alcohol.

"Gin, right?" Isadora asked.

"Yes. I'm good. You?" Gin stopped walking, so I did, too, and Isadora put a foot down on the path.

"I'm all right," the younger woman replied.

A less-than-hearty endorsement. "It's a good morning for some exercise," I said.

She rolled her eyes. "I guess you could call it exercise. Is there anybody anymore who doesn't work out? Anyway, Daddy wanted to see me last night, so I decided to ride up there instead of Lyfting."

If my shop had been attacked last night, she'd be in the clear. But the window had been broken two nights ago. Had Lincoln looked into all of the suspects' whereabouts for Wednesday night? I wasn't positive I'd asked him. I was pretty sure he wouldn't tell me even if he had.

"It's a pretty morning for a ride, though," Isadora went on. "I was going to put in my earbuds, but it's kinda nice to hear the birds singing and stuff."

"How's your father doing?" Gin spoke softly.

"He's all weepy and depressed about Beverly's death, of course." She raised a single eyebrow. "But he's my dad and I love him. He's all I have for family."

Gin and I exchanged a quick look. Except for the half brother, of course.

Isadora sneezed into her elbow. "Excuse me."

"Bless you," Gin said.

Isadora sniffed and drew a tiny bottle out of her jeans pocket, squeezing drops into each eye. "It's too early for ragweed to be blooming." She blinked, carefully wiping away the excess drops from under her eyes. "Something else must be out. My allergies are killing me."

Chapter Forty-two

Heading home from Salty Taffy's after my walk with Gin, I paused when I spied Isadora at one of the round iron sidewalk tables in front of Greta's Grains. Twice in one morning. I had time to say hello, and maybe learn something, too, since we hadn't chatted for long out on the bike trail. She was reading on her phone as she sat, swiping up to scroll down. I paused next to her chair and cleared my throat.

She glanced up. "We have to stop meeting like this, Mac. Have a seat."

"Thanks." I pulled out the other wrought-iron chair.

She set her phone on the table facedown. "I'm on my phone way too much. I lost it once and I was, like, desperate."

I laughed. "I know the feeling. Were you reading a novel?" I didn't care for reading books on a phone, but I knew a lot of people did.

"Yeah, a Brenden DuBois sci-fi. Awesome book. The characters are mostly teenagers."

"I've heard of him. A New England author, right?"

"Yeah. You going to get coffee or anything? You have to go inside for it. They don't have waitstaff."

"I know. My boyfriend Tim owns the bakery."

Her carefully made-up eyes widened. "That hot guy? He's so cute." She eyed me as if she didn't quite believe somebody like me could score someone as gorgeous as Tim.

I smiled. "The same."

"You go, girl. So do you go walking out there every day?" she asked.

"Yep, Gin and I do a morning power walk."

"Power walk," she scoffed. "Everybody's all into how much they exercise, what gym they work out in, how many steps they take every day. I can't be bothered. I watch my weight, that's enough, and I bike a lot." She sipped from the straw in her iced latte. "Did you ever find the dress you were looking for? Because we got some new ones in yesterday. You should totally come by and check them out."

"Thanks, but a friend loaned me one that's perfect." In my dreams, that is.

"You're good, then." She sipped her iced latte. "So I haven't heard that they've arrested anybody yet for Beverly's murder. Doesn't it seem like it's taking the police way too effing long to solve it?" She scrunched up her nose, making her small eyes nearly vanish, the only feature jarring in an otherwise pretty face.

"It's worrisome, for sure. But Detective Haskins is good at his job. He'll catch the killer. Who knows? Maybe even today."

"Hmm." She gazed into the distance. "Hope so."

"Poor Ron," I said, faking sympathy. "He must be worried sick about his grandmother's killer not being caught."

She batted away the suggestion. "He's fine."

The two were about the same age, I thought. "Are you two, you know . . ." I let my voice trail off. It was a possibility, but unlikely. Didn't hurt to ask.

"Hanging out?" she scoffed. "As if. He's a gamer, you know. Anyway, he's all lovey-dovey with Sofia. The Russian who's a waitress." She tapped a black-lacquered fingernail against her phone case. "They're having some kind of service for Beverly this afternoon. Dad told me."

"Oh?"

"Yeah, mostly only family and such. And a weepy would-be admirer named Wesley Farnham—otherwise known as my father. Over at her house."

"Are you going?"

"You kidding? I couldn't stand the lady. Dad asked me to go with him. I don't think so."

One of Tim's employees came out and cleared the table next to us. "You guys good?" he asked us, the stud in his tongue flashing in the sunshine, his green hair down to his ear on one side of his head but shaved up the other.

Isadora nodded. She'd picked up her phone and was tapping away with her left index finger, holding her phone in her right hand. Her nails were so long she probably couldn't text with her thumbs.

"Yes, thanks," I said. "Will you tell Tim I'm here?"

He gave me a thumbs-up and headed back inside. A moment later, Tim stepped out.

"How's everything?" He bent down to kiss the top of my head.

"Great," I said. "Isadora, this is Tim Brunelle, baker. Tim, Isadora Farnham."

Tim's presence wrested her attention away from her phone. She flashed him her brightest smile. "I've been wanting to meet you, Tim. I've heard so much about you, and your pastries are heavenly."

Lay it on a little thicker, girl. *Sheesh.*

"Nice to meet you," Tim said. "You ladies joining us for Breads and Brews tonight? We have a great trio playing."

Tim transformed the bakery into a bar and social hangout certain Friday nights, and always had live music, too.

"Gin and I are planning to come," I said.

"Ooh, it sounds fun." Isadora actually batted her mascaraed and extended eyelashes at him.

"Great." He excused himself and went back inside, but not before giving me a little eye roll, as if to say, "Where'd you pick up that one?"

"I should probably get going," I said. "I need to open the bike shop."

"I'm off, myself." She glanced up from the phone. "Have to do inventory this morning at the shop before we open. My Lyft will be here in three."

"You don't have a car?"

Her lip curled. "Of course I have a car. A sweet Jag convertible with cream leather seats. What I don't have is a license. Third arrest for operating under the influence tends to have that effect."

I remembered Pa saying he knew her from meetings. "Are you in recovery? Like AA or something?"

"They wish. I mean, maybe I should be. But it's fun to

drink, you know?" She shrugged. She glanced over my shoulder. "Speak of the devil. Or devils."

I twisted in my chair. Ron and Sofia walked hand in hand toward us from the direction of Beverly's street. And Danny Rizzoli was the third member of their party.

I sucked in air. I was in big trouble now. They'd already seen us. Ron waved at Isadora, who waved back. If I left now, it would look weird. Might as well see if I could do some damage control.

A moment later, the newcomers stood at our table. I stood, too, and Isadora followed suit, holding her iced coffee.

"Good morning," I said with a bright smile.

"Hey, Mac, Isadora," Ron said. "Do you know Sofia?"

I acknowledged her.

"You've waited on me at Jimmy's," Isadora said.

Sofia smiled but kept silent.

"And this is my father," Ron announced proudly. "Dan Rizzoli."

So he'd dropped the nickname. Because it was associated with his life as a criminal? Possibly.

Ron hesitated a moment. "Dad," he said, as if the simple syllable was awkward to pronounce. "This is Mac Almeida and Isadora Farnham."

"Nice to meet you, ladies." Danny stared at me. "Hey, we talked yesterday, didn't we? Over at the house?"

"So you already met?" Ron asked, gazing from me to his father and back.

"We didn't exactly exchange names. This nice lady said she was a tourist, asked me for directions." He smiled at me.

His eyes were so cold I felt like winter had struck four months early. Or maybe it wasn't an icy wind. Maybe it was fear I felt. Isadora had been following our exchange with raised eyebrows, but they were of interest, not surprise.

"A tourist?" Ron frowned at me. "But you live here and own a bike shop. Why did you say you were a tourist?"

"You must have misunderstood me, Dan." I smiled and left it at that.

"You were wearing a Mac's Bikes shirt." He returned the smile, but it was a cold one.

I groaned to myself. Of course I'd had on a store shirt. How stupid could I be?

"Then we talked about Beverly for a bit, may God rest her soul." Danny solemnly crossed himself. "And Ron's inheritance, didn't we, Mac?" He stressed my name in a mocking tone.

I gave a nervous laugh. "You got that right. Well, I'd better be going. Have a good day, everybody." I was so screwed.

A sedan bearing the Lyft logo pulled up. "Here's my ride," Isadora said. "Nice to meet you, Mr. Rizzoli, Sofia."

Isadora climbed in the back seat. I checked the traffic and crossed the street the minute it was clear. I didn't have to, because my shop was on the same side as Greta's Grains. On the other hand, I did have to. Anything to put distance between me and those arctic eyes.

Chapter Forty-three

I was adjusting the seat height on a rental for a tall man at about eleven that morning when Wesley Farnham hurried in. His face was flushed with the heat of the day, and his neck was sweaty.

"Good morning, Mac. Is Orlean in?" He glanced toward the repair room.

"Hi, Wes. She's in there." I tilted my head. "Feel free." I finished up with the man's seat and told him to have a good ride. I moseyed over to the repair area, ears cocked.

"This afternoon?" Orlean stared at Wes, holding a wrench in her blue-gloved hand.

"Yes, at her house. It's not a funeral—she didn't want one—but a gathering to remember her. Just family and a few friends. You'll come, won't you?"

The gathering Isadora had referred to. What a nice

gesture for Wes to invite Orlean, one of the few people Beverly hadn't been disagreeable to.

Orlean caught sight of me. "I don't know if I can." She gestured down at her dark blue work pants and her T-shirt. "I can't go like this. I'd have to go home and change and come back."

"Of course you'll go, Orlean," I interjected. "Leave however early you need to so you can get home and be back in time."

Orlean gazed at me. She nodded once. "Thanks, Mac."

"Derrick and I can handle the store. If I have to close the repair side early, I will. It's Friday, after all."

"Thank you, Mac," Wes added. "You're welcome to join us, if you can get away."

An interesting prospect. "I'd be happy to go, and I appreciate the invitation." I flashed on what Abo Reba had said. "My grandmother was fond of Beverly. Can I bring her along, if she's free?"

"Of course." Wes spread his hands in magnanimity. "I've ordered in plenty of food and drinks."

"What time does it begin?" I asked.

"Four o'clock." He glanced at the wall clock. "I'd better get going. I have a few more people to notify."

"Thanks, Wesley," Orlean said without looking at him, already focused on her work again.

I walked him out. "Will it be a big crowd?"

He shook his head. "Sadly, she didn't have a lot of friends in Westham. That's why I wanted to be sure to invite Orlean." He smacked his forehead. "I should ask your parents, too. Being neighbors and all."

"That's very nice of you. I can tell them, if you'd like."

His expression lightened at not having one more errand to run. "Please. I hope they're free, especially Reverend Almeida. Even though Beverly wasn't religious, I'd like to have a man of the cloth there." He hesitated but went on. "Have you heard Ron's father is in town?"

"Yes, I met him yesterday, and ran into both Ron and him this morning, too."

Wes's lips pulled to the side. "He's not what one might call a good influence on young Ron, I'd say."

"He seemed confident Ron would inherit the house and property, and intimated he would be moving in soon."

"I think he's in for a big surprise." He cleared his throat. "See you this afternoon, Mac." He hurried to his black Mercedes and drove off.

I wasn't looking forward to seeing Danny Rizzoli again. Those eyes gave me shivers just thinking about them. As I headed back into the shop, I stopped. Lincoln Haskins might be very interested to know about this memorial gathering. I pulled out my phone and tapped a text to him.

FYI. 4 pm memorial gathering at Beverly's house. Wes Farnham invited my mechanic and me, and my family, too.

I copied the message before I sent it. I sent it to the group thread, too. Tulia had posted to it a few minutes earlier.

Fail. My cousin says she didn't see either Sofia or Ron that evening cuz she worked night shift at the hospital. Sorry.

So they could have been together, or Sofia could have been alone. I frowned at the phone. I realized that we, the Cozy Capers, had a logic problem going on. It didn't necessarily matter where anybody was the night of the dinner party. If Beverly was poisoned before or during the meal, the killer could have been tidily tucked into bed by ten o'clock, alone or otherwise. I was about to call Pa when I decided to add that thought to the thread, in case some-body had been tempted to snoop around Isadora's neigh-bors despite Norland's and my cautions not to.

Houston, we have logic problem. If B was poisoned before or during dinner, doesn't matter where killer was overnight.

Bing. A new text from Gin.

Wes asked Eli and me to gathering, too. Kind of creepy? But we're going. See you there.

Interesting. Everybody from the dinner party, plus ex-tras. Would Wes be able to persuade Isadora to go despite her objections? I blew out a breath. Thinking through this stuff was exhausting. But I still needed to call Pa.

After I greeted him, I said, "Wes Farnham wanted to invite you and Mom to a private gathering at Beverly's house this afternoon, since you were neighbors."

He gave a low chuckle. "We were not her favorite abutters, but Mr. Farnham doesn't need to know. I'll check my schedule and will let your mother know. Are you invited, too?"

"Yes, and I'm going to bring Abo Ree if she's free. She said she and Beverly used to talk about roses."

"Good. What time?"

"Four. Oh, and Wes said he'd particularly appreciate having a man of the cloth in attendance, even though he said Beverly wasn't religious."

"I can understand him wishing for a minister's pres-ence. I invited Beverly to join our services more than once, but she always declined."

"I'm not surprised. I'll see you there."

After we disconnected I called Abo Reba, but she didn't answer. I left her a message about the event and asked her to call me back. Mom had said they were planning to go for another ride today, but they could always postpone their excursion or go earlier. I'd let the two of them figure it out.

Now to tell Derrick two thirds of the employees were going to scoot out on him this afternoon. He could manage as long as I posted a notice saying NO REPAIRS AFTER 3 TODAY on the door. He'd have to have Cokey with him from four to six if my parents were going to go to the gathering. It should work out, since my niece loved working in the shop. Of course, "working" meant sitting on the high stool drawing pictures after she'd tired of trying out all the tricycles and bikes her size.

Chapter Forty-four

I needed to pick up Belle's organic pelleted food at the hardware store, so I checked with Derrick at three o'clock. I should have enough time to run my errand, wash up and change my own clothes, and arrive at the memorial gathering by four.

"I'm taking off. You good? The sign about no repairs is on the door."

"I'm good." He sat on the high stool entering rental receipts into our tracking software.

I probably should have started off with a repair software package when I'd opened the store, but I'd already socked so much money into inventory it had seemed easier to stick with the paper repair tickets. By now we had a pretty efficient system going, plus Orlean didn't have to worry about touching a computer screen or keyboard with greasy fingers.

"Pa's dropping Cokey off a few minutes before four," Derrick said.

"Is Mom going with him?"

He shook his head. "She had a client coming."

"Let me guess. A Leo sun with moon in crazy." I smiled.

"And Venus in whacko, with demoted Pluto retrograde." He returned my grin. "Who wants to know if he should buy swamp property in Florida."

We'd been doing this irreverent routine for years, but never in front of our mother. She made her living by working as a professional astrologer and was in demand in the area, especially from all the fresh blood every summer known as tourists. Just because my brother and I didn't buy into the belief system didn't mean she shouldn't profit from it.

"See you tomorrow, brother." I kissed his cheek.

"See you, sis. Stay safe, okay?" His eyes broadcast concern.

"You and me both." I slung on my EpiPen bag, slipped on my lightweight backpack that doubled as handbag, and headed down Main Street. The hardware store was at the far end of town past Gin's. I poked my head into Salty Taffy's, but Gin wasn't at the counter. I'd see her in an hour, anyway.

I gazed at the walkway between the candy shop and the health clinic, where she'd discovered Beverly. The cold, still body. The death grimace on her face. Monday was four days ago now. Why hadn't Lincoln made an arrest? Too many people lying to him, probably. Or at least one. I sent up a little prayer for his success. And that it should happen soon.

Two doors past the clinic was Pete's Westham Mercantile, a vintage name for a good old-fashioned hardware store, which carried anything and everything. Wheelbarrows and rakes decorated the sidewalk, as well as a bushel basket full of brightly colored beach shovels, buckets, and pairs of flip-flops, with a big ONE DOLLAR EACH sign above it. August was already on its way out for retailers.

I headed for the counter in the back. Piet, the Dutch owner, was happy to order Belle's food for me, which meant I neither had to pay postage nor patronize the online giant threatening to take over the world, obliterating small businesses in the process. Piet had anglicized the spelling of his name for the sign out front, but he still spoke with a slight accent. To my ears, the way he said his name wasn't identical with the usual pronunciation of Pete.

He perched on a stool behind the counter, as usual, peering at the screen in front of him with half glasses resting on a scrunched-up nose. He looked up when I approached.

"Ah, Mackenzie. Here to pick up your bird food?"

I smiled. "I am. How are you?"

"All good, all good." He turned and rummaged on the shelf behind me, turning back to set a five-pound bag on the surface between us. "There you are. And a treat for Belle, too." He set a small pouch of mixed dried fruit next to the bag. The cover featured a drawing of an African gray and a scarlet macaw face-to-face.

"Aw, thanks. She'll love it and ask to visit you, I'm sure." I smiled and pushed my credit card into the chip reader.

He eyed me over the top of his readers. "I heard you found the body of a murder victim earlier this week. How are you coping?" His pale-green eyes looked concerned.

I took a deep breath. "I'm all right, thanks. I'd be better if the police had someone in custody."

He glanced both ways and leaned toward me. "Gossip is she was killed with ethylene glycol," he whispered. "Antifreeze."

Where was he going with this? And how had he learned Beverly had been murdered with antifreeze? As far as I knew this detail hadn't been made public.

"Really?" I tried to keep my voice casual. "I haven't heard the means of death on the news."

"My niece, she works for the Bourne police. She heard it in the department."

I raised my eyebrows. Word must travel behind the scenes. "My father had a dog who drank antifreeze accidentally and died from it."

"I know. A young lady, a girl almost, was in here on the weekend." Piet kept his voice low. "She bought some."

My Spidey sensors stood at alert. *Sofia? Isadora?* "She probably bought the new nontoxic kind, right?" The machine beeped and I took the card back, not looking at him as I stashed it in my wallet.

"No, it was the older kind. Ethylene glycol."

"So she drives an older car?"

He shook his head. "That's what got my attention. I saw her park a bicycle out front before she came in."

"What did she look like?" I asked.

"Blonde. Tallish. Never seen her before."

I thought fast. "I know a tall blonde waitress. Works at Jimmy's Harborside. Did she sound Russian?" Of course, Isadora was blonde and tallish, too.

He shook his head. "I didn't wait on her. But I saw what she bought."

Rats. "Who was the cashier the day she came in?" Maybe I could talk to whoever waited on the woman.

"My wife. She left the next day to go help her sister in Leiden. My sister-in-law had major surgery."

Double rats. I loaded Belle's food and treats into my pack and zipped it up. "Belle thanks you for the gift, Piet." I waved and headed out.

I was pretty sure Sofia didn't own a car, and I had fixed her bike for her. Isadora owned a Jaguar, but she'd said she wasn't currently driving it. Anyway, it had to be a late model. She didn't seem like a vintage car sort of girl. Gin and I had seen her riding on the trail, so she clearly also got around locally on a bicycle in addition to summoning a ride service. So what was either of them doing buying antifreeze? I had a feeling I knew the answer. I shuddered to think of Isadora slipping antifreeze into Beverly's drink. Or Sofia providing it to Ron to do the same.

When my phone rang, I paused on the sidewalk outside the mercantile's door.

"I'll go with you to the gathering, Mac, honey," my grandmother said. "Isn't it a nice thing for Mr. Farnham to do?"

"Yes, it is. I'll come by for you a few minutes before four, okay?"

"That'll be fine." She lowered her voice. "Maybe we'll nab the murderer at the service."

"Abo Ree! What are you talking about?"

"I've read my Agatha Christie. Isn't that what they do? Gather all the suspects in one room and lay out the case until the killer is revealed and trapped there?" Her tinkling laugh came over the line.

Geez. I hoped that wouldn't happen. "This isn't a novel or a showdown. It's a social gathering to honor Beverly's memory."

"I'll see you in a bit, sweetie." She disconnected.

I stared at my phone. She could imagine all she wanted. Unless Lincoln and reinforcements attended, I wanted to have nothing to do with a murderer being accused.

Chapter Forty-five

On my way home from Pete's, I passed the library. I changed course and hurried up the wide stone steps. My mind raced from one thought to the next and I craved some order. Maybe a quick chat with Flo would accomplish what I wanted.

Except her office door was closed. I knocked. No answer. I tried the handle. Locked. I sighed and made my way to the central desk.

"Is Flo here?"

A young man looked up. "No, she's gone for the day. Said she had to do some research someplace else before she went home."

I thanked him and turned away. If "research" was making inquiries that might land her in trouble, I didn't want to know about it. I trudged back down the outside steps. I really needed to go home and get ready to go out to a somber occasion. Instead I pulled out my phone. I also needed to check on Flo and make sure she was staying safe. After I texted her I waited but didn't get a response.

I hit Lincoln's number next. By some miracle, he picked up.

"Haskins." His voice was curt.

"Lincoln, I learned something a few minutes ago."

He groaned. "Mac, you have to stop trying to investigate."

"I wasn't! I was picking up a special order in the hardware store, and the owner, Piet, brought up the murder. He said a tall blonde young woman—which fits both Isadora and Sofia—bought some of the toxic kind of antifreeze the other day, but had arrived by bicycle."

"Do you happen to know how many other tall blonde young women are around Westham this month? Riding bicycles you probably rented to them?"

"Fine. Then you won't care that Isadora doesn't drive because she lost her license. And you won't need to inquire if Sofia got her bike fixed recently at my shop." I swallowed, trying to keep my frustration in check. "Did you see my message about the memorial gathering today?"

"Yes, thank you. Listen, Mac, don't get your back up. We're doing our best. I do happen to know Isadora is not currently driving legally, and what model car she owns, but I appreciate the tip." He cleared his throat. "And I might pop by the gathering to pay my respects."

"I'd better get going. See you there." I punched the End button rather harder than I needed to and strode toward home to deliver some treats to one special bird.

When I got there, a box with a certain logo awaited on

the porch. I laughed out loud. Belle's purchases, no doubt. Inside I put away the peanuts and granola bars. Luckily they hadn't shipped anything perishable. Belle and I had a cuddle for a couple of minutes as I sipped a cold beer.

"Piet sent you treats, Belle." I set her on the floor and stood.

"Piet's treats. Belle's a good girl. Snacks, Mac? Piet's treats."

I poured a few treats in her special bowl. "But first, have you been shopping today?"

"No shopping. I like Alexa. Snacks, Mac?"

I laughed and set the bowl on the floor for her. She picked up a piece of fruit in one claw, balancing on the other claw as she brought the treat to her beak. She didn't wobble or fall over and made it look easy. I sure couldn't pick up a snack with the toes on one foot and feed it to myself while I balanced on the other. Not now, not ever.

After I checked the clock, which read three forty-five, I took a moment to text the group.

Piet said tall blonde young woman came in on bike on weekend, bought toxic antifreeze. I told Lincoln. L didn't seem to care.

I added one more note.

Flo, library said you're out doing research. Hope you're being careful.

I scanned the thread, but there was nothing new. What else could I do to sort out my messy thoughts? Nothing was the answer, so I scrubbed my face, hands, and feet, and slipped into a black and turquoise sun dress with a flared skirt. I added my favorite turquoise earrings and a touch of lip gloss, and tied on flat black espadrilles. No strappy, heeled sandals for this girl. My short, curly hair was the same whether I was selling bikes or memorializing a fallen neighbor, so it didn't need any attention except fluffing it up with both hands. I added a silver bracelet and grabbed my EpiPen bag.

"Be good, Belle. I'll be back in a couple of hours."

"Belle's a good girl. Piet's treats." She added a wolf whistle for good measure.

"And no shopping."

"Belle likes Alexa," she muttered. "Belle likes Alexa. Belle likes shopping."

I set my fists on my waist and stared down at her with my firm-mom look. "No shopping."

"No shopping!"

Chapter Forty-six

I had my hand up to knock on Abo Reba's door when it flew open.

"We're almost late, Mac," she scolded. She stepped out and locked the door. My grandmother wore black slacks and a rainbow-colored cardigan over a white top. On her feet were her signature hot-pink sneakers, which were the only shoes she ever wore, even to church. The slouchy beret she also always wore matched her sweater. Reba Almeida was the definition of personal style.

"It's okay, Abo Ree. It's not like a show or a church service."

"We don't want to miss anything, though."

She bustled off down the stairs and I bustled behind her. She was way too excited about this gathering.

It didn't take us more than five minutes to walk to the house. I spied chairs and cloth-covered round tables scattered under the trees in the back, so we let ourselves in through the side gate and joined the gathering. Pa sat at a table with Danny Rizzoli, and Ron and Sofia stood under a big oak, a beer bottle in his hand, a wineglass in hers. I peered at a woman in black pants and a blue top who sat alone at another table, her eyes on her plate. I did a double take. I'd never seen Orlean without her ball cap on. Her reddish hair was chin length and she wore it tucked behind her ears. Two other tables were occupied by people who looked vaguely familiar, so they must be other summer residents who were around town only half the year. No Isadora, no Lincoln. I waved to Pa.

Wes certainly had ordered in abundant food and drink, and had hired a crew of black-clad servers and a bartender, too, from the looks of it. Wes, in a white dress shirt open at the collar and pale linen pants, caught sight of us and hurried our way.

"Welcome, Mac, welcome," he said. "This must be the lovely Reba I've been hearing about." He clasped her hand in both of his and beamed down at my diminutive grandmother. "I'm delighted you could join us, Mrs. Almeida."

"It's fine to meet you, and I appreciate being included. I am sorry it's on such a sad occasion. And please call me Reba."

"Reba it is, and I'm Wes." The smile slid off his ruddy face. "It's a sad occasion, indeed. But I know Beverly wouldn't stand for us moping around, so please help yourselves to refreshments. The caterer made a delicious cool punch, too."

Abo Reba thanked him. Gin and Eli appeared on the driveway at the far side of the house, and Wes headed in their direction to greet them.

"I'm starving." Abo Reba selected a small plate and headed down the line, heaping it with small meatballs and chicken wingettes. "Would you get me a glass of punch, please, Mac?" She made a beeline for Pa's table.

I strolled to the drinks table. The punchbowl was filled with a pale-green mixture, with a creamy shape floating in the middle. Lime and lemon slices floated in it, too. *But . . . green?*

"What's in the punch" I asked the slender bartender, a man in his forties with a weathered face.

"Ginger ale, limeade, pineapple juice, lime sherbet, and rum. It's quite good. Would you like to try some?" He smiled at me and held up a glass ladle.

Green punch at a gathering for a woman killed by green antifreeze? What had Wes been thinking? "Uh, no thanks." I surveyed the array of beer bottles. "I'll take a Shipyard Imperial Pilsner and a glass, please." A cold Pilsner on a hot day was much more my style. But wait. Abo Reba wanted a cup of the punch. Was it safe to drink? "Have you left the table since you assembled the punch?"

He looked at me as if I had a purple horn growing out of my forehead. "Excuse me?"

"Never mind. A glass of the punch, too, please." Surely nobody would dare add poison to a punch in such an open setting.

He handed me the punch and beer bottle with a glass upended on top.

A hand-holding Gin and Eli approached. "Double-fisted drinking, Mac?" Gin asked with a smile, but it looked like a nervous one.

I laughed. "Hi, you guys. The punch is for Abo Reba.

My grandmother," I added for Eli's benefit. "The little woman over there."

"Ah," Eli said. "Good to see you again, Mac."

This was the first time I'd seen him out of running clothes, and he cleaned up pretty nice. He wore crisp khakis and a pale-blue pressed Oxford shirt open at the collar, with the sleeves neatly rolled up on his forearms. The garb of a killer in disguise? I had no idea.

Gin glanced at the punch glass and her eyes widened. "Lime-green punch? Are they crazy?" she whispered, the color going out of her face.

"Insane was my thought, too." I rolled my eyes. I carried the drinks to the table and greeted Pa and Danny as I emptied the bottle into my glass.

"We were having a most interesting conversation," Pa began, "about the dry cleaning business." He smiled at me.

The dry cleaning business? *Huh?* I felt Danny's cold gaze on me even as he smiled.

"I formerly owned a chain of cleaners in New York," he said.

I had nothing to say to that. From the fumes coming from every dry cleaner I'd ever visited, it seemed likely he must be intimately familiar with all kinds of poisonous substances.

"Yes, Mother and I were discussing the trend toward toxin-free cleaning substances with Dan, here," Pa said. "It's an admirable goal, wouldn't you say, Mac?" Pa asked.

"Absolutely. Please excuse me," I said in a bright tone. "I'm going to get something to eat."

Danny gave me the creeps. And I planned to have a

conversation with Pa when this was over to find out what he'd learned from Ron's father. Pa, of course, could chat up a granite ledge, a trait he'd gotten from Abo Reba.

At the food table, I set down my beer. I helped myself to a few meatballs, several cubes of cheese, a couple of wheat crackers, and two strawberries. I stood munching as I watched the group. Gin and Eli talked with the guests at Pa's table. From the looks on their faces, Ron and Sofia appeared to be arguing. I picked up my beer and plate, and joined solo Orlean at her table. She glanced up and gave me a small smile.

"Take a load off, Mac." She rolled the corner of her napkin between her fingers. "Between you and me?" she murmured. "This isn't my kind of gig. But I couldn't say no when Wesley asked."

"I know what you mean." I sipped the cold Pilsner.

Wes walked slowly to the center of the yard. "May I have everyone's attention, please?" He held up both hands as the buzz of conversation ebbed.

A "No!" from Sofia plopped into the silence. Heads turned toward her and Ron. She'd said it to Ron, not to Wes. Ron gripped her elbow and muttered something. Sofia mustered a smile and gave a little wave to the group.

What was up with that? They'd been arguing, but about what?

Wes cleared his throat. "I want to thank you all for coming to honor Beverly's memory. She wouldn't have wanted anything so melancholy as a funeral, but I wondered if the Reverend Joseph Almeida would be willing to offer a few words of prayer?" He gazed at Pa.

Pa stood and strolled to join Wes. "It would be a privilege." He folded his hands and bowed his head, waiting a moment to allow others to quiet and follow suit. "Dear Lord, please watch over our sister Beverly's soul. May she rest in the peace of knowing she was loved. May those of us left on your mortal coil find our own peace, with your divine help, as we make our way forward without her."

I bowed my head, but I peeked at what the others were doing as Pa spoke. Sofia held her hands in prayer position at her chest with her eyes closed. Ron tapped his beer bottle and gazed up into the tree as if he'd rather be anywhere but here. Next to me Orlean sat with hands in her lap and eyes closed. I shifted my clandestine gaze to the waist-high garden gate Abo Reba and I had come through to see Lincoln Haskins standing on the other side of it. He stood somberly, hands clasped at his waist but eyes wide open and gaze roving over the assemblage.

"Amen," Pa finished. A chorus of quiet amens echoed him.

"Thank you, Joseph," Wes said, grasping his hand. "Would anyone like to stand and share a happy memory?"

"I'll begin, if I may," Pa said. "I appreciated Beverly's devotion to her gardens and her work, and her generosity to the health clinic."

I snuck a glance at Ron, who shook his head with a smug look on his face.

Pa continued. "I understand she helped reunite a great many families, yours among them, Wes."

Wes bobbed his head in acknowledgment and smiled.

"She had the blessing of a keen intellect and the discipline to achieve her dreams." Pa headed back to his table.

"Thank you, Joseph," Wes said. "Someone else?"

"Not me," announced Isadora from the driveway.

Orlean gasped, and she wasn't the only one. Wes's face turned dark.

Isadora ignored them all. "Can't share what you don't have. But I'll take a drink while you all wallow in your rosy thoughts." She strutted to the bartender. "Double Scotch on the rocks, darling."

Chapter Forty-seven

So Isadora had decided to come after all. I looked at Orlean next to me. She shook her head, pressing her lips together. Isadora sipped her Scotch and checked out the gathering, a smirk on her face. Her sleeveless sheath was in a bold yellow and black geometric patterned fabric, from Maxine's, no doubt, and her heeled black sandals showed off smooth, tanned legs.

Abo Reba stood and spoke in a louder voice than one might think possible for such a tiny person. "I'd like to share. Beverly loved nature. Look at this beautiful garden. It was all her doing."

"As if," Ron muttered audibly.

But it was her doing. Sure, Beverly had employed a team of gardeners. Still, she'd planned the plantings and overseen their care. Under the trees bloomed masses of impatiens in whites and shades of light pink to dark fuchsia, plus a shiny-leafed low ground cover. The sunny perennial bed had white Shasta daisies, purple phlox, lavender in bloom, and something in a bright yellow, all mixed with different hues of green foliage. I caught a whiff of sweetness from the rose garden near the house. The curving borders were impeccably edged and the lawn was a solid green, no mean feat in sandy soil like ours. And not a weed in sight anywhere.

I glanced over at Haskins. Still there, still observing. He was probably waiting for the testimonies to end before coming in. Isadora turned her back to the gathering and sneezed violently four times. She had a small black bag slung over her shoulder. She grabbed a tissue out of the bag and blew her nose before turning back.

"Beverly and I used to talk about roses for hours. I will miss her." My grandmother sat.

"Thank you, Reba," Wes said. He looked around expectantly.

Did I have anything positive I could say? I wondered.

Ron stepped forward. "My grandma took good care of me when I was younger." He slid his gaze to Eli, to Danny, and away again.

Was he implying Eli hadn't taken good care of him after Ron's mother died? Or saying Beverly had had to replace his parents? Maybe both.

Ron continued. "She wasn't an easy lady to get along with, but she did what she thought was right. May she rest in peace." He rejoined Sofia.

I checked Danny's face. He lifted his chin and drummed his fingers on the table. He didn't look at Ron. Ron nudged Sofia, but she shook her head. I was pretty sure she wouldn't have a single nice thing to say about Beverly. Good for her for keeping her dislike private.

Eli stood. "The death of her daughter hit Beverly hard. It hit us all hard." He glanced at Ron, who didn't meet his gaze. "Mothers aren't supposed to need to bury their children. Still, my mother-in-law kept on going and I admired that in her." Eli sat with a thud.

One of the people I didn't know stood, a woman in her seventies with a white bob and a tasteful outfit from Talbot's, Maxine's, or somewhere similar. "Bev and I played bridge with some other ladies every week. She was a sharp player and a gracious hostess."

The woman of the other couple at the table nodded her agreement.

"May God take her into his arms in heaven. May he bless her and keep her, and bring her peace." The woman sat, and her friend reached over and squeezed her hand.

Wes lowered his head somberly.

I made up my mind and stood. "Beverly was an avid bicyclist and frequented my shop. She supported off-road bike paths, as do I, and I appreciated her devotion to exercising in the fresh air of our beloved Cape." I sat. Not exactly effusive praise, but at least it was positive, and no one else had mentioned the biking part of her life.

Wes moved his gaze slowly over the group. When no one else spoke, he opened his mouth.

Orlean rose so abruptly her chair fell over. Her brow furrowed, she looked from one person to the next to the next, all around the yard, before speaking. "Beverly Ruchart was a good woman. She was generous with her time and talents, and treated me with respect. She's dead. Let no one say a bad word about her." She walked a few steps toward the hedge and folded her arms, her back to the gathering, her shoulders shaking.

I blew out a breath as I righted the chair. I went to my mechanic, venturing my arm around her.

"Thanks, Mac. I'll be okay," she whispered.

I squeezed her shoulder and started back to the table.

"Well, in fact I have a few . . ." Isadora began from her post leaning against the drinks table.

Wes took three fast strides toward her. He grasped her arm. "Don't you dare. Don't you even dare." His deep voice shook. "You'll leave before you'll malign her memory. Have I made myself clear?"

She rolled her eyes. "Yes, Daddy." She drew out his moniker with sarcasm pouring off the word. "Very clear." She shook off his hand and turned away, holding out her glass to the bartender for a refill.

Wes pulled himself up straight and faced the group again. "Thank you all for those dear memories. My own time with Beverly was far too short, but I was blessed with both her talent and her affection." He pulled out a folded lavender handkerchief and wiped his eyes. "Now, please enjoy the refreshments and each other's company."

Lincoln finally stepped through the gate and made his way to Wes, who stood in front of the food table. I moseyed in their direction, too, curious about the conversation that might ensue.

Wes shook Lincoln's hand with vigor. "Please tell me you're here because you have a suspect in custody." His eyes searched Lincoln's face.

"I'm afraid not. We are following up some promising leads, however. Good afternoon, Mac," he said to me when I joined them.

"Promising leads sound, well, promising," I said.

Lincoln glanced at Ron, who had joined his father and

mine at their table. Was Ron the promising lead? Or maybe his father was.

"I'm hoping for a prompt resolution of this case," Wes said.

"You and me both, sir," Lincoln said.

"Detective, please help yourself to food and drink. If you'll excuse me." Wes headed toward the table of summer people.

"So you heard all those testimonies," I said. "What did you think?"

"I think more people liked Beverly than many assume. And I think some had to dig deep to come up with something complimentary to say."

Like me? Like Eli and Ron, for sure. I snagged another piece of cheese. "Have you heard any news on my break-in? Ideas about who the vandal was? Victoria and company haven't told me a thing."

He shook his head once. "Not yet." He hesitated as if he was about to say more, but closed his mouth instead.

My grandmother was sitting and chatting with Orlean. She waved to Lincoln and pointed to an empty chair at their table.

"Catch you later, Mac." He strolled to the table and greeted the women.

Isadora had joined the two couples, smiling and apparently behaving herself. The women were obviously potential customers at Maxine's, or maybe they already shopped there and Isadora knew them. But where were Sofia and Danny? Ron's father no longer sat with his son and Pa.

I surveyed the property, spying them standing in front of the garage. Had Sofia bought the antifreeze for Danny? If so, Ron had to be in the loop, too. Sofia shook her head at something Danny said. He flipped his palms open. I was too far away to eavesdrop. She'd been angry or upset with Ron earlier, too, when Wes had started speaking. Maybe both Danny and his father were trying to get her to agree to something she objected to. But what? Danny glanced in my direction and caught me watching. I gave what I hoped looked like an innocent wave and picked up a carrot from the platter on the table.

The hair on my head pricked. I turned my head. Isadora stared at me with narrowed eyes. It was time for me to clear out of this stew of suspects.

Chapter Forty-eight

I wanted to leave but had to wait around another fifteen minutes until the gathering started to break up, since Abo Reba was chatting with Orlean. My grandmother was holding down most of the conversation, as Orlean had reverted to her native taciturn self.

"Pretty interesting group, wouldn't you say, Mac?" Abo Reba asked when I walked up.

"Very." I'd watched as Lincoln had managed to greet everybody present, stopping by the tables of summer people, as well as saying hello to Danny and Sofia when they'd rejoined the gathering. He'd had a short conversation with Isadora, too. If I didn't know he was a detective, I would have said he was there on a strictly social basis. But I knew better. He had a homicide to solve. This was very much a working visit.

"Are you ready to go?" I asked my grandmother at a

quarter to six. Everyone left was making moves to depart, and the bartender was packing up bottles.

"I'm going to eat at the parsonage. I'll go with your father."

So I hadn't needed to wait, after all.

"Do you want to eat with us, too, honey?" Pa asked me.

"No, thanks," I responded. "I'm going to Breads and Brews tonight."

Ron and Sofia had disappeared into the house, followed by Danny, or I would have said goodbye to them. Isadora seemed to have departed, too, when I wasn't looking. I said my goodbyes to Wes and thanked him.

"Thank you for coming, Mac." He gazed at me, while behind him the two black-clad caterers cleared the round tables now littered with small plates and empty glasses, a crumpled napkin here, an uneaten chicken wing there.

"I'm glad I did. People had some really nice things to say about Beverly."

He breathed out a heavy sigh colored with sadness. "We'll all have to go forward without her."

I trudged toward home, brain full of the conflicts swirling around us here in town. It was going to be good to immerse myself in music, a drink, and Tim's goodies tonight at the bakery. My brain needed a break.

I turned onto Main Street. The road was full of cars creeping in both directions. Tourist traffic could be crazy bad in August, especially on a Friday evening once everybody was off the beach and looking for somewhere to eat dinner. I passed the UU church and was about to walk past the Lobstah Shack. Tulia stepped out and put a key in the lock. She glanced at me.

"Hey, Mac."

I caught up with her. "Hi. I just left a small memorial gathering for Beverly. Wes Farnham held it in her backyard."

"Ooh, interesting. Were all the 'persons of interest' there?" She air quoted the phrase.

"Absolutely, and then some. The detective was, too."

"Really? The same detective who blew you off when you told him the killer was a tall, blonde young woman?"

I laughed. "The same. I mean, he's right. Westham is teeming with women fitting such a description, and I rent them bikes."

"Still would make whoever it was an accessory to murder, right?"

"Only if murder was what the antifreeze was used for. Even if it was Sofia or Isadora, they could have been buying the antifreeze for someone else. For its intended use, an older-model car." I scooted off the sidewalk to let two women pushing double strollers pass by, both occupied by pairs of toddlers looking the same age. Behind them was a mother with a trio of matching babies in a front-to-back three-seater. *Wow*. Must be the Moms of Multiples Club. What if I got pregnant and learned I was carrying triplets? I shuddered at the thought.

"And Isadora was at the event, too?" Tulia asked, jerking me back to the present.

"Yes, she'd told me earlier she wasn't going to go to the gathering. When she showed up, her father had asked for people to share memories of Beverly. Isadora seemed like she was about to say something negative, but Wes stopped her."

She wrinkled her nose. "That's not done. I'm glad he didn't let her."

"Anyway, Lincoln looked—if you didn't know better—like he was there as a friend of the family. I watched him spend a bit of time with every guest."

"You and me both know he was on the job, right?"

"Yep," I said.

She finished locking the door and yawned. "I'm beat. And I'm on Nana duty tonight."

"You have to be the youngest grandmother ever. You're not even fifty, right?"

She shrugged. "Hey, had my daughter when I was twenty, and she gave birth at nineteen. It's good to do it when you're young. You have more energy."

"I guess. It's too late for me to be pregnant at twenty."

She cocked her head. "You have some news you're not sharing?" She grinned.

I stared at her. "Do you mean . . . ? No, actually, I don't. But I'm kinda sorta thinking about it."

"Go for it, Mac. Being a mother is the best and hardest job I've ever had, even counting lobstering. It's completely worth it." She elbowed me. "You stay safe, now."

"Thanks. You too." I watched her climb into her old Suburban and drive off. The best and hardest job, huh? Gin had hinted at the same. But what if I already loved my current best job? I sighed and kicked a thick shard of quahog shell into the gutter.

Chapter Forty-nine

A cloud blew over the low-hanging sun as I approached my house behind the bike shop, now closed for the day. Simply looking at my compact home made me happy. I'd had it built to spec after I moved back to Westham a year and half ago. It had everything I needed and nothing more. The cedar shingles were silvering nicely, a classic Cape Cod look. The transom window in the loft let in lovely light in the mornings and a breeze when I wanted air. The small covered porch under the loft was exactly the right size, with two blue Adirondack chairs I'd assembled from a kit and painted myself. Even the red-painted window boxes matching the front door—all of it was exactly what I'd wanted. What would I do with my tiny house if I combined households with Tim? Could I bear to leave it? On the other hand, it was built on a trailer base so technically it could be moved anywhere.

To Tim's backyard, even. I supposed it could function as an office or guest quarters.

I heard a sound that seemed out of place. I froze. I couldn't place it, but it sounded human. Maybe the snort of someone stifling a sneeze? I turned in a complete circle but didn't see anyone. It was probably a pedestrian out on the sidewalk, or maybe a cyclist on the path leading to the trail, which was on the other side of my hedge of *Rosa rugosa*. It couldn't have been from inside my house. Belle made lots of different sounds, including ringtones, but I'd never heard her imitate a sneeze.

I rummaged in my bag for my house keys, hoping it was only my nerves making me think someone was there. I unlocked the door and stepped over the threshold.

"Hi, Belle. I'm home."

She bobbed her head from the top branch of her perch. "I'm home. Belle's a good girl. Snacks, Mac?"

"Hang on, kid. I'll get your snack in a sec." I bent over to untie my sandals' black ribbons, which wrapped around my ankles. My eyes went wide as I made the connection. If the sound had been a stifled sneeze, it could have been allergic Isadora. It could be Murderer Isadora, who had headed over here after the gathering. *Gah*. I had to get the door locked behind me in a hurry. I swore. One of the ribbons was stuck in a knot. I fumbled with it, which only made things worse. The heck with the shoe-free policy. I could sit down and untangle it after I secured the door.

"Hang on, kid! Hello! Hello! Hello! Hello!" Belle was going nuts. She flapped her wings. "Hello!"

"Hello, Belle. Calm down." I straightened. A cold, hard object poked the back of my neck. My insides turned to ice. I was too late.

Chapter Fifty

A hand from behind grasped my shoulder. The points of long fingernails dug into the fabric of my dress and poked the fleshy muscle. I glanced down. Those were Isadora's nails. They hurt, but my fear was worse. I tried to turn.

"Get inside," Isadora snarled.

I took a step and the cold object went with me.

"Sit down." She shoved me toward the couch and slammed the door closed.

I stumbled but caught myself. Still standing but off balance, wearing only one espadrille, I faced her. From five feet away she pointed a small gun at me with both hands. My hands were sweaty and my throat thick. My heart hammered in my chest.

"I said to sit." Her face was tense. Her lips were flattened and her eyes flinty.

"I'm not sitting." My voice shook. This was bad. Very bad.

She uttered an obscenity in an exasperated tone. "Hands where I can see them," she finally ordered.

I extended my arms a foot away from my body. "Put down the gun, Isadora. Why are you doing this?"

"Hello! Hello! Hello!"

"Tell the bird to shut up," Isadora ordered. She slid her eyes to Belle and quickly looked back at me with a shudder. "I hate big birds like that."

The crow. That was what she'd said about the crow that had crashed into the window at Maxine's. Could I make Belle work to my advantage? "Telling her to be quiet won't work."

"Do it!"

"Belle, please be quiet," I said.

"Belle's a good girl! Hello! Put down the gun!"

"See?" I raised my eyebrows.

"Sit down, Mac." Isadora glared.

I didn't sit. I had to get out of here and it would be a lot harder if she had me trapped on the couch. Did she even know how to use the weapon? It hardly mattered, since she was so close.

"Why are you pointing that gun at me?" I asked. "I didn't do anything."

Her laugh was harsh. "As if. I know you've been asking questions around town. I've heard how much you like to play detective. I know you were getting close."

"Close to what?"

"Come on. You're not stupid. Figuring out who killed Beverly."

"Homicide! Homicide! Hello! Homicide."

"She told you to shut up, bird." Isadora spit out the words.

"Belle, hush," I told her. "Why do you hate parrots so much?" I asked Isadora. Could I stall her enough to escape? But if I got away, she might kill Belle. I couldn't let anything happen to Belle. Ever.

Isadora sniffed. She took her left hand off the gun to rub her nose. "There are a lot of things I hate, including my allergies."

I flashed on seeing her write with her left hand in the dress shop. She might not be able to shoot as well with only her right hand. I could attack her now. But she returned her hand to the gun. I swore silently. On the other hand, if she'd come here to kill me, what was she waiting for?

"You could just leave," I said.

"Really, Mac?" She stared at me, incredulous. "You think I'm an idiot? I need you to sit down right now. I need to get on the road."

"Where are you headed?"

"I'm going to pay a little visit to my father's so-called birth son. He's a scam artist, that's what he is. I'm not having anyone threaten my inheritance. Not Beverly, not him. And definitely not you."

I knew her visit would leave another murder victim behind. Two, if I was to be the next dead. I couldn't let her do that. "How did Beverly threaten what you would inherit?"

"Dad was all ready to propose to her." She shook her head slowly, ominously. "Not on my watch, he wasn't."

"Alexa, call the cops!" Belle said. "Hello! Alexa, call the cops! Hello!"

Isadora whirled. She pointed the gun at Belle. *No!* I clasped my hands, elbows locked, in a volleyball bump stance. I jabbed them under her forearms and drove upward. The gun fired as it flew out of her hands. I grabbed her left wrist and twisted it up and behind her back. She wobbled on her flimsy heeled sandals. I shifted weight onto my bare foot and kicked the back of her knee with my espadrille. She cried out and fell to the floor. I kept a tight grip on her wrist.

I glanced at my bird. "You all right, Belle?"

"Alexa, call the cops!"

Isadora struggled on the floor. She cursed as she tried to turn, but she didn't have enough strength. Her preening about not working out had just come back to bite her. "Let go of me."

"No way." I stomped my shoed foot onto her back, turning her all the way onto her front. I pulled upward on her arm.

Alexa said, "Calling nine-one-one."

My eyes widened. *What?* Belle to the rescue.

"Dispatch," a voice said through Alexa. A human voice. "What is your emergency?"

"This is Mackenzie Almeida in the small house behind Mac's Bikes in Westham," I said to the cylinder, nearly breathless. "I have a suspect in Beverly Ruchart's murder under control, but just barely. She assaulted my pet and me with a gun."

"We'll have officers on the scene as soon as possible. Please stay on the line. Do you feel safe?"

"Take your filthy foot off me." Isadora struggled so much I had trouble keeping it on her.

"Not really!" My voice shook. "Can they hurry?"

"Hello. Belle's a good girl," Belle muttered in a much calmer voice. "Hello. Hello. Alexa, read the shopping list."

"Are you able to leave the premises and wait outside?" the dispatcher asked.

"Not if you want me to keep Isadora Farnham from killing me and my parrot." I wasn't sure where the gun had gone. Even if I knew, I wasn't letting go of Isadora until I saw a uniform.

"Grapes," Alexa began. "Peanuts. Hello. Hello. Grapes."

Geez. Not now. "Alexa, st—"

Isadora reached over her back with her other hand. She tugged at my ankle.

"Oh no, you don't." I pulled up on her arm again until she cried out and let go.

The door flew open. "Police!" Bike cop Jenkins stood there, a decent-sized weapon outstretched in both hands. Lincoln loomed large behind him.

"Thank goodness," I said. "Take over here, okay?" My relief felt better than a cool dive into the bay on a blazing day.

"You cover, I'll cuff," Lincoln said to Officer Jenkins.

"Don't move, Ms. Farnham," Jenkins told Isadora, pointing the gun at her.

She let out a string of obscenities. I winced, hoping Belle didn't add them to her vocabulary.

As a siren whooped its way toward us with increasing amplitude, Lincoln relieved me of Isadora's wrist. I stepped back while he grabbed her other hand even as she struggled. When he clicked on the handcuffs, I'd never heard a more satisfying sound.

"Mac attacked me," she wailed. "She tricked me. You should arrest her."

I checked Lincoln's face. He gave me a little smile and shook his head.

"Isadora Farnham, you are under arrest for the murder of Beverly Ruchart, and for armed assault in a dwelling, assault and battery with a dangerous weapon, and home invasion," he said. He read her rights to her.

Belle gave a wolf whistle. "Hello, handsome."

Chapter Fifty-one

I watched as Jenkins ushered a cuffed and swearing Isadora into the back seat of the cruiser that had sped into my parking area, sirens howling. An officer who had come with Victoria in the police car slid into the driver's seat and took Isadora away.

I sank to sit on my steps, my legs suddenly feeling more like jelly than bones and muscles. I smoothed my dress over my knees and hugged them.

"You all right, Mac?" Victoria asked. She gazed at my single shoe.

I patted my chest. "I will be. It was nothing short of terrifying for a while in there, though." I started to tackle the knotted ribbon with shaking finger but gave up. "I would have been inside a locked door except for this stupid shoe."

Jenkins clicked on his helmet and grabbed the handlebars of his bike, which leaned against the house. "Heading out, Chief. See you around, Haskins."

"Thanks for getting here promptly," Lincoln said. He gave Jenkins a little salute.

"I was a block away. No problemo." He walked his bike through the gap in the hedge.

"Want to fill us in on what went down?" Lincoln asked me.

"Okay. Do we need to go inside?"

"I'm good out here," Lincoln said. "You, Chief?"

"I'm fine." She slid her hands into her pockets and rocked back and forth on her heels.

The detective sank in one movement to sit cross-legged on the ground. I'd been amazed the first time I'd seen him sit that way. He was a big man to be so flexible and elegant in his moves, and not a young one, either. At the time he'd said something about it being in his culture to stay in close contact with the earth.

"Would you like help with that lace?" Lincoln smiled gently. "Untangling knots is one of my superpowers."

I extended my foot. "Have at it." I watched as his big fingers somehow coaxed the knot to loosen and untie. "Thanks, Lincoln." I slid the shoe off with the toes on my other foot.

He nodded his head in acknowledgment.

I swallowed. "Okay. Here's what happened. After the memorial gathering for Beverly broke up a little before six, I walked home. I opened my door and leaned over to take off my sandals. I thought I heard a muffled sneeze. You know Isadora is really allergic?"

Lincoln bobbed his head.

"All of a sudden she was at my back with a gun to my neck," I continued. "She pushed me into my house."

"She didn't fire at you," Lincoln said.

"If she had I wouldn't be sitting here talking to you. I'm not sure she knew what she wanted. She kept the gun pointed at me and said she needed to get on the road. She wanted me to sit, but I didn't."

"Smart move," Lincoln said.

"Yeah, I totally didn't want to be trapped sitting down."

"Then what happened?" Victoria asked.

"She told me her father had been about to propose to Beverly. That if he married her it would dilute Isadora's share of Wes's estate eventually. She said she was headed out to visit the birth son Beverly had helped Wes find, and that nobody was getting in the way of her inheritance, including me. I'm sure she was planning to kill the son, too."

"How did you overpower her?" Lincoln cocked his head. "And what happened to the gun?"

"I'll get to that. My parrot, Belle, was going nuts."

From inside, Belle came out and hopped onto my shoulder. "Belle's a good girl. Snacks, Mac?"

"Belle's a very good girl, but she was really agitated. She knew Isadora was threatening me and she wouldn't shut up." I mustered a wobbly smile for Victoria and Lincoln. "Isadora said she hated big birds. She turned the gun on Belle and away from me. I took the opportunity to whack her arms up from underneath." I raised an eyebrow at Victoria. "One of my best volleyball moves, remember?"

Victoria nodded.

I went on. "The gun went off as it flew out of her hands. I twisted her arm and hit her in the back of the knees." I blew out a breath. "She was wearing heeled sandals. It was easy to get her off balance and force her down."

"Call the cops!" Belle said. "Homicide! Call the cops. Put down the gun!"

Victoria snorted her amusement. Lincoln let out a belly laugh. When he recovered, he prompted, "And you called dispatch?"

"Belle did."

"What?" Victoria asked, her voice rising in disbelief.

"Yep, she told Alexa to call the cops. I didn't know the device could carry out that order, but it worked. I talked to the dispatcher through the device. Jenkins and Lincoln showed up pretty quickly after Belle summoned them."

"Belle's a very good girl." Victoria grinned. "Let me know what her favorite snack is and we'll see she has a lifetime supply."

"Snacks, Mac?" Belle cooed.

"African grays live a really long time, you know," I said.

"She earned it. Can I pet her?" Victoria asked.

"Sure."

She reached out a hand to stroke Belle's head. Belle started bobbing and singing "Happy."

"It's one of her favorite songs," I said.

Victoria laughed, a sound I hadn't heard from her in decades.

I gazed at Lincoln. "How did you get here so quickly?"

He grimaced. "I had a guy tailing Ms. Farnham. We had several avenues pointing at her for the murder."

"Avenues?" I asked. "But not evidence?"

"We were getting there. I'm afraid her alcoholism led her to cut some corners in covering up her crime. An hour ago, the lab identified her fingerprints on a container of antifreeze in Beverly's shed."

"And on the one in Gin's garage?" I asked. "Which she had planted there."

"Yes," Lincoln confirmed.

Victoria gave a single nod. "A container which she would have no conceivable reason to touch."

"What a stupid move. No gloves?" I asked.

"Apparently not." Lincoln shook his head.

"You think she dosed Beverly's drinks at the dinner?" I asked.

"She completed a bartending course a couple of years ago," Lincoln said. "Mr. Farnham told me Isadora convinced the deceased to let her prepare and pour all the drinks for the dinner."

"That's a critical piece of the puzzle." I stared at him. "When did you learn that?"

His smile was wistful. "Only this afternoon. I think Farnham had been sitting on the information, afraid of the truth. He finally got his nerve up to tell me."

Condemning his own daughter. "Why didn't anyone else mention that Isadora had made the drinks?"

"Your guess is as good as mine, Mac."

"We can ask them for every tiny detail a million times," Victoria said. "Sometimes people don't see what's right in front of them."

"Anyway," Lincoln said, "my guy who was following Isadora got stuck in a major traffic jam."

"I walked by all those cars going nowhere," I said. "It's crazy at the end of the day this time of year, and on a Friday, no less."

"Isadora was riding a bike and he was driving." He

shook his head. "When he told me, I had a Spidey sense to head over here on foot, and I heard the call from dispatch as I came."

"Detective Haskins is well-known for his Spidey sense," Victoria said with only a hint of sarcasm.

"Seems like it's a good thing to pay attention to. This time it was, anyway." I gazed at him. "Do you think Isadora acted alone?"

"It seems so," he said. "Ron Ruchart and Danny Rizzoli aren't the most upstanding citizens around, but in this case they appear to be innocent." He cleared his throat. "I need to apologize for the way I reacted to your hardware store tip. If I was brusque, it was out of caution. I do not want to encourage you and your friends to become unlicensed private investigators."

I held up both hands, palms out. "I told you, Piet supplied the information totally unsolicited. He was the one who brought up the murder, and he volunteered about the tall, young, blonde woman on a bicycle who bought the antifreeze. All I did was pass along the news." I folded my arms.

Victoria had been following our conversation as if she were watching a game of table tennis. "He did apologize, Mac." She pointed at him.

True. "Thank you, Lincoln."

My parents hurried through the gap in the low hedge.

"We heard the siren and saw the lights, Mac. Are you all right?" My father's gaze searched my face, then Lincoln's and Victoria's.

Mom moved to my side and sank down next to me. Her arm around my shoulders had never felt so good.

"I'm fine, Pa. It was kind of a close call, but . . ." I swallowed away emotion. "I'm fine."

"I think we're done here for now," Lincoln said as he pushed up to standing. "I'll need you to sign a statement, Mac, but it can wait until tomorrow. Please stop by the station at your convenience. I'll have it ready."

I stood, too, and held out my hand. "Thank you both." I shook Lincoln's big, warm hand. Victoria's petite hand was half the size, but she had almost as firm a grip.

"Goodbye, Belle," Victoria said.

"Call the cops!" Belle cried.

I laughed. "Belle, they are the cops." I watched the tall and the short of them head for the sidewalk. I smiled at my parents, then turned to my avian rescuer. "How about a snack?"

Chapter Fifty-two

I'd never been so happy to sit and tap my foot to some excellent tunes. The bakery-turned-bar was packed at eight that night. The lively music tonight was from a local Celtic group with a fiddler, a guitarist, someone playing a small accordion type of instrument, and a musician who alternately played a tin whistle, an Irish drum, and uilleann pipes, which gave off a haunting sound similar to bagpipes.

I perched on a stool, a half-full glass of IPA at my elbow on the counter and the remains of one of Tim's scrumptious mini pizzas on a plate next to it. The basil pesto, soft goat cheese, and artichoke hearts he'd topped it with had been nothing short of perfect. Gin sat next to me, holding a glass of white wine, the strain of being considered a person of interest smoothed off her face. I'd relayed the bones of Isadora's attack and capture when we'd met out front half an hour ago. I was still jittery. It was going to take a while to come down off this week's tension and recover from being threatened with my life, however briefly.

Tim, meanwhile, was a two-handed wonder. Pouring beer and wine, bringing out plates of savory bacon muffins and three kinds of mini pizza, and schmoozing with one and all. I'd had a quick chat with him when I'd arrived.

"They arrested Isadora Farnham for the murder today," I'd whispered.

His big baby blues went wide. "Yeah?"

"Truth. What a relief."

Somebody waved at him for a drink refill.

"I'll tell you more later."

He was about to turn away but paused, his brow knit. "You're all right, aren't you?"

I smiled. "I am."

Now Gin leaned toward me. "Eli told me something funny when I was talking to him earlier today, after the gathering."

"Oh?"

"Remember you asked about that look he gave you when you came in with me the other night?"

I nodded.

"He confessed that he had a kind of messy thing in his past. Well, not messy so much as bad. He was arrested for drug dealing."

Which I already knew.

"The charges were dismissed, but he's still jumpy, even though it was a long time ago. When I said that you were with me, he thought I'd said, 'Cop's here,' and it spooked him."

I wrinkled my nose. "I guess you could hear 'cop' for 'Mac' if you were feeling jumpy."

"Plus he has tinnitus. He's always mishearing things."

For my friend's sake, I was glad that's all it was and that Eli hadn't been involved in Beverly's murder.

I spied Flo and Norland weaving through the crowd toward us. "Look who's here."

"Cool." Gin gestured for them to join us.

After we'd exchanged greetings and they'd ordered drinks, Norland said, "I heard something pretty interesting on the scanner. A couple of somethings, actually." A little smile played at the corner of his mouth.

"You have to fill me in, Mac," Flo said. "Norland wouldn't tell me a chicken-pickin' thing."

I glanced around. The music was loud enough I didn't think anyone would overhear.

"Isadora came to my house and held me at gunpoint."

Flo's mouth formed an O. "She didn't."

Norland gazed at me with what looked a lot like admiration.

"She sure did." I told them what Isadora had said about the birth son while she pointed the weapon at me, and how Belle had told Alexa to call the police.

"I didn't know you could use one of those devices to call the police," Norland said.

"I didn't either, obviously, or I would have done it myself, and sooner," I said. "I have a new model. Maybe it's a feature they added recently."

"How did the police get the gun away from her?" Norland raised his snowy eyebrows.

"I managed to before they got there."

Flo's mouth dropped farther open. Norland nodded as if he already knew, which he probably did.

"How'd you do it?" Flo asked.

I raised a shoulder and dropped it. "Ever play volley-ball?"

She shook her head. "But I've seen it played on TV in the summer Olympics."

"I used to play during high school and college." I set down my beer, joined my hands, and straightened my arms into the bump position. "Comes in handy when your attacker's attention is distracted by a manic bird."

"Here's to Belle." Gin held up her glass.

We all clinked our drinks and echoed the sentiment.

"Isadora must have been attacked by a parrot at some point," Gin said.

"She was totally freaked out by Belle." I thought back. "Or maybe it was another kind of bird. A few days ago, when I stopped by the shop where she works? A big crow flew into the front window and it was like it had attacked her personally. She said she hated big birds."

"Even on *Sesame Street*?" Gin asked with a wicked grin.

I laughed at the thought of anyone being afraid of gentle yellow Big Bird.

"People can have all kinds of trauma in their past," Norland said in a somber tone.

"True enough," I agreed.

"So it had to have been Isadora who vandalized your store," Flo said. "Remember how you said you were on the phone with your mom Wednesday night and Belle kept saying hello at the window?"

"Exactly," I said. "Isadora must have thought I was getting too close. I think she'd planned to break into my house, but then Belle raised the alarm and freaked her out. Anyway, I'll bet Lincoln will get the story out of her.

The door to the street opened. Ron stalked in, followed by his father, and they headed straight for our little group.

"Here comes trouble," I said, gesturing toward them with my head.

A moment later, Ron faced me, arms folded. "You knew I wasn't getting the money."

"What are you talking about?" I asked. "What money?" I sort of did know, but not officially.

"My grandma's. You ruined everything," he shouted.

People near us quieted and stared. Tim moved behind me on the other side of the bar, but the band played on.

"He means he got a call about the will," Danny offered with a smirk. "My late mother-in-law left everything but a couple thou to some charity."

So what Abo Reba had told me was true.

"How exactly is Mac supposed to have ruined anything?" Norland asked in his deep, authoritative voice. "She didn't write your grandmother's will. Beverly wrote it herself."

"She's been snooping around, asking questions," Ron said, still glaring at me.

His logic escaped me.

Danny appeared to agree with me. He laid a hand on his son's arm. "Listen, son, I told you this was a bad idea."

I glanced at the music lovers nearest us until they looked away. I kept my voice soft. "Isadora Farnham killed Beverly. She's the one who had reason to be mad at anyone asking questions about the death."

"I was going to kill the old broad myself." Ron lifted his chin.

I sucked in air and glanced over at Gin for a second, whose hand had flown to her mouth.

Ron's tone dared anyone to challenge him. "Isadora just beat me to it."

Chapter Fifty-three

Cokey jumped up and down at a little before ten the next morning, her eyes shining, her curls bouncing under her Red Sox cap. She had five minutes to go before the Fun Run started. Derrick and I had handed over the retail and rental side of the shop to Norland so we could be here. He'd offered to help out last night after the shock of Ron's announcement had ebbed. Danny had nearly dragged Ron out of the bakery muttering what a stupid jerk he was to say such a thing in public.

"You can't arrest somebody for considering murder if they don't do anything about it," Norland had pointed out after they left.

"Is it time, Titi Mac?" Cokey now lisped. "Is it time?" She clapped her hands and patted the paper race number pinned to the front of her yellow T-shirt.

"It's almost time, Cokester, almost," I said.

"I'm number two-one-one, Daddy, see?" She pointed to her little belly.

Pa and Mom had brought her to the race site and met Derrick and me here. Mom wore a race number, too, and a yellow shirt matching her granddaughter's. She'd said she needed the exercise, but I knew she wanted to keep Cokey company. Now the rest of us stood on the side-walk, including Tucker in his harness yipping at all the excitement.

"Tio Tim!" Cokey cried. "You made it!"

I turned my head to see Tim. He hurried up beside me and slung his arm around my shoulders.

"I wouldn't have missed this for anything, sweetie," he told her, holding up his other hand. "Gimme five for luck."

She slapped his hand. "And another for thpeed."

"And for speed." They low-fived this time.

"Now remember to pace yourself, Coquille," Pa said. "You have a whole mile to run. You'll get out of breath if you go real fast at the start."

"Abo." She rolled her eyes like a mini teenager. "Tio Tim and I have been training. He already told me."

I covered a laugh.

A race official with a megaphone had a classic deep announcer's voice. "One minute to start in the Falmouth Family Fun Run!" he said with great drama. "Runners, get ready."

Cokey darted to the curb and kissed the top of Tucker's head before joining Astra again. Yards of kids and parents were ahead of them, with as many behind.

"On your marks," the announcer said.

"Like this, Abo Astra." Cokey bent her front knee, pushed back her rear foot, and set her hands on her knee, leaning forward.

Mom did the same.

"Have a good one. See you at the finish line!" Pa called. Since it was a circle route with identical start and finish lines, we didn't have to go anywhere.

"Get set," blared the announcer. "Go!"

A cheer went up from all the loved ones watching and from the runners in like measure. The mid-pack racers got off to a slow start, but finally our two yellow- shirted blondies disappeared down the road. I checked my phone for the time.

"What'll it take them, maybe fifteen minutes?" I asked.

"Depends on how tired Cokey gets," Tim said. "The winners will be in a lot sooner than that."

Pa laughed. "Coquille was pretty wound up this morning."

"Are you ready for tomorrow?" I gazed up at Tim. The adult race was held the day after the Family Fun Run.

"As ready as I'll ever be. I'm not looking for any gold medals, believe me."

Pa turned serious and faced me. "How are you recovering from yesterday, Mackenzie?"

"It's over," I said. "I'm safe, Belle's fine. It's all good."

"You were extraordinarily brave, Mac." Tim squeezed my shoulder. He had come over after closing the bakery last night, and I'd filled him in on the details of the attack.

I gazed up at him. "We do what we have to do. I sure am glad I used to play volleyball."

Tim bobbed his head. He wasn't smiling, but the expression on his face, his eyes, his mouth as he looked at me? The definition of caring.

"That poor young woman was deeply troubled, I fear," Pa said. "It's a tragedy she felt she had to hurt others in order to heal."

Tim nodded. "Last night Ron Ruchart came into the bakery. He told Mac he was thinking of killing Beverly himself."

"You don't say?" Pa's grizzled eyebrows flew up.

"He did," I said. "I didn't get a chance to tell you. Ron said Isadora beat him to it. He seemed mad at me about Beverly leaving her money to the clinic, too."

"He's missing a step or five, wouldn't you say?" Tim asked.

"No kidding." I shook my head. "Like I had anything to do with it."

"Mother told us about the will last night over dinner," Pa said. "Beverly made quite a generous bequest."

"The clinic can really use it, too," I said.

We spent the next few minutes talking about anything but murder. I watched the race organizers string a yellow ribbon across the yellow mat that had become the finish line. Two runners came into view down the road, a boy and a girl more than twice as old as Cokey, maybe eleven or twelve. They were red-faced and sprinting, clearly a race to the finish. The crowd cheered them on. Three yards before the end the girl put on a burst of speed and crossed with a huge smile, breaking the ribbon. A roar of applause went up.

"Those two are twins," Pa said, beaming. "They compete at everything."

I checked the time. "Wow, seven minutes. That seems fast for kids."

"You can tell they're both built to be runners," Tim said. "They've probably been training."

A flood of racing children followed, but it was five more minutes before I spied the two yellow shirts who were dear to our hearts. Cokey put on her own burst of short-legged speed and crossed the finish line a few seconds before Mom. My niece pumped both fists into the air, then grabbed Mom's hand and nearly dragged her over to us.

"Did you see me?" she asked, her cheeks flushed. "I beat Astra!"

"You sure did." Tim hoisted her in the air and gave her a big hug. "What a champion."

I exchanged a high five with her before he handed her to Derrick. My throat was thick, and not from being stung or from fear. Family was more important than anything.

RECIPES

Zane's Summer Cooler

Distiller Zane King suggests this drink to Mac.

Ingredients
Pineapple juice
Cuban rum
Tonic water
Lime
Fresh mint

Directions

For one drink, mix 2 ounces each of pineapple juice, a good rum, and tonic water.

Squeeze half a lime into the drink. Crush a mint sprig and swirl it through the drink.

Add more juice if you like it sweeter, or substitute seltzer water for the tonic if you prefer it less sweet.

Tulia's Cod Cakes

Tulia brings these to Mac from the Lobstah Shack.

Ingredients
4 peppercorns
1 bay leaf
1 lemon, cut into eighths
1 pound cod fillets, or other white flaky fish
2 tablespoons unsalted butter
2 ribs celery, trimmed, peeled, and diced
1 medium-size yellow onion, peeled and diced
2 cloves garlic, peeled and minced
1 heaping tablespoon mayonnaise
2 teaspoons Dijon mustard
1 tablespoon fresh dill
2 eggs
1½ teaspoons kosher salt
½ teaspoon freshly ground black pepper
1 teaspoon smoked paprika, or to taste
1 teaspoon red pepper flakes, or to taste
1 heaping cup Panko breadcrumbs or crushed crackers
½ bunch parsley, roughly chopped
2 tablespoons vegetable oil
Any good salsa

Directions
Fill a shallow, wide pan with high sides with about an inch of water and set it over high heat. Add the peppercorns, bay leaf, and one section of the lemon to the water, and allow it to come to a bare simmer. Place the fish into this poaching liquid and cook, barely simmering, until the flesh has just begun to whiten all the way through, ap-

proximately 6 to 8 minutes. Using a wide spatula, carefully remove the fish from the water and set it aside to cool. Reserve the poaching water to include in a fish soup at another time.

Empty the pan and return it to the stove. Over medium-high heat, add the butter and allow it to melt, swirling it around the pan. When the butter to the pan foams, add the celery, onions, and garlic, and sauté, stirring often, until the vegetables soften and the onions turn translucent. Then remove from heat.

In a large bowl, mix together the mayonnaise, mustard, dill, eggs, salt, pepper, paprika, and red pepper flakes. Add sautéed vegetables and mix. Pour the Panko crumbs or crushed crackers over all and stir to combine. Add the parsley and stir again.

Flake the cooked fish into the binding sauce carefully, keeping the flakes as whole as you can manage. Gather the mixture into balls and flatten them into patties: 4 to 6 for a main course, 6 to 8 for an appetizer. Place them on a sheet pan or platter, cover loosely with plastic wrap, and transfer them to the refrigerator for at least 30 minutes to set.

Set a large sauté pan over high heat and add the oil to it. When the oil is shimmering, remove the fish cakes from the refrigerator. Turn the heat to medium and carefully sauté the patties until they are golden brown, approximately 4 to 5 minutes per side. Work in batches if necessary. (A small smear of mayonnaise on the exterior of the patties will give them a crisp crust.)

Serve with salsa as a topping or with lemon wedges.

Avocado Deviled Eggs

Mac makes these to bring to book group.

Ingredients
8 hard-cooked eggs, shelled
2 ripe avocados
1 teaspoon fresh cilantro or dill, minced (Some people
    have a severe aversion to cilantro, so consider your
    diners.)
3 teaspoons lime juice
1 tablespoon capers, chopped finely
Habanero or jalapeño hot sauce
Salt and pepper to taste
Smoked paprika or chili powder

Directions
Halve eggs lengthwise and remove yolks to a bowl.
Mash avocado with yolks. Add capers, cilantro or dill,
lime juice, a few drops of hot sauce, and a pinch each salt
and pepper. Mix gently and season to taste.

Fill egg-white halves. Sprinkle smoked paprika or
chili powder on top. Cover and refrigerate if you won't be
serving immediately.

Parmesan Polenta Disks

Mac enjoys these cheesy disks with her scallops at Jimmy's Harborside.

Ingredients
3½ cups water
¾ teaspoon salt
1 cup yellow cornmeal
2 tablespoons butter
½ cup grated fresh Parmesan cheese
About ¼ cup olive oil

Directions
Oil a 9" × 13" baking dish and set aside.

Add the water and salt to a sauce pot and bring to a boil over high heat.

Add the cornmeal while continuously whisking to prevent lumps. Turn the heat down to low and let simmer until thickened, around 10 minutes.

Stir in the butter and grated Parmesan until smooth. Spread the mixture onto the oiled dish in an even layer. Cool in the refrigerator, uncovered, until solid.

Cut the solid polenta into disks with a biscuit cutter.

Add 2 tablespoons oil to a nonstick skillet and warm over medium heat. Once the oil is hot and glistening, but not smoking, add the polenta slices and cook until golden on each side. Add more oil as needed to fry the remaining slices. Serve hot. (Fry up the odd-shaped bits later for a tasty treat.)

Option: If you don't want to make the polenta from scratch, slice rounds from a premade log of polenta, fry, and top with a teaspoon of cheese while still hot.

Bear Claws

Tim's alteration of the standard bear claw is better than the original. Tim's version has cinnamon and ground pecans throughout, and chopped pecans and sugar on top. You can make the yeasted dough yourself, or use puff pastry if you don't feel confident to make the dough.

Yield: Makes 16 pastries

Ingredients
2 cups pecans ground, plus 1 cup roughly chopped
2 eggs
½ cup plus 4 tablespoons granulated sugar
Yeasted dough (see recipe below), or 2 sheets puff pastry, thawed
1 egg beaten with 1 tablespoon water (the egg wash)

Directions
Preheat oven to 350°F. Line two baking sheets with parchment paper.

Mix together the nuts, eggs, and sugar until they are well combined.

Roll half of the yeasted dough or one sheet thawed puff pastry into an 8" × 16" rectangle (give or take) and make 8 (4-inch) squares.

Apply egg wash to the top of each square.

Plop about 2 tablespoons of filling onto each square and form it into a log on the bottom end.

Roll the bottom about one third of the way to the top and then fold the top down to meet it. Press gently to seal.

Make four diagonal slits into the bear claws-in-progress.

Pinch to form the traditional shape with cuts spreading apart. Brush the egg wash on the top, and sprinkle with roughly chopped pecans and with sugar. Repeat with the other half of the dough or a second sheet of puff pastry. Bake for 10 to 15 minutes or until nicely browned.

Slide the parchment paper and claws from the baking sheet onto a wire rack. Serve warm with coffee or mimosas.

Yeasted Dough

Ingredients
Dough mixture:
1 package (¼ ounce) active dry yeast
½ cup warm 2 percent or whole milk (110° to 115°)
2 tablespoons sugar
¾ teaspoon salt
1 egg, lightly beaten
1 tablespoon cinammon
1½ cups plus 2 tablespoons unbleached white flour

Butter mixture:
2 tablespoons unbleached white flour, divided
¾ cup cold butter, cut into tablespoon-size pieces

Directions
In a large bowl, dissolve yeast in warm milk. Stir in sugar, salt, and egg; mix well. Mix the cinnamon into the flour and add it all at once, stirring until mixed. Set aside.

For butter mixture, sprinkle 1 tablespoon flour on a work surface; place butter on surface and sprinkle with 1 tablespoon flour. Press and roll out with a rolling pin. Scrape butter from rolling pin and continue to work the butter until it forms a smooth mass without any hard lumps. Knead in remaining flour, working quickly to keep butter cold.

Place butter mixture on a sheet of plastic wrap and shape into a small rectangle. Cover with another sheet of plastic wrap; roll into a 9" × 6" rectangle. Refrigerate for 20 minutes.

Turn dough onto a floured work surface; roll into a 14" × 10" rectangle, with 10-inch side toward the bottom. Unwrap butter mixture; place on dough 1 inch above bottom edge and ½ inch from each side edge. Fold top half of dough over butter and pinch edges to seal.

Turn dough a quarter to the right; sprinkle lightly with additional flour. Lightly roll into a 16" × 8" rectangle. Fold bottom third of rectangle up and top third down, as when folding a business letter, making a 5.5" × 8" rectangle (this is called one turn). Rotate dough a quarter to the right. Lightly roll into a 16" × 8" rectangle and again fold into thirds, finishing the second turn. Repeat rotating, rolling, and folding two more times for a total of four times. Cut in half, wrap loosely in plastic wrap, and refrigerate for 30 minutes or up to overnight.